PRAISE FOR EILEEN GOUDGE P9-ELD-555
THE CYPRESS BAY MYSTERIES

"Eileen Goudge writes like a house on fire, creating characters you come to love and hate to leave." —Nora Roberts, *New York Times*–bestselling author

SWIMSUIT BODY

"Clever, fast-paced, and filled with as many laughs as twists and turns, *Swimsuit Body* is sure to delight cozy fans. Eileen Goudge breathes life into her lovably flawed and fearless heroine Tish Ballard and all the quirky characters that populate this killer tale." —Lisa Unger, *New York Times*–bestselling author of *Ink and Bone*

"Eileen Goudge does everything right in this new mystery. The amateur sleuth is irresistible. . . . The dialogue crackles with wit. The plot is twisty and surprising. The northern California small-town setting is fun and charming. You'll delight in reading this master storyteller's master work." —Jane K. Cleland, author of the Josie Prescott Antiques Mysteries

BONES AND ROSES

"Expect to become immersed with the indomitable heroine, Tish Ballard, the cast of colorful secondary characters, and Eileen Goudge's trademark storytelling." —Sandra Brown, *New York Times*–bestselling author

"A sophisticated, cleverly crafted mystery with complex, intricately drawn characters . . . I was fascinated by everyone in this story, and never saw the ending coming." —Donna Ball, author of the Raine Stockton Dog Mysteries

Bones
and
Roses

Bones and Roses

A CYPRESS BAY MYSTERY

EILEEN GOUDGE

OPEN ROAD

INTEGRATED MEDIA

NEW YORK

Cover design by Amanda Shaffer

978-1-5040-3553-8

This edition published in 2016 by Open Road Integrated Media, Inc.
180 Maiden Lane
New York, NY 10038
www.openroadmedia.com

Bones
and
Roses

CHAPTER ONE

S ince when is stealing dead bugs a crime?"

Officer James is smirking as he says this. Like he can already see himself recounting the incident over a round of beers at the Tide's Inn for the amusement of his buddies. I want to smack him. But I can't because he's a cop and the last time I took a swing at a cop it didn't end well. That was before I got sober, three and a half years ago, when my definition of a marathon wasn't the kind that had you powering to the finish line with a number on your chest, shrink-wrapped in Lycra and dripping sweat. Mine had me chasing shots as opposed to other runners, while being egged on by fellow bar patrons. Suffice it to say, I was lucky I didn't spend the night behind bars.

But that was then and this is now. The current situation involves the theft of a valuable collectible by a shoplifter and not the loss of my alleged virtue at the hands of a guy who thought I'd be too drunk to notice him grabbing my ass. We're at the Gilded Lily, the shop in downtown Cypress Bay that sells decorative items and high-end household goods, where my best friend, Ivy, works part-time and sells her artwork on commission. One of her pieces was stolen, and Officer Friendly here is doing little to convince me "the long arm of the law" isn't just a figure of speech.

Ivy draws herself up to look him in the eye, which takes some doing as she stands scarcely higher than his shoulder at five foot two. "You think the theft of valuable artwork is funny?" *Atta girl.*

He's unrepentant. "Pardon me for saying so, but this ain't exactly the Louvre." He pronounces it "louver" as in "shutters." He glances around at the displays—everything from table linens embroidered by French nuns and glassware hand-blown by local artisans to vintage items, like the Victorian brass birdcage and Art Deco martini shaker—with pointedly raised eyebrows. *Jerk.* Okay, so the Gilded Lily's wares aren't museum quality, but they're carefully curated nonetheless, by the owner, Parker Lane, the only gay man I know who prefers clutter to clean lines.

"Seriously, you call this art?" His beady-eyed gaze settles on one of Ivy's dioramas and he leans in to take a closer look. The piece happens to be one of my favorites: green-backed beetles—from an honest-to-God insect emporium, in LA, where Ivy buys her preserved bugs—picnicking in the park. The "wicker" basket is fashioned from toothpicks, the blanket from a checkered cloth napkin; the greenery is so natural-looking it looks real at a glance. All of it contained on a pedestal, under a glass dome, small enough to fit in the palm of a hand. Part of a grouping, it sits between dioramas of a cricket jazz quartet and a bespectacled caterpillar peering at an optometrist's eye chart.

Ivy's aquamarine eyes flash and I jump in with, "Good question. And one I'm sure the artist would be happy to answer." I gesture toward Ivy. He has the decency to blush, and do I detect a hint of a smile on the face of his female partner? An attractive dark-haired woman in her twenties, Officer Ruiz appears to be taking pleasure in seeing him squirm.

"Well, are you going to just stand there or are you going to fill out a report?" Ivy demands of Officer James. Her cheeks are flushed and her shoulder-length raven curls make me think of a thunderstorm brewing. "Honestly, what if it was a dead body!"

This prompts him into finally flipping open his notepad. He

looks to be in his mid-thirties, the same age as Ivy and me, with police-issue brown hair, a mustache, and acne scars on his cheeks that give him a certain rugged appeal. From the neck down he's Barney Rubble: on the tubby side with rolls of fat slopping over his belt that speak of frequent Dunkin' Donuts runs. He also looks familiar—our paths must've crossed at some point, which tends to happen when you've lived in the same community your entire life. Except for the four years I was at San Diego State I've resided in the Northern California seaside town I call home since I first had my butt smacked, in the delivery room at Cypress Bay Community. Down the street from the Catholic church where I attended Mass when I was growing up and where these days I attend AA meetings.

"Can you describe this individual?" Officer James inquires, all officious-like.

"Mid-forties, medium height, dark brown hair, blue eyes. Kind of heavyset, though I wouldn't call him fat." Ivy describes the man she suspects of having made off with her diorama of ladybugs frolicking on the beach. "He was wearing tan slacks, Merrells, and a light blue O'Neil T-shirt."

Officer James whistles, impressed. "Sounds like you got a good look at him."

"He went out of his way to chat me up," she explains.

"I'll bet." He waggles his eyebrows suggestively.

Suddenly I remember where I know him from. He was in Ivy's and my class at Harbor High. Jordan James. I'd have recognized him sooner if not for the mustache and fifty pounds he's gained since then. It was Jordan who pulled that cruel prank on Rachel Shuck, asking her to the junior prom so she'd be humiliated when he stood her up. I had overheard him laughing about it with his buddies at the prom, saying stuff like, "I should've made it a bucket of pig's blood."

I'd been having a crappy evening to begin with—my own date, Adam Ricci, was in the john puking up his guts from the vodka we'd spiked our punch with (amateurs are such wusses)—and this had really gotten me riled. So I'd come up with a plan to teach Jordan a lesson. Armed with my Kodak Instamatic, which I'd brought to take candid shots of the prom for the yearbook (I was on the committee), I'd then enlisted the help of my friend Evan McDougal, the "Carson Kressley" of Harbor High, who was out and proud, sporting guyliner and sequined high-tops before it was socially acceptable. The photo of Evan planting a big wet one on a surprised-looking Jordan became an instant classic when it appeared in the yearbook on the "Most Memorable Couples" page.

"Hey, didn't we go to school together?" I say to him now, a big, fake smile on my face.

"Yeah, come to think of it, you look kinda familiar." He gives me a funny look, like maybe he suspects I was behind his most humiliating moment in high school. Or maybe it's because of what happened with Spence Breedlove later on that year when I was the talk of our junior class. "*Her* I remember." Her jerks his head toward my best friend. How could he not? Ivy was a standout then as she is now: a Scarlett O'Hara doll from Franklin Mint with the soul of a rocker chick who liked it loud and fast, whether it was partying, cars, or boys. "Didn't you two used to hang out?"

I nod and stick out my hand. "Tish Ballard." My full name is Leticia, but everyone calls me Tish. (My parents, in naming me after my grandmother—thus dooming me to a lifetime of grief, from teasing in school to being hounded by telemarketers who've mistaken me for an old lady these days—at least knew better than to compound their error with the nickname Letty.) I drop my gaze to his ring finger as we shake hands. "You're married, I see. Good for you. Commitment ceremony or did you make it legal?" I also make a point of mentioning I voted for Proposition Eight.

He flushes bright red at the implication. "I'm not *gay*," he chokes out after he's regained the ability to speak. "I'm married to Teresa. Teresa Winkler." He names another former classmate of ours; they were a couple senior year—it's coming back to me now. "We have three kids," he adds, lest there be any doubt about his virility, deepening his voice and puffing out his chest.

"Oh. I see. I just assumed . . ."

Ivy flashes me a grin behind his back. She looks like a demented revolutionary dressed in a ruffled pink skirt, flip-flops with big sparkly daisies on them, and a black Che Guevara T-shirt. Heaps of silver necklaces and bracelets, from her jewelry-making phase, adorn her slender wrists and throat.

Not until they're headed out does Officer Ruiz break rank. She slows her steps to let Jordan get ahead of her, then pauses to murmur to Ivy, "Don't mind him. I love your . . . whatever they are. They're beautiful." She studies the diorama of grasshoppers sipping tea from miniature cups around a "wrought-iron" table fashioned from wires. "Strange but beautiful."

Parker Lane blows in minutes later, dapper as ever in a Colonel Sanders suit and striped pink shirt, his thick, wavy mane, the yellowing ivory of old piano keys, blown about as if he dashed here on foot. He hugs Ivy so hard you'd have thought she was the victim of a mugging. "Are you all right? Did he hurt you?" Parker was born and raised in Huntsville, Alabama, his accent so pronounced his mellifluous baritone, if it were a tree, would be dripping with Spanish moss.

Ivy makes light of it, to spare him further grief. "Who, the cop or the robber? Don't worry," she assures him. "I wasn't held at gunpoint. And my virtue is still intact. Mostly," she adds with a wicked grin.

We leave him to flutter around the shop like an agitated magpie putting its disturbed nest to rights, and head out to grab a bite to eat for lunch. You'd never guess, from the way Parker carries on, that he doesn't depend on his income from the Gilded Lily. In fact he's independently wealthy and lives with his partner of fifty-odd years, Desmond, in a spectacular oceanfront home that has every realtor in town salivating, awaiting the day when one or both of them dies off and it goes on the market. Before I traded my dress shoes for sneakers and went into business for myself, I think I was the only real estate broker in town who didn't covet the listing. I could never want someone else's loss to be my gain. I know what it is to experience a devastating loss—when I was eleven, my mom ran off with her lover, never to be seen or heard from again—and it's not something I'd wish on my worst enemy. It left me damaged. It made me who I am today: a person you wouldn't have wanted to encounter after I'd had too many vodka martinis. There's something inside of me that, when let loose, can be like that one kid at a birthday party who ruins it for everyone. Drunk, I was a human wrecking ball. Sober, I'm nicer but never more than one step from blowing it, for myself or someone else, with a mouthy remark or raised middle finger. I don't take well to being told what to do and I don't bow to authority figures.

"I'm starved," Ivy announces as we make our way up the street to the Bluejay Café, where it's the tail end of the lunch hour.

"Nothing like a police incident for working up an appetite," I tease. The truth is, she's always starved. I read that on average a bird consumes half its weight in food per day; if that's true then it's fair to say Ivy eats like a bird. Where she puts it is anyone's guess—she's a size zero petite and living proof that life isn't fair. At five feet, nine inches and a hundred fifty pounds, I'm the opposite of dainty and have the metabolism of a three-toed sloth. It's a constant battle to keep my weight in check. Fortunately I have a job that keeps me perpetually on the move.

I'm proprietor and sole employee of Rest Easy Property Management, the business I launched three and a half years ago, after I flamed out as a broker in a blaze of ingloriousness. I look after other people's vacation homes. I see to upkeep and repairs. I supervise domestics and maintenance people. I make sure the homes that double as vacation rentals don't get trashed by college kids on spring break. I'm also the soul of discretion. If you're cheating on your spouse, your secret is safe with me. I'll even go the extra mile, like when I replaced the previously unopened box of tampons in the master bath at the Stones' after Mr. Stone's romantic tryst with his mistress. Who but me would have thought to do so? It comes from being no stranger to secrets myself.

"In a weird way it's a compliment." Ivy waxes philosophic over lunch. "I mean the guy must really have wanted it. I don't imagine there's much of a black market for stolen insect dioramas."

"Whatever, it still pisses me off that he's getting away with it." Many hours of painstaking work go into each of Ivy's pieces. It's not fair she should be out the commission.

"Yeah, well, what can you do?" She sighs in resignation. "It's not like the cops are going to put out an APB. They won't lift a finger. Especially not after you insulted Jordan's manhood. Totally worth it, by the way," she adds with a giggle. "The look on his face? Oh my God, *priceless*."

I shrug. "Nothing wrong with being gay."

"Tell *him* that."

Our waitress arrives with the sandwiches we ordered—the turkey club for Ivy, avocado-and-hummus on whole-wheat for me. (I'm doing penance for the party leftovers—an assortment of finger sandwiches, crab puffs, bite-sized mushroom quiches, and petit fours—I was given by clients of mine, the Willetts.) The dense fog of morning has burned off, giving way to sunny skies that has every outdoor table at the Bluejay filled. Housed in what was once a cottage—the orphan child of the Painted Ladies that line the block—it's a favorite of locals and tourists alike, always packed even during non-peak hours. We were lucky to snag a table on the patio, under the grape arbor that forms a leafy canopy at one end. I bask in the warmth from the dappled sunlight.

Mark Twain is quoted as having once said the coldest winter he ever knew was the summer he spent in San Francisco. The same could be said of Cypress Bay, a two-hour drive down the coast. This time of year the fog rolls in every morning like the tide, usually not burning off until midday. When I left my house at 6:30 a.m. to go to work, it was chilly and gray. Now it's warm enough for me to have peeled off the sweatshirt and Henley shirt I'd been wearing over my tank top.

"How was the meeting last night?" Ivy changes the subject. She means the AA meeting I attended. When I was newly sober, I used to go to one a day, but nowadays I go to one a week. That I felt the need for more than my regular Thursday night meeting this week is clearly cause for concern. I could tell from her overly casual tone.

"Good." I don't elaborate. What goes on in the "rooms" stays in the rooms. Ivy is well aware of this; that's not why she was asking. She's worried I'll fall off the wagon.

"You didn't return my call."

I extract a clump of sprouts from my sandwich before taking a bite. You'd think Cypress Bay was the birthplace of the alfalfa sprout from its prevalence in these parts—it's the kudzu of crunchy land. I'd be happy if I never saw another sprout. "Yeah, it was too late by the time I got your message."

"I thought the meeting got out at nine."

"I went out afterwards with some friends," I lie.

"Really. Is that why all the lights were on at your house?"

I narrow my eyes at her. "What, so now you're spying on me?"

"I was checking up on you. That's not the same as spying. I was worried, okay? I thought something had happened to you." I can't say I blame her, after what I put her through during my Lost Weekend years. She was the first person to whom I made amends after I got sober.

"I'm perfectly fine as you can see." I spread my arms to show I have nothing to hide—as in no bruises from having fallen down while in a drunken stupor, no bandages from having slit my wrists.

Ivy says nothing.

I munch on my sandwich as if I hadn't a care in the world, swallowing what's in my mouth before delivering another whopper. "Today is just another day as far as I'm concerned."

She returns her sandwich to her plate and pushes her aviator sunglasses onto her head to look me in the eye. "It's no use, Tish. I've known you since we were in sixth grade. You can't fool me."

I shrug. "It's been twenty-five years. Believe me, I'm over it."

"No, you're not," she insists. "You're only saying that so I'll shut up. But this isn't one of those fake-it-till-you-make-it things." I hate it when she does that, quotes AA scripture she learned from me.

"What do you want from me? Do you expect me to moan and wail?"

"No, but you could mark the occasion—you know, to get closure. Have some sort of ceremony."

"What, you mean like scatter her ashes? Visit her grave?" An edge creeps into my voice. "My mom isn't dead, Ivy. She ran out on us."

She ignores my biting tone. "Tish, it's time. You'll never get past it if you don't deal with it."

"I've dealt with it plenty, trust me."

"Oh, really. Is that why you're glaring at me like I just confessed I slept with your boyfriend?"

"You don't even like Daniel," I remind her, seizing the chance to change the subject. I take a sip of my Perrier, wishing it was a gin and tonic. I haven't touched a drop in three and a half years, but right now it feels like the first thirty days when every hour of every day was an uphill battle.

"I never said I didn't like him," she corrects me. "All I said was I didn't think he was right for you."

"Like you're such an expert. You've never been in a relationship that lasted longer than the milk cartons in your fridge."

"It's no use trying to pick a fight," she replies with maddening calm. She does know me too well—that much is true. "We're not talking about me. Or men. We're talking about *you*."

I give a sigh of surrender. "All right, I admit it's been on my mind. But I'm not doing some stupid ceremony." Why bother when each year the anniversary of my mother's defection is marked by the black cloud that descends on me? "Even if I saw the point, it's not just me—there's Arthur to consider. You know how he gets." My brother is unpredictable to say the least.

"She's his mom, too." I'm grateful for her use of the present tense. It's easy to imagine the worst when you haven't heard from someone in twenty-five years. "He might want to say his own good-byes."

"He talks to her all the time." Along with the other voices in his head.

"It doesn't have to be a huge deal. Light a candle, say a prayer."

"I stopped going to church when I was twelve." I guess Dad didn't see the point after Mom went away. God didn't want to be his friend? Fine, he wasn't going to play over at God's house.

"Say a prayer to your Higher Power, then."

I only pray to my Higher Power for the strength to resist temptation, but no point getting into that. I reply grudgingly, "I'll think about it." We go back to eating our sandwiches—or rather, Ivy eats while I pick. "I didn't have it so bad, you know," I point out, as if in saying it, I can make it so. "Dad did the best he could." Never mind it was what the Big Book of AA calls "half measures." As in *Half measures availed us nothing.* The truth is, my brother and I would have been better off if we'd gone to live with our grandparents. "Lots of kids had it way worse."

"Yeah, I know. Macaulay Culkin and the poor kids in Africa."

"Funny you should mention Africa." Ivy's mom is a doctor who gave up her private practice some years ago to start a free clinic in a remote village in Malawi, leaving then twelve-year-old Ivy in the care of her dad and grandmother. Ivy sees her only once or twice a year, when she visits Malawi or on the rare occasion when Dr. Ladeaux can fly home between cholera outbreaks and dengue fever epidemics.

If my intention was to point out that Ivy might have abandonment issues of her own, I'm not getting any traction. "At least I always knew where my mom was," she says with a sanguine shrug. She isn't being cruel, just stating a fact, but I feel a dull throb nonetheless. "Okay, so mine cared more about her boyfriend than about us. That doesn't make her Mommie Dearest."

"No," she agrees, adding gently, "but you don't have to be beaten with a coat hanger to have scars."

I have nothing to say to that; I can only swallow against the lump in my throat.

The last time I saw my mother was when she was waving good-bye as I ran to catch the school bus that day. She was dressed for work, in a yellow wraparound dress with poppies on it that matched her bright red lipstick and red slingback heels: an outfit more appropriate for a pool party than place of employment. Her blond hair was in a French braid, curly tendrils trailing around her heart-shaped face. From a distance she looked like Marilyn Monroe. I was at an age when my friends were embarrassed by their parents, but I never felt that way about my mom. I was proud of her. Proud to be her daughter, even though I felt I could never measure up. I had been told I was pretty, but I wasn't beautiful like her. My hair was dirty-blond rather than golden; my flat chest and boyish hips showed no hint of coming attractions the likes of which she boasted. The only thing I got from her was my eyes: gray-green and thick-lashed. (My boyfriend, Daniel, once said gazing into them was like gazing into a tide pool, which was a compliment coming from him: He's an associate professor of marine biology.)

I had noticed at breakfast she seemed preoccupied, as if something were weighing on her, but I didn't think too much of it. My parents hadn't been getting along, so I chalked it up to another argument with Dad. When I arrived home from school later that day, she was gone, along with her suitcase. She'd left a note saying she had to go away for a little while, but she'd be back for Arthur and me as soon as she could. *Don't worry. Everything will be okay. Love, Mom.* I didn't know then about her lover, whom she'd met at work—Stan was on the construction crew building the new wing at the Fontana Spa and Wellness Center, where my mom ran the gift shop. I didn't find out until much later when a kid in my class, Cam Pressley, called my mom a whore. After I was sent to the principal's office for slugging Cam with my backpack hard enough to give him a bloody nose, my dad had to come pick me up. I asked him about Mom on the way home. He was careful not to lay blame, saying only that she had found someone else who made her happier than he could. To his credit, he never once said a bad thing about her. Whatever he might have felt or thought, he took those feelings to his grave.

My mother was far from perfect. She drank too much and flirted with other men. She was always buying stuff my parents couldn't afford and she'd pout when Dad made her return it. She was famous for starting and abandoning projects. When I finally got around to clearing out the basement of our old house after Dad died, I found boxes with half-completed scrapbooks; squares for a quilt that was never stitched; fabric from bolts, folded but not cut, and dress patterns never opened; recipe books with page after page of bookmarked recipes she'd never gotten around to trying. Yet she could light up a room just walking into it. She had a laugh so infectious random passersby on the street would often pause and smile at hearing it. She was generous in her affections, too, always pulling me or Arthur into a hug and snuggling up next to us on the bed before tucking us in at night. That's what made it so hard to believe she would abandon us. For years I clung to the hope that, if we hadn't heard from her, it was due to circumstances beyond her control: amnesia from a blow to the head, or that she was being held prisoner by Stan, who'd turned out to be a bad guy. It was a long time before I had reason to doubt her love.

Ten years ago, I got a postcard from a cheesy theme park in Florida. On the front was a photo of a burly guy wrestling an alligator. On the back was a brief message that read "Sorry for everything." It was signed "Stan Cruikshank." It was only then I had learned Stan's name. A subsequent Google search turned up nothing but a couple of misdemeanor arrests, one for driving with a suspended license, the other for assault and battery. But it dispelled the notion that my mom was being held prisoner or that she had amnesia. Or that she was dead—if he felt bad enough to contact me, surely he would have informed me. Which left the inescapable conclusion: She'd abandoned us. Maybe it was out of shame that she hadn't contacted us. Maybe her drinking had gotten out of control, like mine was starting to. Whatever the reason, it hurt all the same.

To this day I can't think about it without feeling as if I've had the air knocked out of my lungs. Lighting a candle or saying a prayer wasn't going to change a damn thing. I stare down at the sandwich on my plate, oozing hummus and bristling with sprouts. Suddenly I want to throw up.

I must look a little green, because Ivy takes pity on me. She steers the conversation onto other topics. We talk about her show at the Headwinds Gallery in two weeks' time, for which she's been frantically preparing. I tell her about my fun morning getting sprayed with woodchips at the Caswells'—the tree-trimmer I hired to limb their trees wielded his chainsaw as if it were a six-shooter and he a Wild West gunslinger—and then fishing a dead possum out of the swimming pool at the Russos.' Finally I get around to dishing the latest on the Trousdale divorce.

Douglas and Joan Trousdale are the wealthiest of my clients by a couple of zeros. Douglas is CEO of Trousdale Realty, where I worked as a broker; it's easily the most successful realty in town, judging by the signs with his grinning mug marking every other property for sale in these parts. He also owns the Fontana Spa and Wellness Center, where my mom worked, which he inherited from his father when the old man died ten years ago, and which is now world renowned due to his promotional efforts, with franchises in several other locations—Palm Springs, La Jolla, and Las Vegas. Joan is a prominent socialite and on the board of several charities.

They own three homes: their primary residence in the tony San Francisco neighborhood of Pacific Heights, where Joan now lives alone; the condo in Pacifica, where Douglas is currently shacked up with his twenty-five-year-old mistress; and the oceanfront estate in La Mar that I manage. The latter sits on ten acres and boasts an Olympic-sized swimming pool, tennis court, and not one but two guesthouses, one of which my boyfriend Daniel occupies rent-free in exchange for maintaining the grounds. (His meager salary as a tenure track assistant professor at the university wouldn't cover his living expenses otherwise). Meanwhile, Douglas and Joan are so busy fighting over who gets what and when each should have use of it—in a divorce so epic it makes all others seem like minor squabbles in comparison—the La Mar house sits empty for the most part. Not for much longer, however; their son Bradley is due to arrive soon for an extended stay.

I have yet to meet the man. All I know about him is that he's a combat cameraman for CNN based in the Middle East—and an only child, the apple of his mother's eye. He's flying in tomorrow from New York, after three months in Afghanistan. One of the items on my to-do list for today is to ready the house for his arrival.

"Who cares if he's stuck up? He's hot," says Ivy after I've expressed my low expectations regarding the only son of billionaires. A while back, I made the mistake of mentioning he was good-looking, which I know from the photos of him scattered throughout the house.

"What's that got to do with it?"

"Everything. But if you two fall in love, it'll be kind of awkward with him and Daniel living on the same property. Then I guess he'll have to find another place to live. Daniel, I mean."

I frown at her. "Seriously, what has he ever done to make you dislike him?"

"Nothing. And I repeat, I don't dislike him." She retrieves a piece of bacon that's fallen out of her sandwich and pops it in her mouth. "He's a perfectly nice guy. He's also intelligent and kind-hearted and environmentally conscious. But face it, Tish, you're not in love with him. And he's not in love with you."

"How can you say that? We have a very loving relationship."

"You have a loving relationship with your cat. I should hope you want more from your boyfriend than to have him curl up next to you."

"Nothing wrong with that. When you've been together as long as we have—" going on two years now— "you don't go from zero to sixty in a heartbeat. You take it slow."

She scoffs at this. "I have two words for you: rug burns."

I roll my eyes. "Jesus. What is it with you?" The bedroom was an amusement park, in Ivy's view, and anything less than Six Flags-worthy was beneath consideration. "No, I don't get rug burns with Daniel, but—"

"Enough said."

I sigh. It's no use arguing with Ivy. She has no idea what it is to be in a long-term relationship. She's seldom without a boyfriend, but she checks out as soon as he lets her know he wants more than sex and companionship. She always says she's perfectly content with her life as it is. She has me and her other friends, a career she loves, and the rambling Victorian a half mile from my house she calls home. Personally I think her problem with men is related to the abandonment issues she won't admit to. On the other hand, maybe she just hasn't met the right guy.

Not until after lunch, as we're headed back to work, do I remember what else is on my to-do list. The other day I heard from a man named Tom McGee, the manager of the White Oaks self-storage facility out on Old County Road, who informed me he'd been instructed to release the contents of one of the units to me. It was all very mysterious. He didn't have the name of the lessee, just the entity listed on the contract: Starfish Enterprises.

At first I couldn't think who my mystery benefactor might be, but I've since come to suspect it's a former neighbor of mine, old Mrs. Appleby, who died a couple of months ago. She used to say I was more of a daughter to her than her own daughter because I took her grocery shopping or to the drugstore to get her prescriptions filled, that kind of thing. Her own daughter rarely visited and only when she needed money. Probably this was Mrs. Appleby's way of ensuring Ms. Greedy Graspy didn't get it all. I can't imagine what she might have left me, though, since she was far from rich. Some old furnishings or a set of china? A painting she thought was valuable? I'll know soon enough. I'm scheduled to meet with Mr. McGee later this afternoon for the big "reveal." I'm not optimistic.

"It's probably just a pile of junk," I speculate aloud to Ivy.

We're strolling along the pedestrian mall at the heart of the business district, a street lined with stucco storefronts painted in beach-umbrella shades and adorned with decorative wrought-iron and terra-cotta planters from which bright blooms spill. We pass a homeless man begging outside the Hang Ten Surf Shop. He looks sporty if unkempt in banana-yellow board shorts and blue-tinted Oakleys. I toss a quarter in his cup and he glances up from the battered paperback he's reading to smile at me from his recumbent position on the sidewalk where he sits with his legs outstretched, reclining against his backpack. I only wish I were as content as he appears to be.

Ivy smiles and says, "You know what they say. One man's junk . . ."

". . . is another man's treasure," I finish for her. "We'll see. Just don't expect a lost Rembrandt."

I spend the next hour at the Noels' vacation rental readying it for the paying guests due to arrive later in the day. One of my nicer properties, its desirable location overlooking one of the prettiest beaches in Cypress Bay, has it much in demand. So far I've been lucky with renters. No broken dishes, no towels or linens that "mysteriously" go missing. No overflowing toilet not reported in a timely fashion, or carpet stains resulting from someone having ignored the no-pet policy. (Believe me, I've seen it all in my line of work.)

I open windows to let in fresh air. I arrange the cut flowers I picked up at Trader Joe's in vases and distribute them throughout the house. Finally I see to the small details that escaped the cleaning lady's attention: I change a light bulb that was burned out, clean out the lint trap in the clothes dryer, and replace the used soap bars in the bathrooms. The house is as welcoming as a smile and a handshake by the time I leave. I pause to gaze out the picture window in the living room on my way out. The beach spread out below, dotted with sunbathers and their colorful accouterment, looks like a giant sheet cake from this distance. Gentle waves roll in to lick the shore.

I lock up and head back to my trusty green Ford Explorer, which I bought new with the commission from my first home sale. I climb in and start the engine. Two more stops before I have to be at the White Oaks self-storage facility. I can swing by the Trousdales' after I'm done there; it's on my way home.

By four o'clock I'm winding my way along Old County Road, in the wooded hills above Cypress Bay. The breeze blowing in my open window brings the sharp menthol scent of the tall, shaggy-barked eucalyptus trees that line the road on either side. I love the peace and quiet out here, away from the bustle of the more touristy areas: the beaches; the Boardwalk that dates back to the 1920s and municipal pier with its souvenir shops and fish shacks; the marine center with its aquarium; and popular surfing and sightseeing spots. During the cold-weather months Cypress Bay is home to a population of roughly thirty thousand, but from late spring through early fall that number triples with the tourists who flock to our fair shores. Traffic along the main thoroughfares slows to a crawl and you'll have an easier time scoring ganga from one of our local pot dealers than finding a parking space. At my favorite coffee shop, Higher Ground, that's normally grab and go, it's not unusual to have to wait in line for fifteen minutes. Normally I don't mind the inconvenience, because I never lose sight of the fact that tourism is the lifeblood of this town and small business owners like myself; it's the tourists themselves I find objectionable. The majority are law-abiding and respectful, but there are those who light fires on public lands in defiance of local ordinances, who don't clean up after their dogs, who use our garden hoses without permission to wash the sand from their bodies after a day at the beach, and who block our driveways with their illegally parked vehicles. And that's when they're behaving themselves.

I wonder again about my mysterious bequest and feel a flutter of anticipation. I could certainly use the extra cash if it's anything of value. The renovations on my Craftsman bungalow wiped out the bulk of my savings, and the last vet bill for my tom after he got torn up in a fight with another cat took most of what was left.

A few minutes later I'm turning through the gated entrance of the White Oaks self-storage facility—which consists of prefab metal units set in rows on a slope like risers on a staircase and a two-story gray cinderblock building that houses an office and what looks to be living quarters above—where I find Ivy waiting. I brake to a stop in front of the office, next to where her orange VW Bug, aka the Pumpkin—an ironic take on Cinderella's coach—is parked.

"It doesn't look too promising," I remark, looking around me.

"Just remember. A lost Rembrandt wouldn't stay lost if it was somewhere obvious," she says.

Inside we find a man tapping away at a desktop computer as ancient-looking as the office's sparse furnishings. "You're late," he says in a gravelly voice without looking up. He speaks with a pronounced New York accent that matches the Yankees jersey he has on. Clearly he's not from around here. Nor does he appear to have a pressing appointment I'm keeping him from.

I glance at my watch. "Five minutes. But I didn't think it was a big—"

"Come with me." He stands up and grabs a key from the wooden pegboard above the desk. We're out the door before he bothers to introduce himself. "Tom McGee." A calloused hand wraps around mine, then he's plowing ahead of me. I have to practically run to catch up to him.

As he leads the way to my unit in the uppermost row, I find myself studying McGee surreptitiously. He reminds me of guys you see in AA meetings, scruffy and unshaven with puffy eyes, though from the odor of stale beer that wafts toward me it's obvious he's not in the program. He looks to be in his mid-forties, with a gaunt face and dark brown hair slicked back in a ponytail that more closely resembles a rat's tail. The only thing about him that isn't dull or worn-looking is his eyes: they're as black and sharp as a raptor's. A corner of his thin-lipped mouth hooks up in a half-smile as he hands me the key to the padlock when we finally arrive at my unit.

"Have at it. But don't blame me if there's a dead body in there." He has a sense of humor at least.

My first thought as I peer into the darkened interior is that this has to be somebody's idea of a joke. Because at first glance the unit appears to be empty. Only when my eyes adjust do I spot the footlocker in the shadowy recesses at one end.

"Well, what do you know," Ivy comments dryly. "I always wondered what happened to D. B. Cooper's loot."

I move in to get a closer look. The footlocker is army-issue and coated with at least three inches of dust. I stare at it without moving. It's not padlocked, but it might as well be. For some reason I'm hesitant to open it. I begin to shiver, feeling chilled to the bone; I could be standing in a meat locker. I was so busy guarding against false hope, it didn't occur to me I might be in for a nasty surprise. I pissed off a lot of people during my drinking days, and I haven't gotten around to making amends to all of them. What if one of them is harboring a grudge and this is their way of getting back at me? When I finally turn the key that's in the lock and lift the lid with a haunted-house groan of rusted hinges, I'm relieved when a rattlesnake doesn't jump out at me. Instead I'm met with something bulky wrapped in a filthy, blue, plastic tarp bound with nylon rope. The unpleasant odor that wafts my way tells me it hasn't seen the light of day in some time. McGee assists me in pulling the bundle onto the concrete floor. He uses the box cutter he produced from his back pocket to cut the rope. I peel back the layers of tarp to reveal what it holds.

Then I start to scream.

CHAPTER TWO

The remains are clearly human: a grinning skull with matted hair, a skeleton curled in a fetal position. A half-crumbled bouquet of roses is the final grisly touch. The world goes black at the edges and my knees buckle. I'm distantly aware of arms catching me before the blackness closes over me.

When I regain consciousness, I'm lying on the ground looking up at blue sky. Two faces hover over me, one gaunt and whiskery, the other pale, framed with a riot of black curls. Ivy and McGee are peering down at me like a pair of concerned parents at a child who'd fallen down and bumped her head. I struggle into an upright position, dry-mouthed, head swimming. I'm sitting on the strip of stubbly grass that borders the row of units. Ivy helps me up. Every ounce of my being wants to run away. Instead I stagger back to my gruesome find. I need to know if it's what I think it is.

"Fuck me," mutters McGee as I shine my phone's flashlight over what appears to have been an adult female, judging from what's left of her clothing.

"Tish, is that—?" Ivy's voice penetrates the buzzing in my ears.

"Yeah." I nod, a sharp jerk of my head. The rotted fabric that forms her shroud, once-yellow, now a dull ochre, printed with poppies, confirms my suspicion: The woman whose remains I'm looking at are those of my mother. She was wearing that dress the last time I saw her. I gulp hard against my rising gorge. "I think I need to sit down," I hear myself say in a shaky voice.

"Would one of you ladies mind telling me what the fuck is going on?" barks McGee after Ivy has phoned 911 and I'm once more seated on the grass, gulping in fresh air to combat my spinning head. I turn to look up at him, an action that seems to take place in slow motion underwater.

I can't speak. Ivy answers instead.

She didn't run out on us. All this time she was dead. Moldering away.

Next thing I know, I'm tossing my cookies onto the grass. "Tish . . ." At the sound of Ivy's voice I look up to find her squatting beside me and holding out a handkerchief, from McGee's pocket. The faint odor of cigarettes invades my nostrils when I use it to wipe my mouth.

I'm feeling a little less shaky by the time the cops get there. Though it doesn't help matters that the first responders are none other than officers James and Ruiz. "Anything you want to tell us?" asks a narrow-eyed Jordan as he stands before me working a wad of gum.

"Like what? That someone with a sick sense of humor played a practical joke on me? I should think that would be pretty obvious," I snap.

"It's just," he pauses to give his jaws a rest, long enough for me to get a good look at the grayish wad protruding from his molars, "I gotta say, it doesn't look good. Two crime scenes in one day?" Either he's especially dense or he gets off on making other people suffer. My guess is the latter.

"Show some respect," Ivy snarls. "That's her mom." She gestures toward the yellow crime scene tape strung across the open door to the unit. The ME and CSI team have arrived and are busy photographing and combing the scene for forensic evidence.

It was clearly the wrong thing to say. Jordan shifts his gaze from

Ivy to me, his eyes narrowing further until they're little more than slits in his pitted face. "And you know this because . . . ?"

Before I can reply, a deep male voice interrupts. "Tish. Got a minute?"

I turn around slowly to find myself face-to-face with another unwelcome blast from my past, in the form of one Spence Breedlove. My former nemesis, one-time crush, destroyer of my reputation in high school, and now, the lead detective on this case. "Sure," I say as though to a stranger who'd stopped me on the sidewalk to ask directions. Defense mechanisms are a wonderful thing.

Too bad they have a short battery life. "Listen, I know how it must look, but it's not what you think," I find myself babbling a minute later. "I didn't know she was in there. I didn't even know she was dead! Ask him. He'll tell you." I gesture wildly toward McGee, who takes a step back and throws his hands up.

"Don't look at me," he says with his Brooklyn accent that makes him sound like Joe Pesci in *My Cousin Vinny*. "I don't know nothing about it." He explains how it all went down, in clear, concise language that tells me there's more to this guy than meets the eye. Then it's my turn to speak.

"Do I need a lawyer?"

"I don't know. You tell me," Spence answers mildly, his eyes boring into me.

Spence Breedlove towers over me at six foot four, which I know to be his height because, when he was star linebacker for the Harbor High Sea Lions, his stats were well documented. The school paper, *The Harbor Mouth*, reported his every triumph in minute detail (it speaks volumes that I have a better recollection of the winning touchdown he scored in the season playoff than I do of the drunken encounter that led to my deflowering that same year) complete with photo coverage. He was our very own Tom Brady. I see that same face, a bit older but no less handsome, looking at me now: square jaw, cleft chin, hair worn shorter than in high school, so thick it's like blond turf. Only his eye color is different, a blue not found in nature or his yearbook photo—he's wearing tinted contacts. Ugh. I wonder if the personal vehicle he drives has vanity plates.

This, I reflect, is the downside to living your whole life in the same community: Former classmates, whom you would go out of your way to avoid if you were sharing a jail cell with them, have a way of resurfacing like turds in a toilet bowl. The jerky boyfriend you dumped is today's bank manager with the paperwork for your home loan on his desk. The mean girl who took pleasure in humiliating you for four years straight is the maid of honor at your coworker's wedding. And the campus stud who lured you upstairs with him while you were drunk at Stacey Schwabacher's sweet sixteen? He's the detective in charge of investigating your mother's murder.

"I have nothing to hide," I declare, tilting my chin up at him.

"Good. Then how about we continue this conversation down at the station," he suggests in a voice that tells me I have little choice in the matter. I take a jab at him even so.

"Gee, I don't know. My dance card is kind of full at the moment."

He looks taken aback by my sarcasm, then he smiles and spreads his hands in a conciliatory gesture. Hands as big and manly as the rest of him, sporting a sprinkling of hairs the gold of the wedding band on his ring finger. I feel my cheeks warm, thinking about the places they went on my body twenty years ago. "I'm asking nicely." He speaks in a low voice. "Let's not make this personal."

"Too late," I retort sharply. A few minutes ago, he arrived on the scene without so much as acknowledging my presence. He walked right by me, not saying a word. What was up with *that*?

His eyebrows draw together in a frown. "Look, I'm not the enemy. I'm just doing my job."

"Really? Do you always show such compassion to bereaved family members or is it just me?"

"Tish. Come on now." I detect a vein of iron ore running through his reasoning tone. "I understand this has been a shock, but I'm sure you're just as eager to get to the bottom of this as I am."

We stare at each other for a beat or two. I'm the first to break eye contact. This is silly. We're not in high school anymore. And yes, I do want to get to the bottom of this. I blow out a breath, relaxing my stance. "Fine."

Ivy steps up alongside me, intervening. "Can't it wait? She's in shock."

"Yes, I can see that." He studies me, and I feel myself grow self-conscious under his gaze. I must look much the same as I did after the regrettable experience of that night I wish I could forget: pale and clammy, my dirty-blond hair hanging in strings around my face, the front of my shirt stained with vomit. "But it'd be best if we went over it while it's still fresh in your mind," he says to me.

"You call that fresh?" I gesticulate wildly in the direction of the two crime scene guys who're carrying out the body-bagged grisly cargo on a stretcher.

His voice is the calm eye of the hurricane howling inside me. "If this was foul play, any information you could provide would be useful."

"*If* it was foul play?" I stare at him in disbelief. "Is there any doubt?"

"He's a cop," McGee supplies with a shrug.

I give a nod of acquiescence, blinking back tears. Spence and I head downhill toward our respective vehicles, Ivy and McGee trailing behind. The years have not been unkind to Spence Breedlove, I observe dispassionately as I trudge alongside him. If anything, he's gotten better looking with age. He's still buff with a set of guns more impressive than what's in his holster. His blond hair, which he used to wear chin-length, is cut short but not too short, and any remnants of baby fat he had as a teenager have been stripped away, leaving a face that's all hard planes and angles. The one discordant note is the tinted contacts. There are a lot of not-nice things I could say about Spence, but I wouldn't have labeled him vain. In high school he wore his mantle of glory with the easy grace of a prince born to the throne. Speaking of which, those unnaturally blue eyes are also an uncomfortable reminder of the many nights I'd spent hugging the porcelain throne, staring into toilet water tinted the same chemical shade, before I cleaned up my act.

I'm also reminded that he's not my friend. He betrayed me once before. How do I know he won't do so again?

The police station is located in the large and unlovely municipal building on Center Street that also houses the courthouse, county jail, and DA's offices. A gray concrete cube of a structure that stands three stories high, it has all the curb appeal of a Soviet-bloc government building from the Cold War era. I'm escorted to a cramped and windowless space with walls painted a shade of green reminiscent of a sputum sample. Its only furnishings are a metal table and two chairs, bolted to the floor. I sit down in one of the chairs. Spence sits down opposite me. I gesture toward the tape recorder on the table. "Is that really necessary?"

"Standard procedure," he explains. "Nothing to worry about."

I narrow my eyes at him. "How do I know you won't use it against me?"

"Let's not get ahead of ourselves. I'll ask the questions, you answer, and we'll see where we're at."

I settle back in my chair. "How do I know you won't make me look bad?"

"Why would I do that?"

"It wouldn't be the first time."

His expression hardens. "I thought we weren't going to make this personal."

"You started it." I cringe inwardly at my childish tone. *Grow up*, I tell myself. The trouble is, I'm not feeling very mature right now.

He stares at me unflinchingly. "Do you really want to go there, Tish?"

"You should ask yourself the same question."

"Fine. Let's talk about it, then," he says, a note of anger creeping in his voice. "Tell me what the hell you're so pissed about. *I'm* the one who should be pissed."

"Aha!" I jab my index finger in his direction. "I knew it. You're still mad that I torched your car." I speak of the 1972 maroon Camaro that was his pride and joy in high school and that I set fire to in retaliation for his having trashed my reputation. Not my finest hour, I admit.

He folds his arms over his chest in a gesture that has his bulging arm muscles straining the shoulder seams of his navy sports coat. He stares at me stonily, his Tidy-Bowl blue eyes flashing. "I *was* mad, yes. At the time. But I'm over it," he says in a tone of voice that suggests otherwise. "Though you *do* owe me an apology. Isn't that one of the steps in AA? Making amends."

I feel a rush of heat to my face. It's a wonder my hair doesn't catch fire, it's so intense. My voice is pure ice, in contrast. "I'm not going to ask how you know I'm in AA, because I'd have to kill whoever told you and then you really would have something on me."

"So that's how it is, huh? You're playing the injured party?"

"It's not an act." I haven't given much thought to this stuff in years, but my gruesome discovery, it seems, has caused it to resurface like the gunk I fished from a clogged drain earlier in the day.

"I'm sorry you feel that way. My memory of our . . . whatever you want to call it . . . is different. I remember it as consensual. So if that's what you're pissed about, I still don't get it."

I snort. "You think I'm mad about *that*? I hate to break it to you, but it wasn't all that memorable. "

Red stripes form along the ridges of his cheekbones. "Then what is it, huh? What did I ever do to you?"

"Like you don't know." The last semester of my junior year had been a living hell. Everywhere I went I'd had classmates whispering and snickering. School was a Roman amphitheater into which I'd been tossed, only it wasn't just one lion out to maul me, it was dozens. There the lies and taunts; the nasty things written about me on blackboards and bathroom walls; the condoms stuffed in my locker. It was rumored I'd had sex with half the players on the football team, not just its star linebacker. All because of Spence. "You trashed my reputation!"

"Seemed to me you were doing a pretty good job of that all by yourself."

Fury boils up inside me. "Right. Like I went around telling everyone I was a slut. Fuck you."

He looks confused. No doubt it's genuine—after all, I'd been only one of his many conquests; how could he be expected to keep them all straight much less recall his every callow act? "I meant that everyone knew about your drinking. What did you think I meant?" Before I can answer, the door opens and the pretty, dark-haired Officer Ruiz enters carrying a steaming Styrofoam cup. She places it on the table in front of me and I inhale the fragrance of hot coffee.

"On the house," she says with a smile.

I almost burst into tears at the small kindness.

Spence gets down to business after that. He punches a button on the tape recorder and states the time and date and both our names for the record before proceeding with the interview. I'm thrown for a loop with his first question. He asks the name of my mother's dentist. "So we can confirm the identity of the victim."

"I told you already. It—she's my mother." I swallow hard. "*Was,* I mean."

He nods and only then do I see a flicker of compassion. "It's not that I doubt you, but we still need her dental records to make it official." I give him the name of our family dentist, Dr. Hanson.

What follows is a blur of questions. I struggle to answer as best I can in my shell-shocked state. I dredge up memories I'd spent the past twenty-five years trying to forget.

"What can you tell me about him?" Spence asks when I get to the part about Stan.

"Nothing other than what I just told you. I didn't even know his last name until I got that postcard."

"When was that?"

"I don't recall the exact date, but it's on the postmark."

"You saved it?" His gaze sharpens.

I nod. "I'll look for it when I get home." I'd tucked it in one of my drawers.

"I'll have one of my men stop by later on."

"There's no ne—" I start to say before I note the expression on his face. Clearly it's not optional.

"You're certain of what he wrote?"

"Yeah. Just those three words. 'Sorry for everything.'"

"You have no idea what he was sorry for?"

"At the time I assumed it was because he felt guilty for robbing me and my brother of our mom. Now I'm wondering if it was a confession. I mean, isn't it obvious he killed her?"

Spence shrugs. "That remains to be seen."

"Who else could it have been?"

"Where's the motive? They'd planned to run off together. Presumably they loved each other."

"Maybe she got cold feet. They fought over it and he lashed out in a moment of anger. She fell and hit her head, or he hit her harder than he'd meant to. Then he disposed of the body so he could make it like they'd run off together."

"It's one theory."

"What I can't figure out is why he contacted me. Or why he'd arrange for me to find her, if it was him. Unless it was eating at his conscience. You know, like in that Edgar Allen Poe story."

"*The Telltale Heart.* We studied it in English sophomore year," he reminds me. "Miss Whitson's class?"

I ignore the comment. The less I dwell on memories from our high school years the better. "Are you going to bring him in for questioning?"

"As soon as we can locate his whereabouts. But keep in mind he's only a person of interest at this point. I'd need to see enough evidence to charge him. And that's going to be tough. I won't lie to you. We don't know yet if it was foul play, and even if we can prove it, we're looking at a murder that took place decades ago, for which there are no witnesses, no timeline, and forensic evidence so degraded it probably can't be used in court. Also, we can't rule out other suspects."

"Everyone loved my mom."

"Your dad couldn't have been too happy with her."

His words send a jolt through me, causing my hand to tremble as I'm sipping my coffee. I wince as some of the hot liquid sloshes over the rim to splash my knuckles. I stare at him in disbelief. "Are you saying my *dad* is a suspect?"

"Usually it's the husband. And he had a motive. She'd left him for another man."

I suck on my scalded knuckles where they're throbbing. "No way. He wasn't like that. He was . . ." I rethink what I was about to say. *Ball-less* was the word I was going to use. "Mom used to complain she could never get a rise out of him. She'd accuse him of being unfeeling. But I don't think he was. He was just a really private guy." My father had his faults, God knows, but he wasn't mean or vindictive. "He never said a bad word about her even after she left us. He was a gentle soul."

"Or a bomb waiting to go off."

I bristle at his words. "Oh well, in that case, you can add me to the list of suspects while you're at it."

He studies me for a moment. "You're not a suspect. Not at this point in time. Although," he adds thoughtfully, "you've been known to be violent."

I push my coffee aside. Otherwise, I'd be sorely tempted to throw it in his face, which would only prove his point. "Are we done here or is there some other personal failing of mine you'd like to dissect?" We've covered my short fuse and weakness for alcohol. What's next, my rumored promiscuousness? I use my hands, flat against the table, to push myself into a standing position.

"You're free to go," he says as though it were up to him.

"Thank you," I snap.

My head is throbbing, the sunlight like needles stabbing my eyeballs, when I finally climb in behind the wheel of my Explorer. I phone Ivy to let her know I'm all right and not under arrest for assaulting a police officer, which I came close to doing with Spence. Had I been in my right mind I'd have driven straight home. Instead I take a different route. I have one last item on my to-do list.

Twenty minutes later I'm turning onto the private drive to the Trousdale estate, fifteen miles south of town in the village of La Mar. I think about the less-than-cozy family reunion in store for Bradley Trousdale, which in turn leads to thoughts of my brother. I dread breaking the news to him about our mom. Arthur's brain isn't wired like other people's; it has no shock absorber—in stressful situations he tends to shut down. There's no telling what this could do to him.

The drive meanders for a half mile through landscaped grounds maintained by my boyfriend, Daniel. The setting sun casts a sparkly net over the ocean visible in the distance. Minutes later I'm pulling up in front of the house, a sprawling cedar and glass structure. Inspired by Frank Lloyd Wright's designs, it's built to blend with the landscape rather than dominate it; from a distance, partially hidden by the surrounding greenery, it's barely distinguishable from the bluff on which it sits. The wraparound deck and floor-to-ceiling picture windows offer unobstructed ocean views from every angle. It's so quiet out here that when I pull to a stop and cut the engine, there's only the sound of the wind blowing off the ocean, whistling amid the rock formations.

Daniel occupies the smaller of the two guest cottages. Small being a relative term: each one boasts a fireplace, galley kitchen, and bedroom. I don't see his Jeep in the driveway, so he must still be at work. He has a part-time job, as research assistant to Professor Gruen, the head of the marine biology department, in addition to his teaching position, which means he often works until late in the evenings. I don't know much about the research, except that it has to do with the nervous system of lobsters; I only know I'm the happy beneficiary of the by-product. Daniel makes a mean lobster bisque.

I let myself in the front door of the main house with my key, but when I go to punch in the passcode, I notice the system is disarmed. The housekeeper must've forgotten to set it when she was leaving earlier today. I make a mental note to speak to Lupe about it. Luckily no harm was done. I see no evidence of a forced entry. The house is silent, the only sound the squeaking of my rubber soles against the tiled floor as I make my way down the hall.

I pause on the threshold of the great room, but I don't notice its majestic proportions or open-beamed cathedral ceiling, Mission-style furnishings, and museum-quality artwork. It's the view through the floor-to-ceiling windows that draws my eye. It's like I'm standing on a ship's deck with the ocean all around me. The sun is setting, the sky along the horizon painted with brushstrokes of gold and coral. Breakers roll in toward the cliff below the house. It's a shame the Trousdales don't get to enjoy it more often, but I can't say I mind having it all to myself. Especially feeling as I do now, like my head is about to split open and I've been stripped of my skin.

In the kitchen, with its acres of granite countertop and center island ringed with hanging copper pots, I grab a vase from the walk-in pantry. I fill it with water and arrange the remaining flowers from Trader Joe's, then head for the largest of the two guest suites. Bradley Trousdale isn't due to arrive until tomorrow, which is why I'm startled by the sound of the shower running in the en suite bathroom as I enter the room. I see no evidence of a newly arrived houseguest. No clothes in the closet, no luggage even, just the frayed and filthy backpack on the floor by the king-sized bed. In that moment all I can think of is the recent break-in at one of my other properties, where I arrived after having been alerted by a neighbor to find the intruder, a homeless man, in the kitchen making himself a sandwich. My heart starts to pound. My shot nerves are humming like a jarful of bees. I react unthinkingly when the door to the bathroom swings opens and a male figure emerges amid a cloud of steam, naked except for the towel around his waist.

I hurl the vase at him.

CHAPTER THREE

The sound of glass shattering is accompanied by a sharp cry. I'm not certain which one of us cried out; I'm as stunned as he is. Then I realize to my horror that the man at whom I hurled the vase, who fortunately ducked in time to keep from getting nailed, is none other than Bradley Trousdale.

He's staring at me like I'm a crazy person. And believe me, from being around my brother, I'm well acquainted with the looks crazy people get. I glance down at the shards of glass and gladioli strewn across the floor at his feet, and blood rushes to my cheeks. "Oh my God. I'm so sorry. I thought you were—" I break off. No need to add insult to injury. "You . . . you must be Bradley."

"You were expecting someone else?" he replies in a deadpan voice.

"No. Um. It's just . . ." I motion toward the frayed backpack at the foot of the bed as if it's somehow to blame for my rash act. "I wasn't expecting you until tomorrow."

"I caught an earlier flight." He states the obvious. "You must be Tish."

"That would be me." I grimace.

"My mom told me you'd be stopping by. She didn't say you were armed and dangerous."

At his expression of wry amusement I feel myself go weak with relief. At least he's not picking up the phone to let his mother know she has a lunatic working for her. "Really, I'm so sorry," I apologize again. "I know it's no excuse, but it's been one of those days." To put it mildly.

"Tell me about it," he mutters, looking down at the wreckage.

I watch as he bends to collect the shards. I'm thinking I should fetch a broom and mop before the puddle on the hardwood floor leaves a stain, but I can only stand rooted to the spot, staring at him. In his early thirties, he's good-looking with a face that, if you were to examine each feature individually—the hawk nose, the wide mouth with its crooked eyetooth, the prominent brow—you might not think handsome but which somehow works as a whole. His cobalt eyes, the color of a twilight desert sky, stand out against a swarthy complexion deepened by long exposure to the Middle Eastern sun. His curly dark-brown hair gives him a vaguely Dionysian look. He's average height, but that's the only thing about him that's average. The nomadic life he leads is evident in his lean, muscled frame, marred only by the wicked scar on his left shoulder.

He dumps the shards in the wastebasket and straightens. I must have looked unsteady on my feet because the next thing I know he has me by the arm and he's leading me down the hallway. Depositing me on the leather sofa in the great room opposite the fireplace, he murmurs, "Be right back."

He reappears shortly, dressed in worn denim jeans and a blue chambray shirt equally faded from many washings. He's carrying a bottle of red wine and pair of wine goblets. "Thanks, but I don't drink," I inform him, not without regret, as he places them on the coffee table. I could use a glass of wine right now, or five. "I used to, but . . ." *Too much information.* "Anyway, I should really go clean up that mess . . ." I start to get up, and he gently pushes me back down into the little nest I've made for myself amid the sofa's kilim throw pillows. I'm in no shape to protest.

"All taken care of. Sit tight," he orders in a firm voice. He leaves the room again and returns minutes later with a steaming mug of tea. "Chamomile," he says, handing it to me. "It's supposed to have a calming effect." He pours himself a glass of wine—a Chateau Lafleur Burgundy, I note with approval—before sinking down on the sofa. A remote control device sits on the glass-and-wrought-iron coffee table; he picks it up and, with the push of a button, we have a nice fire flickering in the gas fireplace. "Feeling any better?" he inquires after I've taken a few sips of my tea.

"Why are you being so nice?" I blurt.

"Something tells me walking in on a strange man getting out of the shower wasn't the worst thing that happened to you today."

"You got that right," I reply with a grimace.

"If you feel like talking about it, I'm a good listener."

I'm sure he's only being polite, so I demur. "Trust me, you don't want to know. Let's just say I'm not in the habit of walking in on strange men getting out of the shower. You caught me by surprise."

"Next time you could try knocking," he says lightly.

"I thought you were an intruder!"

"I see. So you were expecting monogrammed luggage and an entourage?" He chuckles at the notion. "Well, no harm done."

"To you. But your mom will kill me when she finds out I broke her vase." It was one of the expensive crystal ones, too.

"No, she won't."

"Easy for you to say." At the sharpness of my tone, I wince inwardly. God, what's *wrong* with me?

"If she notices it's missing, I'll tell her I broke it," he replies calmly.

"You would do that?" I stare at him in astonishment.

He shrugs. "Accidents happen."

"I owe you big time, in that case."

"You don't owe me a thing. Just promise to go easy on me next time." His wry gaze drops to my throwing arm.

"I used to get hit on a lot in bars," I explain, hinting at why I don't drink—one reason, anyway. "Some guys won't take no for an answer. You have to be more forceful in getting the message across."

He breaks into a grin. "I pity the poor slobs."

"Luckily you have quicker reflexes than they did."

"Where I just came from, if you don't duck when you see something coming, you're likely to go home in a coffin." I feel the blood drain from my face at the gruesome image that surfaces in my mind of my mom's remains. Bradley peers at me with concern. "Hey, are you okay?"

I have no choice then but to tell him. About my mother turning up dead after all these years and my subsequent questioning by the cops. "All this time we thought she was off living her life in some other place. You know, the life she would've had if she hadn't gotten married or had kids." I choke up and wipe my tear-filled eyes, apologizing, "I'm sorry I'm such a mess."

His expression is a mixture of shock and sympathy. "Who wouldn't be? Jesus. What are you even doing here? You should be home taking it easy."

"Good question. I guess I wasn't thinking too clearly. But you're absolutely right, and I've imposed on you long enough." I start to get up, and he seizes my arm, pulling me back down. His grip on my elbow suffuses my whole body with warmth. I feel like I'm sinking into a warm bath.

"You're not going anywhere. You're in no shape to drive."

"Been a while since I've heard that one. Never mind," I say at the questioning look he gives me. He doesn't need to know about all the times I had my car keys confiscated by conscientious bartenders.

"I'd give you a ride," he says, "but I probably shouldn't risk it, either." He indicates his empty wineglass. "Why don't you stay for supper? I'm sure we can rustle up something to eat." He adds, with a smile, when I don't answer right away, "I promise you're safe with me. I'm not one of those guys."

I rouse from my stupor, remembering my place. I'm the property manager, not an old friend who'd dropped by unexpectedly.

"Thanks, I appreciate the offer, but really, there's no need. I'll be fine in a minute. This stuff seems to be working." I lift my tea mug. "I feel calmer already."

I can't bear to talk about my mom, so we talk about his job as a combat cameraman. "It's dangerous at times, and not always fun," he says, "but I can't imagine doing anything else. I'd rather take a bullet doing what I love than be miserable trying to make my parents happy. Though right now I'm the least of their worries." His expression clouds over at the reference to their divorce.

It's not my place to comment, so I only say, "I'm sure they're glad to have you back. How long are you staying?"

"Two, three weeks, maybe longer. I never know when or where my next assignment will be."

"Where's home?"

"You mean as in permanent address? Nowhere, really. I used to keep an apartment in the city, but when it came time to renew my lease, I realized there was no point. I was almost never there."

"It helps to have parents with vacation homes." Besides this one, there's the condo in Aspen.

"True. Though I usually stay with my girlfriend in New York whenever I'm between assignments."

So he has a girlfriend. That explains why we haven't met before now. It doesn't surprise me, though I feel strangely let down. Which is ridiculous. I have a boyfriend. Whose consoling arms will soon be around me. At that precise moment I hear Daniel's voice call my name as if I'd conjured him up.

"There you are!" he cries, his gaze falling on me as he comes striding into the room. "I've been looking all over for you." He comes to an abrupt halt when he notices I'm not alone, his gaze flicking from me to Bradley and then back to me. I can imagine what's going through his head.

"Daniel, I was just . . ." I trail off, not sure what I wanted to say.

"You weren't answering your phone. I've only left about a

million messages on your voicemail," he goes on as if I hadn't spoken, closing the distance between me and him. I've never seen him so agitated; normally he's the calm voice of reason. "Ivy told me what happened. I was worried when I didn't hear from you. Thank God you're all right." What he means is, I'm not drowning my sorrows in some seedy bar. Daniel's never seen me drunk, but he knows my history.

"I'm sorry. I had my phone off when I was at the police station. I forgot to check my messages. Daniel, this is—"

He remembers his manners then and turns to our host before I can make the introductions. "Oh, hey. You must be Bradley. I'm Daniel. Resident groundskeeper and boyfriend." Bradley rises and the two men shake hands. "Sorry for barging in like this, but when I saw Tish's Explorer in the driveway . . ." His gaze drops to the bottle of Bordeaux and two glasses sitting on the coffee table, and I feel another flutter of apprehension, imagining what it must look like to him. Another man would demand an explanation or stomp off in a fit of jealousy, but Daniel merely inquires pleasantly, with a nod toward the wine, "Mind if I join you?"

I don't know whether to be relieved or annoyed.

I'd been sober a little over a year when I first met Daniel. One sunny fall day I was taking a stroll out at Paradise Point when I spied a stocky, sandy-haired guy around my age, dressed in olive cargo shorts and a Greenpeace T-shirt, chasing after a seagull that wasn't flying away for some reason. They made such a comical sight—the seagull hopping along on one leg, flapping its wings, pursued by the guy waving a butterfly net at it—I stopped to watch. He didn't see me until he almost ran into me.

"Oh, hey," he said as we stood facing each other after the seagull had hop-flapped down the path. He explained that the bird had a plastic ring from a six-pack holder caught on one of its feet. "Happens all the time. I rescue the ones I can catch so they won't die of starvation." Seagulls feed mainly on fish and mollusks, he explained.

I helped him catch the gull and we wrapped it in my windbreaker before removing the plastic ring and setting it free. After we'd watched it fly off, we sat on of the benches alongside the path and talked. I learned his name was Daniel Gunderson. He'd moved here from Racine, Wisconsin, after he was accepted into the graduate program at the university. The minute he'd set foot on this rugged and largely unspoiled stretch of coastline, he knew he was here to stay. "This is my spiritual home," he said, and coming from him it didn't sound like trite New Age blather.

I warmed to him right away. I mean, how can you not like a guy who goes around rescuing birds that are generally referred to in these parts as flying rats? (If you've ever been pooped on by a seagull, you'd know why.) I also found him attractive, with his broad Scandinavian face, lively blue-green eyes, and sandy hair that flopped over his forehead. Romantic relationships are generally frowned on in the first year of sobriety, besides which, pretty much the only guys with whom I came into contact in those days were the ones at AA meetings. Before that, my romantic life had been a distant second to my drinking. Suffice it to say I didn't need to have my arm twisted when he phoned the next day to invite me over for a lobster dinner.

One week later we were lovers and a month after that he was living in one of the guest cottages at the Trousdales.' Their previous groundskeeper had been deported to Mexico. (This was before I learned to be scrupulous in checking green cards) and Daniel had experience, having worked summers for a landscaper throughout high school, so it was the ideal arrangement for all concerned.

This evening as we stroll hand-in-hand down the path to the guest cottages after saying our good-byes, I feel something settle inside me. Where I'd once taken solace in drinking, he's hot cocoa with marshmallows on top. I know what Ivy would say about that:

there's nothing sexy about hot cocoa with marshmallows. Which is fine, because right now I'm not feeling very sexy. I'm content just to have him at my side.

Daniel's cottage is the farthest from the house and closest to the swimming pool and tennis court. The exterior is shingled in cedar shakes silvered by exposure to the sea air. Inside it's decorated with light-colored wood furnishings and fabrics from the Ralph Lauren California Romantic collection, and there are touches of whimsy such as the fireplace mantle fashioned from a piece of driftwood and re-purposed factory skid that serves as a coffee table. I release a breath as I step through the doorway, and Daniel puts his arms around me, pulling me close. "I'm sorry about your mom," he murmurs into my hair. "I know you never lost hope that she'd turn up one day."

"And guess what? She did." I choke out a laugh.

"Have you told Arthur?" I feel a tightening in my belly at the mention of my brother.

"Not yet." I draw back and cross the room to sink into the chintz armchair by the fireplace. "I'll tell him tomorrow when I see him." I drop by my brother's every other day on my way home from work to make sure he's taking his meds, keeping his place clean, and not neglecting his personal hygiene. Often I cook him supper or we just hang out playing video games. Saturday mornings are for grocery shopping and errands.

"What if he finds out before then?" Trust Daniel to think of that.

"He won't." Arthur rarely goes out in the evenings. He's usually at his computer working on some program.

"Well, you know best."

"When it comes to my brother, yeah I do." I grow prickly at the understated disapproval in his voice.

Daniel and I get along for the most part although we're polar opposites in most respects: He thinks like a scientist whereas I'm driven by emotions. He's slow to anger and I have a short fuse. He watches PBS documentaries for fun and my favorite TV show is *The Good Wife*. We only butt heads where Arthur is concerned. Daniel thinks he'd be better off in a group home and I know for a fact my brother would sooner be homeless. He's weird about sharing a bathroom and he'd hate having to follow a bunch of rules. Living independently, he can stay up all night, eat Cocoa Puffs for supper, or smoke indoors if he so chooses. No, it's not ideal, but the alternative would be worse; he'd be miserable. But whenever I point this out to Daniel, he argues—correctly—that the problem with schizophrenics is they often forget to take their meds, which wouldn't be the case with proper supervision. He'll quote stats about improved mental and physical health and increased life expectancy. I, in turn, point out that *I* make sure Arthur takes his meds, and who cares if he showers regularly as long as he's happy? At which Daniel will shrug and say, "Well, you know best," in a tone that implies the opposite. This has led to some heated arguments.

Tonight Daniel ignores my snappishness to give me a patient look that says, *I know you're under a lot of stress so I'll try not to take it personally that you're being a bitch.* "Why don't I fix you something to eat?" he offers. "I could warm up some of the lobster bisque from last night."

"Sounds good." I suddenly realize I'm starving, having only picked at my sandwich at lunch.

He heads for the kitchen, leaving me to gaze out the window at the darkened landscape, the lights of the swimming pool glowing in the near distance. Arthur was only eight when Mom left, but he remembers details about her I'd forgotten—that's how his mind works. On any given day if you ask what he did that morning, he can't always tell you, but he remembers the mincemeat pie Mom baked for Thanksgiving one year. How will he react when I tell him she turned up dead? Lately he's been on an even keel, but this could send him veering off course. He could even capsize. I pray it won't come to that. Because there's no mayday like an Arthur-related mayday.

CHAPTER FOUR

Arthur," I say to my brother as he tosses another economy-size box of Honey Roasted Cheerios in the shopping cart he's pushing down the cereal aisle at Albertson's, "can you afford all this?"

It's Saturday morning and we're doing his weekly grocery shopping. The day before yesterday when I broke the news about our mom, I thought he handled it pretty well—he smoked three cigarettes in a row without saying a word. When he finally spoke, it was to ask, calmly, if I thought a memorial service would be appropriate—but now I'm not so sure. He's acting so squirrely I don't need his shrink to tell me he's verging on another one of his psychotic episodes. For one thing, he's loaded the cart with enough food to feed a family of ten and we're only on aisle two.

Arthur regards me as though I'm the one who's being unreasonable. "Tish," he answers with exaggerated patience, "I *need* all this stuff. I have to keep up my energy." He drops his voice to a confidential whisper. *"For the project I'm working on."*

No doubt a top-secret government project aimed at averting global nuclear annihilation or some such. My heart sinks. Next he'll be phoning me in the middle of the night to tell me he's being "watched" and that "they" are after him. The most maddening thing about it is he's really good at what he does. He has a genius IQ and the programs he designs work when he's firing on all cylinders. Tech stuff that confounds me is for him effortless, and he writes code like I do shopping lists. I know who to call whenever my computer is acting up or I need to install a new program. When his meds—an anti-psychotic cocktail, with drugs to counteract the side effects that would dwarf the reputed contents of Michael Jackson's medicine chest—are working, there's nothing he can't handle. When he's off on one of his tangents, he's a loose cog spinning aimlessly.

Today is one of those days.

"Arthur." I adopt a firmer tone, pulling the box of cereal from the shopping cart and returning it to the shelf. "You don't need *three* Honey Bunches of Oats, besides which you've already maxed out your budget. We talked about this, remember? You can't blow your entire allowance and then expect me to bail you out. You *do* realize I'm not made of money?"

He puts on his haughty professor's face. "I'm well aware of that. I don't need you to lecture me." A lanky six-foot-two, he looks like an elongated exclamation mark in the black raincoat he's wearing (never mind it's sunny outside). His square, black-framed glasses are smudged and his brown mop more unruly than usual—he's overdue for the haircut that's next up. I want to sock him and hug him all at once. Instead I give him my sternest look, at which he caves. "I'm sorry, Tish. I promise I'll do better." He hangs his head, looking up at me with puppy-dog eyes, then his long arm snakes past me to retrieve the box of cereal. "Starting next week."

I sigh. Arthur is hopeless with money. Put a dollar sign in front of a number and his mathematical brain utterly fails him. Which is why I'm his fiduciary in addition to the other hats I wear with him: big sister, chief handler, and health advocate. I pay the bills from his monthly SSDI check and give him a weekly allowance for groceries and incidentals. I try not to interfere with how he spends it because I want him to have as much independence as possible.

He'll find out soon enough, when he comes up short at the cash register, how serious I was about not bailing him out.

"Listen, about Mom," I broach, picking up the pace as he energetically steers the cart down the canned beverage aisle. This probably isn't the best time to bring up a delicate subject, but with my brother there's never a good time—you just have to jump in and hope for the best. "I've been thinking about what you said. About . . . you know." My voice cracks. "A memorial service."

"Uh huh," he answers distractedly. "Sure, whatever."

I blow out an exasperated breath. "Did you hear what I just said?"

"Yes, of course." He cocks his head up at me as he's bending down to pull a case of Mountain Dew from the lower shelf. "It's just that I'm really busy right now. With this project. So it's kind of hard to focus on anything else."

"Let me guess. It's a matter of national security."

He nods gravely as he straightens. "Yes, and it's highly sensitive, so I would appreciate it if you didn't mention it to anyone, not even Doctor Sandefur." Dr. Sandefur is his psychiatrist. "If it were to get back to the people I'm working for . . ." He trails off, shaking his head as if to say, *You don't want to know.*

My heart sinks further. "Arthur." I grab his arm as he's turning away, forcing him to look at me. "You know there's no government agency, right? That it's all in your head?"

I see a flash of the old Arthur in that instant. It's hard to believe, looking at him now, but my brother was once normal. That was before he started hearing voices in his head and subliminal messages on the radio and TV. It began the year after he graduated Stanford University when he was working in research and development at Microsoft. I got him to a shrink—it wasn't easy, let me tell you; he can be really stubborn—and after a battery of tests, we had a diagnosis: paranoid schizophrenia. Eight years later, thanks to a regimen of meds and regular monitoring by Dr. Sandefur, he holds his own for the most part, if his hold is shaky at best.

Arthur stares at me, green eyes blinking rapidly behind his Clark Kent glasses. It's not that he's unfeeling, but stressful situations cause him to retreat into his fantasy world. "You think I'm making this up? I assure you I am not. Our lives would be in danger if you spoke to anyone about this. You MUST keep it confidential."

I suppress a sigh. "Fine. But if I find out I'm being followed by some spook in a trench coat, I'll know who to blame." I extract the case of Mountain Dew from the cart and replace it with a six-pack.

"Any theories?" he asks in a thoughtful voice as we're rounding the corner into the next aisle.

"About what?" I ask warily, not sure if he was referencing the "spooks" or yet another crackpot theory.

"Who killed Mom."

I'm startled by his reply. Arthur's mind is like a Jack-in-the-box: You never know what's going to pop out. "Her boyfriend, who else?" I lower my voice. "He was probably the last person to see her alive."

Arthur pauses, wearing a troubled look. "Detective Breedlove asked about Dad, too."

I bristle at the mention of Spence. "Detective Breedlove can kiss my ass," I say, tossing a roll of paper towels in the cart as Arthur watches distractedly. If it's not edible, he's not interested. "He's not even convinced it was foul play. Hello. Like a dead body ends up in a trunk by *accident.*"

"Sounds as if you don't like him very much," he observes mildly.

I pluck a spray bottle of Windex from a shelf of cleaning supplies, throwing it in the cart with enough vigor to have its contents— the blue of Spence's artificially-enhanced eyes—foaming. "We went to school together. He was a jerk back then and he still is."

"So it wasn't personal?"

"Oh, it was personal all right."

"Why, what happened?"

"We hooked up at a party one time. Biggest mistake of my life."

"Oh." Thankfully Arthur doesn't press for details.

"It doesn't matter. It was a long time ago." I'm betrayed by the bitterness in my voice. "Though tell *him* that. Spence Breedlove would love nothing more than an excuse to pin Mom's murder on me." A gray-haired lady pushing her shopping cart shoots me an alarmed look before hurrying past us.

"Interesting. Most males find sexual encounters to be a pleasurable experience, so if he's angry at you, there must be another reason." Arthur is logical to a fault when his mind isn't on one of its tangents.

I pause, lowering my voice. "You could say that. I torched his car."

Arthur's eyes widen. "Why?"

"In retaliation. And because I was sixteen and sixteen-year-olds aren't known for doing the mature thing." *I was also drunk at the time.* "Look, I'm not proud of it. I was lucky he didn't have me arrested then."

"Did Dad know?"

"No." If our dad had been paying attention at all, he might have noticed I had a problem, and not just with Spence. A problem involving the fake I.D. I used to carry in my purse along with Visine and the breath mints I was always sucking on. "The only one who knows besides you is Ivy. And Spence." What amazes me is that he never told. Maybe he has a shred of decency after all, or he felt it evened the score. "You won't tell anyone, will you?"

"I might be persuaded to remain silent if you could slide me a little extra for groceries this week." He breaks into a sly grin.

"You're incorrigible." I shake my head and sigh. "Fine. But it's not a bribe, only because I'm a good sister."

As we head for the checkout stand I wonder if insanity runs in our family. I know one thing: I'm not sitting on my ass waiting for Spence Breedlove to find out who murdered my mom. I'm going to do some investigating of my own. Starting with the prime suspect, Stan Cruikshank.

＊ ＊ ＊ ＊

"Hi. I'm Tish B. and I'm an alcoholic . . ."

Thursday night of the following week and I'm at my weekly AA meeting at St. Anthony's church. It's a speaker meeting and I'm tonight's speaker. I look out at the sea of faces before me. Some I know, others are new to me. I spot old-timer Henry W. looking natty in a plaid vest and bowtie; the aptly named "Big Mike" in his biker leathers and signature red bandana; nerdy, balding Steve B., who runs an insurance agency; soccer mom Nicole B. with her wash-and-wear bob and microfiber track suit. Seated to the right of Nicole is the formerly homeless woman known only to us as "Mustang Sally," wearing one of her colorful getups: a flounced ankle-length print skirt and pink turtleneck with a black see-through blouse over it, heaped with so many beaded necklaces she looks like she just came from a Mardi Gras. We make eye contact and she flashes me a grin that showcases her remaining teeth, all half dozen of them.

I used to feel self-conscious sharing at meetings, but it's gotten easier over time. Plus, after some of the stories I've heard in this room, mine doesn't seem so awful. I'm your average garden-variety alcoholic, as in luckier than most. No felony arrests or permanent injuries from driving under the influence. I'm not on a waiting list for an organ transplant and, in addition to two functioning kidneys and a liver, I still have a roof over my head. Drinking may have cost me my career as a realtor, but I found one that suited me better. In AA we have a term: terminally unique. That was me. I thought I was special, and not in a good way, until I found out I wasn't so special after all.

I was twelve years old when I got drunk for the first time. I'd been spending the night at my friend Sarah's house where her parents were throwing a party. After the guests had departed and Sarah's parents had gone to bed, she and I had drained the dregs from the wineglasses. Sarah had become so sick, she'd sworn she would never touch another drop. For me it had been akin to a spiritual awakening: Jesus in a bottle. Parties in high school had been little more than an excuse to get hammered. In college I'd regularly hosted all-nighters just so I wouldn't have to drink alone. By the time I was in my mid-twenties I was a full-blown alcoholic, consuming a case of wine each week and hitting the bars on weekends. Naturally I was in denial. I was a successful career woman; I had money in the bank; I owned my own home. How could I be a drunk?

I ignored the growing evidence to the contrary: Ivy's frequently expressed concern and my brother's increasing agitation at having his big sister, who was supposed to be the responsible party, out in the Big Blue along with him; the boyfriends who broke up with me because they couldn't handle my drinking; the prospective buyers who went from hot to cold overnight (I was deluded enough to believe Tic-Tacs masked the booze on my breath.) My "bottom" was an incident so shameful, I can only speak of it in meetings. What happened was this: I went off on a client, a single mom named Elena Marquette, after she'd informed me by email she was pulling her listing due to what she called my "erratic behavior." That night I'd driven over to her house, shit-faced, and had torn into her in an expletive-laced rant that had culminated in my hurling the keys to her house and remote control device to the gated community it was in, into her koi pond. Only then had I noticed Elena's five-year-old daughter standing in the doorway. I'll never forget the look of horror on her face: like she'd just seen Santa Claus come down the chimney and get popped with a .22.

I went to my first AA meeting the very next day and I've been going regularly ever since. That was almost four years ago. I won't say it's been easy, but I've stayed the course, by the grace of my higher power and my own stubborn determination. With sobriety came the realization that I didn't enjoy being a broker. So I went into business for myself, ditching my skirts and pantyhose for jeans and sneakers and trading the demands and quirks of sellers and prospective buyers with whom I'd been forced into close contact, often for days and weeks on end, for mostly absentee homeowners I only have to talk to over the phone. I can't say all of my problems were solved by AA, but at least I no longer hate myself, nor do I hate going to work in the mornings.

Tonight as I tell my story I spot a familiar face that gives me a jolt. Tom McGee, manager of the White Oaks self-storage facility. Recalling the odor of stale beer that had wafted from him when we'd first met, I wonder if he's here for the same reason that I've been having trouble sleeping nights lately. The hideous sight of my mother's remains was perhaps a wakeup call for him; whereas for me it was why I stood up tonight in front of all these people—to gain strength from sharing about my downfall. Whatever, I'm not happy to see him. I don't need any reminders.

He comes up to me after the meeting, following the usual round of handshakes and affirmations accorded me as tonight's speaker, which has me lingering after almost everyone else has left. He looks scruffier than I remembered, unshaven, wearing ill-fitting gray cords and an even baggier desert camouflage jacket, a Yankees ball cap pulled low over his head, his poor excuse for a ponytail dribbling from in back. "Funny meeting you here." He greets me in his gravelly voice as I'm pouring myself a cup of coffee to-go at the refreshment table.

"Funny in what way?" I stir a spoonful of creamer into my coffee. Anna D., who was in charge of refreshments for this meeting, forgot the milk. Again. Drunks, they can be so unreliable.

"Hell if I know. But it's gotta mean something, right?"

"Yeah. That we're both alcoholics."

"What makes you think I'm here for the same reason you are?" he replies testily.

"Gee, I don't know. Chalk it up to my brilliant powers of deduction."

He regards me impassively with his dark, hooded eyes. "I

gotta say, for a spokesperson, you're not doing such a good job selling me on this AA thing. If what you see is what you get, I ain't buying."

I drop the sarcastic tone. "Okay, so tell me: Why *are* you here?"

He stands there scratching the back of his neck as he considers this. "Dunno. Curiosity, I guess."

"Well, you know what they say: Curiosity killed the cat. So good luck with that." I start to move past him, but he clamps a hand over my arm.

"Wait. You got a problem, let's hear it."

"I don't have a problem with you, Mr. McGee. Don't take this the wrong way, but the less I see of you the better. I don't need any more reminders. I'm having trouble sleeping nights as it is."

"Yeah, I can see that. Pardon me for saying so, but you look like shit."

"Good. Maybe it'll scare off some of the reporters." The story snowballed after it came out in the local paper. Now it's all over the Internet. I've had the press calling at all hours and showing up at my door.

"I've been getting some of that, too. Fucking ghouls." He shakes his head in disgust. "They don't generally stick around after I've fired off a couple shots." I can only hope he means that figuratively.

I take a sip of my coffee and make a face. The coffee at AA meetings is pretty dreadful as a rule. I don't know why; maybe it's some sort of metaphor, the whole dregs of society thing and all. "The other morning I got a call from a reporter in New York. Woke me out of a sound sleep at five freaking a.m. I just hope I wasn't quoted, because the language I used wasn't fit to print."

McGee chuckles, a sound like pebbles rattling in the tire well of a moving vehicle. "I don't doubt it. You got a mouth on you like the perps I used to haul in." I guess I didn't react in such a ladylike fashion to the horror show at White Oaks. But that's not what I'm keying into right now.

"You're a cop?" I eye him with interest.

"Retired." He grabs a Styrofoam cup from the stack and fills it at the dispenser, dumping in enough sugar for the spoon with which he's stirring his coffee to stand up on its own. We alcoholics are notorious for our sweet tooth. I doubt I would have stayed sober if not for Reese's Pieces. "I was with the NYPD twenty-two years. Homicide division. The other day? Not my first D. B."

I can only assume "D. B." stands for dead body.

I ought to be disturbed by his talk of homicide, but instead I feel a tickle of excitement. Maybe this is a sign that I'm on the right track. I look into his eyes. Cop's eyes. He may be retired—either by choice, or, more likely, because blue wall or no, his colleagues could no longer turn a blind eye to his drinking—but it's in his blood. I picked up on it the first time we were together. Now it has me wondering. I might not be the instrument of McGee's salvation—he didn't seem too interested in my story when I was telling it tonight—but he could well be mine.

If I'm to find and bring my mother's killer to justice, I'm going to need all the help I can get. And who better than a former NYPD detective? "Interesting," I remark. "It must have seemed like déjà vu."

"That's one way of putting it."

"What do you make of our local talent?"

His eyes fix on me above the rim of the cup as he sips his coffee. "In general or Detective Hard-on in particular?"

I cringe inwardly. He doesn't miss much. "There's bad blood between Sp—Detective Breedlove and me," I explain. "I wouldn't want it to affect his judgment."

"You want my advice, you'll keep it zipped."

I feel myself stiffen at the obvious implication. "It's not like that with us. We were never—" I break off before I can reveal too much, my cheeks warming.

McGee gives another throaty chuckle. "I was talking about your mouth. What did you think I meant?"

"Nothing. Forget it." I suddenly get busy screwing the lid on the creamer, taking my time until the heat in my face has abated. When I glance at him out of the corner of my eye, he's still smirking.

It's fully dark out by the time we emerge from the church basement and climb the steps to the sidewalk. I pause to look up at the familiar façade of St. Anthony's, where I used to go to Mass every Sunday growing up. It's a classic example of 1930s Spanish colonial architecture with its plain stucco exterior and twin bell towers flanking a rounded cupola. As a child, I prayed in the sanctuary; nowadays, I seek redemption on the floor below. My mom, from whom I inherited my dark sense of humor, would have appreciated the irony. I turn to McGee as we're nearing the parking lot.

"Listen, I was wondering—"

"Not happening," he interrupts me.

"You don't know what I was going to say!"

"Sure I do." He doesn't look at me or so much as slow his steps. "You think your old pal Detective Hard-on is doing a crap job on account of he can't see past his own dick, and if you had a real live big-city cop to assist you, you could solve this case on your own. That about sum it up?"

"Well, I wouldn't put it quite that way, but . . ."

"Fuggedaboutit." He fishes a set of keys from one of the pockets of his camo jacket as he heads for his car, an older-model blue Ford Focus that looks as if it hasn't seen the inside of a car wash in quite some time.

"She died of a broken neck!" I call after him. "They're calling it 'suspicious' but they're not saying it was foul play. How does someone who died of natural causes end up stuffed in a trunk?"

He slows to a halt and turns to face me, a dark figure amid the shadows of the parking lot and an uninspiring one at that. "Illegal disposal of human remains. It happens. Someone panics, worried they'll take the rap for something they didn't do." I notice his Brooklyn accent isn't quite so pronounced when he's speaking in a professional capacity. "It's fucked up, but it's not murder."

"I don't believe it was an accident and nor do you." I'm guessing about the last part, but would we be having this conversation if he didn't have doubts of his own? "It was no accident, either, she turned up after all these years. Someone wanted me to find her. I need to know who and why."

"Knock yourself out." He turns and continues on.

"Let me buy you dinner at least!"

He utters a derisive laugh and calls over his shoulder, "What, suddenly I'm your new best friend? A minute ago, I was persona non grata. Should Detective Hard-on be worried?"

I bite my lip against the growl that surfaces. "It's just dinner."

He halts in mid-stride, jingling his keys.

"There's a café down the street that serves the world's greatest tacos. House-made tortillas, the works. You like Mexican?" My grandma always said the way to a man's heart was through his stomach.

"Sure. What I don't like is the heartburn."

"You can tell them to hold back on the hot sauce."

He deliberates another second or two and then, with an audible exhalation, pockets his keys as he reverses his steps, glowering at me. "Something tells me I'm gonna have heartburn either way."

McGee, I soon learn, comes from a large Irish clan of which seemingly every member is in law enforcement, a family tradition dating all the way back to the Plug Ugly era. He followed in his father's and grandfather's footsteps as had his brothers and cousins. Brooklyn born and bred, he moved to Rockland County when he made detective, where, as he put it, "a man can take the wife and kids out for pizza without breaking the bank." Neither of which he has. He's never been married, he informs me, and as far as he knows the only "little McGees" are his nieces and nephews.

At Rosalita's, after he's plowed through the complimentary basket of tortilla chips and salsa and a combo plate with the works, he reiterates what he said earlier: He's not interested in helping me. I have to play on his sympathies in addition to buying him dinner before he finally relents and agrees to make some inquiries on my behalf. His brother-in-law Pete works in Internal Affairs, it turns out; he can get access to the national police and FBI databases. A day later I'm looking at a faxed copy of a driver's license with the current address of one Stanley A. Cruikshank.

They always come back, someone once told me, and it's true: However far a native Californian might roam, he always comes back in the end, drawn by the mild climate, natural wonders, and abundant produce of the Golden State. Stan's peregrinations have brought him full circle. He's a live-in ranch hand at the Four Chimneys Ranch in nearby Watsonville, not a fifteen minute drive from my house. I'd pictured him living in some godforsaken town at the other end of the continent. Now I'm wondering if I'm on the wrong track. Why would a guilty man return to the scene of his crime? There's no statute of limitations for murder.

I pull up images of the ranch on Google Earth. One shows an older man on horseback whom I recognize as Stan from the one photo Mom kept of him—I found it tucked in the lining of her jewelry box when I was packing up her things after Dad died. His face is more lined now and his hair silver when it had then been light brown, but he's still lean and rangy. Still handsome if you go for the Marlboro Man type. I bet he's a real lady killer. The question is, did he kill my mom?

Only one way to find out.

The following morning I awaken, at my customary early hour, to the sight of my striped tom, Hercules, curled asleep next to me. He looks so peaceful you'd never guess he'd been out all night hunting for small furry and feathered critters to maim and slaughter—he's the Dr. Mengele of the cat world. I stroke his fur and he cracks open one yellow eye and purrs. "Enjoy it while it lasts," I murmur. He follows me when I get up and head down the hallway, drawn by the aroma of coffee. I have the timer on my coffeemaker set for the same time every morning.

In the kitchen, I look around me with satisfaction as I wait for the coffee to finish brewing. My housekeeper, Esmeralda, was in yesterday to clean and every surface gleams. I take in the black and white checkerboard flooring, original glass-front cabinetry and green tile counters, deep porcelain sink, and vintage Formica dinette. My 1930s Craftsman bungalow isn't grand or luxurious like the homes I manage, but what it lacks in square footage it makes up for in charm. It still has many of its original features, which previous owners had either covered with sheetrock or painted over, and I was able to restore when I bought and reno-vated this place eight years ago. It was worth every drop of sweat equity and savings it took to make it shine.

I pour myself a cup of coffee and sit down at the table with my laptop to check my email. A half hour later I'm headed out the door, showered and dressed, with my travel mug and a banana. The sun hasn't yet risen, and there's just the rosy tinge in the sky above the rooftops of my quiet residential neighborhood, which is a five-minute walk from the beach. My first stop is the Willets' Cape Cod on Opal Cliff Drive, then it's on to the Voakes' split-level on Sea Breeze Court, both routine walk-throughs with no surprises. At the Blank-enships' oceanfront villa in Casa Linda Estates I oversee the installa-tion of a new alarm system. At the Oliveiras' shingled two-story on Swallow Lane I meet with the pool guy to discuss a remedy for the black algae infestation. I spend the better part of an hour at the Mar-tinson's duplex by the yacht harbor conducting a thorough search for eight-year-old Grady Martinson's hamster that's on the lam. I don't break for breakfast or lunch; I bolt the banana and a protein bar on the run. I'm hurrying through my to-do list so as to be done by four o'clock, in time to pick up Ivy for our trip to Four Chimneys Ranch.

She's waiting on the porch when I pull up in front of the Victorian white elephant she inherited from her late grandmother. She waves to me and comes trotting down the walk. She's my "wingman," a role she's taking seriously I see, after she's climbed in and we're en route, when she pulls a gun from her straw handbag. It's the pearl-handled derringer that had belonged to Ivy's great-grandfather, Beauregard Ladeaux, a notorious bootlegger in his day. I've never seen it outside its glass display case in the parlor. "Um. I don't think we'll be needing that," I say, eyeing it nervously.

"You never know."

"When was the last time it was even fired? Jesus. Put that thing away before you do some damage!" I cry as she cocks the hammer.

"Relax, it's not loaded," she assures me. "It's just for show. In case he tries anything." She's wearing sixties bellbottom jeans and an embroidered peasant top, cork-heeled wedgies on her dainty feet. Bonnie and Clyde meets the Summer of Love.

"He wouldn't dare. Not in broad daylight," I state with more confidence than I feel.

"He's a murderer. God knows what he's capable of."

"We don't know that he's a murderer." *Not yet.* "That's what I have to find out. I'm only going to feel him out a bit. Ask some questions."

"He could abduct you and take you to where it's just you, him, and the rattlesnakes." When Ivy gets an idea in her head, there's no prying it loose. "You'll be glad then I came prepared."

"Don't worry, I've got it covered." I brake at the next stoplight and rummage in my canvas messenger bag, producing a small black object roughly the size and shape of a cigarette pack. "Behold the Tornado five-in-one personal defense system. Pepper spray, strobe light, and high-frequency alarm all in one." I bought it yesterday at Markey's Gun Shop, on Old County Road a few miles from the White Oaks self-storage facility, at McGee's recommendation. Markey's also carries a full selection of firearms, but I decided to hold off on getting a gun until I learn how to shoot.

Ivy examines the device with interest. "Cool. Does it come in any other colors?"

"Not as far as I know, but as long as it does the job, right?"

"So you *do* think he's dangerous."

"No," I lie. "It's just a precaution."

Ivy is flushed with excitement, eyes sparkling. To say she's adventurous is putting it mildly. She'll scale heights in rock-climbing that would have me peeing my pants. She's gone hang-gliding and sky-diving. She once traveled through India by train and spent the summer after college backpacking around Europe. She'll try any food, however exotic. The other day she allowed a street performer to drape his pet python over her shoulders, never mind it could've crushed her like a soda can.

As we head south on Highway 1 I think back to when I first met Ivy, in seventh grade. She'd just moved to town with her dad from Seattle, Washington. I was intrigued as soon as our teacher, Miss Cherry, introduced her to the class. Ivy was a living, breathing Madame Alexander doll in all her dainty perfection, except instead of ruffles and bows she was dressed in torn jeans, midi top, and platform shoes. The only thing we had in common, that I could see, was that we'd both been saddled with old-lady names. When I remarked on this, rolling my eyes, as I was walking with her to our next class, she only commented, with a shrug, "It beats Tiffany or Brandy."

"I'd rather be a Brandy than have a name that belongs on a mossy gravestone," I declared.

Ivy ignored my attempt to draw her into a discussion of my favorite topic: the many and varied ways in which my life sucked. "I'll show you mine sometime if you like. My grave rubbings," she added at my questioning look. "I have tons of them from all over. It's kind of my thing."

I was fascinated. Miss Cherry was probably thinking we could both use a friend, which was certainly true in my case, and she assigned me to show Ivy around. Ivy would have every other kid in our class vying to be her friend by the end of the week, but I was kind of a loner in those days. My mom had seemingly fallen off the planet and my dad might as well have—he moved through our lives as a ghost; my brother and I would have starved to death had we waited for him to remember to feed us. I felt alienated from the girls I used to hang out with. They were from homes with a mom and a dad and a fully-stocked fridge, where there was always someone to help with their homework and the family gathered for supper every evening. There were two girls in my class, Sarah and Caitlin, with whom I was friendly, but I never asked them over to my house and made excuses whenever they invited me to theirs. Ivy, I suspected, was anything but normal.

She told me her parents were getting a divorce and that she and her dad were living with her grandmother. When she told me who her grandmother was, I couldn't contain myself. "No way. Old la—I mean, Mrs. Ladeaux, is your *grandmother*?" If I'd been paying attention when Ivy was introduced to the class, I would've made the connection. Ladeaux wasn't a common name in these parts.

She nodded, entirely too blasé. "Ghosts?" she echoed with a laugh, after I'd sheepishly explained my stunned reaction. Every neighborhood has one and the Ladeaux house was ours: the one door you don't knock on when trick-or-treating on Halloween. A rambling Victorian with turrets and gingerbread and a widow walk, it was rumored to be haunted by the ghost of a previous owner. "I don't know about that—I've never seen one—but it'd be pretty cool if it was true."

"Why don't you live with your mom?" I asked her.

That was when she told me about her mom, that she was a doctor who ran a free clinic in Malawi. "We discussed it as a family," she answered, in the voice of someone mature beyond her years, "and decided the best thing would be for me to live with Dad and Grandma. It was that or boarding school." I asked if she missed having her mom around, and she said, with a sanguine shrug, "Sure, but it's not like I'll never see her. She'll come for visits and I'll visit her in the summers."

"It won't be the same." I missed my own mom so much it was like a hole in my gut.

"No," she agreed. "But she waited until I was old enough to handle it. Plus, she's over there saving lives, which is pretty awesome. And she said I could help out at the clinic when I visit. How cool is that?" Her aquamarine eyes glowed like a swimming pool at night lit from within.

I failed to see the appeal. "Doing what?" I asked skeptically.

"Life-and-death stuff. They have diseases over there you never heard of and tons of poisonous snakes. Did you know you can die from a mosquito bite? Oh, yeah, and there's these worms that get into your bloodstream through your feet. Those can kill you, too."

Grave rubbings, divorced parents, deadly worms. It was official: Ivy was as weird as I was. Weirder, even.

We were inseparable from that day on. The fact that she lived in the Ladeaux mansion only added to her appeal. I'd always been curious about the old lady. I used to see her around town, dressed as if for a garden party hosted by the Rockefellers, in silks and linens, gloves and high heels. I'd imagined her to be mysterious and remote, but she was really sweet once I got to know her.

Grandmother Ladeaux is long gone and Ivy's dad has since remarried—he lives across the bay in Carmel with his new wife. Now it's just Ivy living in the big, old gingerbread house on Seabright Avenue. (Which might seem Dickensian if you didn't know her. She's more Elizabeth Bennett than Miss Havisham.) One thing hasn't changed, though. She's still my best friend.

Twenty minutes later we're bumping over the rutted two-lane road to Four Chimneys Ranch. Situated in the Pajaro valley, it boasts a hundred acres and is one of the top breeders in the country for Arabian horses. They also train horses and offer riding instruction. It's been under the ownership of the same family, the Valparaisos, since the days of the early pioneer settlers, and vestiges from that bygone era remain, most notably in the crumbling chimneys that give the ranch its name. It's all that's left of the original homestead that was destroyed by fire in the late 1800s. I can see the cairn-like chimney tops peeking over the trees in the distance as we rattle along.

I pull into the parking area behind the barn and stables, matching red-painted post-and-beam structures as well-maintained as the road is not. It's an impressive operation, I see after I've had a look around. The facility has four riding rings—three outdoor, one indoor—a grooming area that could accommodate a whole herd of horses and state of-the-art tack room with more floor space than the average house. The majority of the riding students are tween and teenage girls. I'm reminded of when I was briefly enamored with horses at that age, before I discovered that boys were way more fun and a lot less work. I buttonhole one of the ranch hands, a short, stocky guy with swarthy skin and a Hispanic accent, wearing a green polo shirt with the Four Chimneys logo, and ask if he knows where I can find Stan. He directs me to the staff quarters down the road, a cluster of cheaply constructed cabins reminiscent of a fifties-era motor court.

Minutes later I'm knocking on the door to Stan's cabin. To Ivy's disappointment, I'd decided it would be best if I went in alone. Suspected murderer or no, he's my only source of information at this point; if he felt he was being ganged up on, he might shut down. My heart is pounding and I'm sweating profusely. What does he know? What secrets is he keeping? Was his the last face my mom saw before she died?

The door swings open. Before me stands a tall man, long and lean as a whip with cropped silver hair and a spare, weathered face from which bright blue eyes leap like sparks from a blacksmith's anvil. He's wearing what appears to be the ranch uniform, jeans and the green polo shirt with the Four Chimneys logo, with a pair of dusty cowboy boots. "What can I do for you?" he asks.

"Stan Cruikshank? Hi, I'm Tish," I introduce myself when I finally find my tongue.

Recognition kicks in as we're shaking hands. His gaze sharpens and he stares at me for a long moment, then says softly, "You look like her."

"So I've been I told. Do you have a minute?"

"This isn't a good time." His expression closes against me as surely as if he'd slammed the door in my face. "I was just headed back to work. Don't get off for another hour." He speaks with a Texas drawl.

"Fine. I'll wait." I fold my arms over my chest.

He regards me warily, appearing to debate with himself before finally coming to a decision. Stepping back, he holds the door open for me. "I guess I can spare a few minutes. Come on in."

"If you don't mind, I'd rather we talked outside." I gesture toward the pair of folding lawn chairs on the postage-stamp porch to my right. Even armed with my Tornado five-in-one device, I have no desire to be behind a closed door with him. I may be reckless, but I'm not stupid.

He shrugs. "Suit yourself." I sit down, and after moment or two, Stan lowers his lanky frame into the other chair. He leaves the door to the cabin open, and from where I sit I can see inside. The room holds a neatly made double bed, cheap set of dresser drawers, and floating desk. A rifle is propped against the wall by the dresser, the sight of which has my stomach clenching. "I know why you're here," he says, "but you're wasting your time. I don't have any answers for you. I didn't even know she was dead 'till I read about it in the paper."

I sense he's lying. The expression on his face is that of a veteran poker player: a tell so hard to detect that in itself is telling. No one who'd loved my mom enough to run away with her could be so devoid of emotion. "I'll take your word for it." I play along. "But at least tell me what you *do* know."

He ignores the question to gaze out at the scruffy yard where a dog snoozes in the shade of a loquat tree, until finally he says, without turning to look at me, "We had plans, her and me. We were looking to get a fresh start. I had a job lined up in Sacramento. But at the last minute she had a change of heart. Told me she couldn't go through with it. She couldn't do that to her kids."

Suddenly I have trouble catching my breath. "What happened after that?"

"Nothing. She went her way. I went mine. Never saw or heard from her again. End of story."

I don't believe a word of it and I'm not fooled by his poker face. I deliver a jolt, in an attempt to shake him up. "Then you wouldn't know how her body ended up in a footlocker?"

The color drains from his face, leaving it the ashy gray of a cold campfire. "No, ma'am, I wouldn't." I notice his hand is trembling as he pulls a pack of Marlboros from his shirt pocket and taps out a cigarette.

I worry I may have pushed too hard, but I've gone too far to stop now. Also I'm not one to give up easily. There's a bumper sticker that reads "Rehab Is For Quitters," which would be funny in an ironic way if it weren't so representative of my kind—we're an obstinate bunch. "Then I guess you wouldn't know, either, how that footlocker ended up in a storage unit with my name on it."

He lights the cigarette and expels a jet of smoke. I study his profile as he squints into the middle distance. I'm loath to admit it, but in the interest of full disclosure, I have to admit he's good-looking for an older dude. In the photo of him when he was younger he resembles Clint Eastwood when he starred in those Dirty Harry movies my grandpa used to love to watch (when Grandpa had

Alzheimer's, toward the end of his life, and couldn't remember anyone's names, I had only to utter the immortal line "Make my day," for him to break into a grin of recognition). Now he looks like the Clint who fathered a child with a woman thirty years younger than himself.

I know his age from the birth date on his driver's license, and when he finally turns to me, I can see every one of those sixty-three years on his face. "I'm sorry for your loss, Miz Ballard. Hell, I'm sorry for a lot of things. But, like I said, if you want answers, you came to the wrong person."

I stare at him. "I don't think so."

He takes another drag off his cigarette. "I told you what I know. Same as I told the cops." At the look of surprise I must have worn, he adds, with a glint in his eye, "Yeah, that's right. They were out here the other day. The fact that they didn't see fit to arrest me should tell you all you need to know. If they had so much as a shred of evidence against me, would I be sitting here talking to you?"

"That doesn't mean they won't find any," I burst out.

"I never laid a hand on her."

"Then why did you send me that postcard? Why say you were sorry?"

A flicker of emotion crosses his face. He leans forward, elbows propped on his knees, smoke curling from the cigarette that smolders, forgotten, in the fork of his first and middle fingers as he gazes into the distance. I'd about given up on getting any more out of him when he answers, "I felt bad for you and your brother. You being motherless and all. I wanted you to know, is all."

A jolt goes through me at his words. Because now I *know* he's lying. A minute ago, he claimed he didn't know my mom was dead. If that was true, how had he known I was motherless?

CHAPTER FIVE

"Are you all right? What happened? What did he say?" Ivy peppers me with questions as I climb back in the Explorer.

"I'm fine," I answer in a surprisingly calm voice as I start the engine and shift into reverse. "Nothing happened. We just talked." I recount my unnerving conversation with Stan as the cabins recede in my rearview mirror. "Don't you see? It proves he was lying if he knew all along she was dead."

"You think he killed her?"

"Why lie if he was innocent?"

"Okay, but somebody else had to have been in on it, or at least known about it. Stan wouldn't have arranged for you to find the remains. It makes no sense. Why put himself at risk?"

"Good point," I reply, mulling it over.

"What I don't get is why this other person, if he exists, wouldn't have just gone to the police."

"Maybe he was an accomplice." I turn onto the main road, where ranchlands give way to strawberry fields in which day laborers toil, their shadows stretching over the neatly planted rows in the late afternoon sun.

"Why would Stan have an accomplice? If it was a crime of passion, it means it wasn't premeditated."

"All the more reason. What would you do if you killed someone by accident? You'd freak out and call me, of course. And me being the loyal friend I am, I'd help you get rid of the body."

"You'd do that for me? Gee, I'm touched," she remarks dryly.

"So, anyway," I go on, warming to my theory, "let's say he calls his buddy in a panic and the buddy comes through. Then years later they have a falling out. Maybe he slept with the guy's wife or screwed him out of some money. At any rate, Stan figures he's safe because the guy can't go to the cops without implicating himself."

"But the friend is crafty." Ivy picks up where I left off. "He fixes it so the shit will hit the fan without any of the shit landing on him." Starfish Enterprises, the entity to which the storage unit was leased, had turned out to be a dummy corporation with no physical mailing address, to no one's surprise.

"It's the only explanation that makes sense." I wonder how I can find out if this hypothetical friend exists.

"Are you going to share this theory of yours with Spence?" Ivy's voice breaks into my reverie.

"No way. He'd only accuse me of interfering."

"Well, you kind of are," she points out, not so helpfully.

"True, but at least I'm getting somewhere, which is more than I can say for him."

"I doubt he'd see it that way," she remarks wryly.

"Even if I went to him with this, what good would it do? He wouldn't follow up on it."

"What makes you so sure?"

"For one thing, it's not officially a murder investigation, which means he'll go through the motions, but he won't knock himself out. He told me himself the chances of his making an arrest, without a single witness or DNA evidence that'd hold up in court, are slim to none. Add the fact that he has it in for me, and you've got a recipe for my butt getting kicked out the door. I'm telling you, he hates me."

"Because you torched his Camaro? Don't tell me he's still

holding a grudge after all this time? Over a little thing like that?" Ivy never misses an opportunity to make me regret having confided in her about my brief and inglorious career as an arsonist. "Though, in hindsight, maybe you should've slashed his tires instead. You know guys and their cars. They'd sooner lose a nut."

I shoot her a dirty look, then heave a sigh. "I would've told him I was sorry if he'd given me the chance." Or if he'd ever made amends for what he did to me.

"You'd go to him if you had actual evidence, though?" Ivy's jocular tone gives way to a serious one.

"Of course. I'm not authorized to make an arrest, so I wouldn't really have a choice."

"Well then, we'll just have to find some. Evidence, that is. What's our next move, Sherlock?"

"I'll let you know when I've figured it out. In the meantime I'm keeping my eye on Stan."

"You mean spy on him?" she asks excitedly. When I glance over at her, her eyes are glowing and her cheeks pink at the prospect of some covert activity. Now I'm talking her language.

"Sorry to disappoint you, but I think it's best if we leave any spying to my brother's imaginary cohorts," I reply archly. "I'll see what McGee can come up with. He's got more connections than a Mafia don. The kind that are on the right side of the law, that is," I hasten to add.

"Whatever, count me in."

"Are you sure? It could get dangerous." I realize who I'm talking to—the kind of person who takes pleasure in bungee-jumping and packs a derringer—only after the words have passed my lips.

Ivy laughs. "Please. It's the least I can do, if you'd help me dispose of a dead body."

My Craftsman bungalow is a welcome sight when I pull into my driveway after dropping Ivy off at her house. I glance around me, to make sure no one's lurking about, before getting out. But it seems the press has moved on. It's been days since I've seen or heard from a reporter. The only eyes peering out at me are those of my cat, from the hydrangea bushes that border the porch.

Hercules streaks past me into the house when I let myself in the front door. Normally he comes and goes through his cat door, and as soon as I enter the kitchen, I see he was up to some mischief while I was out. He's gotten into the African violet again. Potting soil is scattered over the windowsill and sink below. Typically he's accomplished this feat without disturbing the plant itself or the ceramic pot it's in—he's nothing if not fastidious. "Bad kitty," I scold him as I clean up the mess, but my heart's not in it and he knows it. He purrs loudly, rubbing against my ankles.

I pop a frozen pot pie in the oven and shake some premixed salad greens into a bowl. Hercules's dinner is a more elaborate affair: a mixture of dry and canned food and diced chicken livers. The house is quiet. The only sounds are the rhythmic clinking of my cat's bowl against the fridge as he licks it clean and the soft tinkling of the wind chimes outside—one of Ivy's creations, made from bits of sea glass and seashells strung on lengths of fishing line. Normally I'd be unwinding, but instead I feel unsettled. A feeling that in the old days could only have been remedied by a belt of something stronger than the Fresca I'm sipping. I pick up the phone and call my sponsor, a no-nonsense older woman named Ann Petty who used to practice family law and now runs the garden center where I buy my gardening supplies—annuals and varietals are less likely to drive her to drink than combative husbands and wives, as she's fond of saying. "Go to a meeting," she advises in her clipped, New Englander voice. "Then get your butt over here. Haven't seen you in ages." She attends the Early Bird morning meetings, so we don't see each other as often as we had in the early days of my sobriety when I went to two meetings a day. I promise to stop by for a visit and, after we've chatted a few more minutes, I hang up and call McGee.

I tell him my theory about Stan. "He's hiding something, that much I know. What I don't know is if he acted alone or he had help."

"Let me guess—this is where I come in," he replies in a flat voice. I hear the muted clink of a dead soldier joining the ranks of its fallen comrades followed by the *pop siss* of a fresh recruit taking its place. I refrain from commenting. "You remember the part where I told you I was retired? I wasn't kidding. I'm done with all that, and not just because I turned in my badge and service revolver. I'm fucking tired of all that shit. Peace and quiet, that's all I want. Is that too much to ask?"

"You can't let a murderer walk free."

"You know for a fact he's a murderer?"

"He wouldn't look me in the eye, and he contradicted himself after claiming not to have known she was dead until he read about it in the paper." I use my shoulder to hold the phone to my ear as I set the table—placemat, napkin, cutlery. *When ones lives alone, it's easy to let one's standards slip.* I hear Grandmother Ladeaux's voice in my mind. *All the more reason to observe the niceties.*

"That's some ace detective work there." McGee's tone is mocking. But what had I expected, a gold star and pat on the back? "Sorry to burst your bubble, but you'll have to do better than that."

"What if I can prove he's lying?"

"Knock yourself out. With any luck you'll find another body or two buried in his backyard. Or you'll sweet-talk him into submitting to a lie detector test—which, by the way, wouldn't be admissible in court."

"No need to be sarcastic. I'm not an idiot. I know there's no smoking gun. But there could be circumstantial evidence. And if this hypothetical accomplice exists—"

"This ain't no Nancy Drew mystery." He cuts me off.

"I *know* that," I reply irritably. "And if you don't want to help me, fine. For some reason I got the impression you missed the action, but I guess I was wrong. I'll leave you to your Reader's

Digests and your rocking chair. And your Coors," I add pointedly. My dig is met with silence.

"You're something else, Ballard," he growls, at last.

"I'll take that as a compliment." I press on while I have the advantage. "Look at it this way: Your being retired could work in our favor. When you wore a badge, you had to play by the rules. That's no longer the case—we can bend the rules without breaking them, go places cops can't."

"Yeah, like the county jail."

"I'm not talking about doing anything illegal or even unethical. We'd just be thinking outside the box." I argue my case. "'By any means necessary.' Isn't that a term used in law enforcement?"

"Actually, it was Malcolm X that said it. And as you may recall, things didn't turn out so good for him."

"This isn't about staging a revolution. What's the harm in doing a little digging? Anything we find, we turn over to the cops. All we need is enough evidence to justify their launching a full-fledged investigation."

"You keep saying 'we.' It's making me uncomfortable."

I ignore him to go on, "You helped me once already, and not just because you're a good guy. You miss the action. Admit it." He's quiet, which I take as a positive sign. "Let's say I'm right about the accomplice. Suppose we were to track him down and convince him to testify against Stan in exchange for immunity."

"You watch too much TV," he scoffs.

"And you drink too much." I don't miss a beat. "Which is why we'd make a good team. We can keep each other honest."

"Jesus. You're like stray cat, Ballard. I toss you a scrap and now I'm your meal ticket?"

"If you won't do it for me, then do it for the sake of justice. You can't let a killer go free."

The silence that ensues is so lengthy I wonder if the connection's been broken. Then he growls: "Just so you know, I'm holding you personally responsible if another dead body turns up on my watch."

"Even if it's mine?"

"*Especially* if it's yours."

I smile. "I'll take that as a yes. Oh, and by the way, I'm saving you a chair." It's an AA expression. And judging by his muttered expletive, you don't have to be an AAer to know what it means.

CHAPTER SIX

It's . . . um . . . very avant-garde," observes the big-haired lady to my right, diamond earrings flashing like hazard lights as she leans in for a closer look at the diorama on display in front of us. It's my personal favorite from Ivy's current collection—a daddy long legs spider and monarch caterpillar exchanging vows under a bridal canopy fashioned from twigs and dried flowers—titled "Midsummer Night's Dream." Though I get the feeling the artistry is lost on Big Hair.

It's Tuesday evening of the following week, the opening of Ivy's show at the Headwinds Gallery. A nice turnout, I'm pleased to note. Invited guests and walk-ins alike mill around the loft-like space where each of Ivy's pieces is showcased by a blown-up photo mounted on the wall above. Ivy, resplendent in an ankle-length batik halter dress made of lightweight cotton that flutters around her when she walks, her hair spilling over her shoulders in a torrent of dark curls, looks every inch the woman of the hour. At the moment she's being squired around by the gallery owner, Rick Swannack, a short, energetic man with clipped salt-and-pepper hair, wearing what appears to be a velvet smoking jacket. He's introducing her to the VIPs in attendance, which I pray will lead to bigger and better things. Not that Ivy cares about fame or fortune; she's content as long as she's earning enough to pay the bills. I watch her break away from Rick and the well-dressed older man with whom she'd been chatting to greet my brother. He's just walked in with his friend and fellow computer nerd, Ray Zimmer (hacker name: "Zorro.") It may have cost her a sale, but she'll always go with her heart before her head, and I love her for that.

My brother's face lights up. He adores Ivy—she's like the nicer sister he wishes I was. I'm pleased to note he's wearing a sports coat for the occasion, never mind the shirt it's paired with hasn't been ironed and has a button missing. "Did you know a high-density image has four thousand eight hundred pixels per inch?" she says to me when I catch up to them. She gestures toward the photo on the exposed-brick wall above a diorama of line-dancing caterpillars. "Your brother—" she gives Arthur an affectionate nudge with her elbow—"is a walking factoid factory."

"Actually, your usage of 'factoid' is incorrect," Arthur instructs her. "By definition it's a piece of information that becomes accepted as true because it's repeated often."

"Dude. That is so random." Ray regards Arthur with the admiration of a mere mortal in the presence of genius. He may be a gifted hacker, but with him it's one of those savant things—he's just a regular guy in every other respect. His most endearing quality is that he doesn't see Arthur as crazy. "Did he tell you about the video game we're working on?" he says to Ivy and me. "Aliens from cyberspace take over the Earth. Can't you see it?" He makes a picture frame with his hands. "Arthur came up with the idea. It's gonna be awesome. Dude's a freaking genius."

Ray is as short and round as Arthur is tall and reedy, sporting a beard two shades redder than the curly ginger hair on his head. He has so many freckles on his face, he looks as though he's been hit by a paintball through a screen door. They met online a few years ago, two hitchhikers on the virtual highway who'd randomly encountered each other and struck up a friendship, despite their having little in common besides a talent for writing and cracking code. Ray shares a house with three other guys, has an eye for the ladies, and works as a T-Mobile salesman when he isn't pursuing his hobby of hacking, which he does merely for the fun of it and not for profit or to wreak havoc.

"That he is." I tuck my arm through Arthur's. "Thanks for coming, bro." Only I know what a sacrifice it was. This is so not my brother's thing. He'd sooner be abducted and anal-probed by aliens than attend a social gathering. He's here only because he didn't want to let Ivy down.

"No problem," he murmurs, blushing furiously. He's been better since Dr. Sandefur upped the dosage on his meds. I haven't heard any talk lately of top-secret government projects; I'll take aliens from cyberspace any day over that, as long as it's rooted in reality. "The show appears to be a success." He points toward the red "sold" dot on a diorama of badminton-playing beetles.

"I've sold six pieces so far," Ivy announces delightedly. "Can you believe it?"

"Why wouldn't I?" he answers as though it weren't a rhetorical question.

"Any luck at the Fontana?" she asks me after the men have gone off in search of refreshments.

"Total waste of time," I report. I paid a visit to my mom's former place of employment, thinking, if I could get the names of the people she'd worked with, it might yield some leads. At least one of those people had to remember the hunky construction worker who'd been on the crew building the new wing at the time and who'd been so enamored of the pretty, blond Ava Ballard. I told the office manager, a scarily efficient woman named Mrs. Bouchard, I was planning a memorial service for my mother and wanted to invite any of her former coworkers who still lived in the area. She was pleasant enough but told me she wasn't authorized to give out employee contact info. She'd offered to send out the invitations on my behalf instead. "Looks like the only way I'll get that information is by having Arthur and Ray hack into the database."

"I'm sure they'd love nothing more. But they'd get into trouble if they were caught." It's my brother she's worried about, not Ray. Arthur's psychotic episodes have landed him in hot water on more than one occasion—most recently when he accosted a fellow pedestrian whom he'd mistaken for a CIA operative—the last thing he needs is for me to create more problems for him.

"There might be another way," I say when I spy Joan Trousdale. Every year in July the Trousdales host a gala fundraiser at the Fontana for one of the charities on whose board Joan sits. If I could score a ticket to this year's, it would provide a golden opportunity to do some sleuthing. Because it wouldn't be just wealthy donors in attendance. One of the employee perks at the Fontana, I know from when my mom worked there, is an invitation to its annual summer gala. The same goes for former employees of long standing who enjoy lifetime privileges.

I hurry over to Joan after Ivy has rejoined Rick Swannack. "Joan, hi! Glad you could make it. I didn't know if you'd be in town." Her visits have become infrequent since she and her husband split up, so I didn't expect to see her. I'd sent her an invitation more as a courtesy than anything.

She greets me warmly. "You caught me at a good time. I'm here visiting with my son. He should be along any minute, in fact," she says with a glance at her slim, gold Piaget wristwatch. "We have an eight o'clock dinner reservation at Bouche." She names a popular restaurant down the street.

"It must be nice having him back," I remark.

"Yes, and thankfully in one piece." Her light tone doesn't mask the relief in her voice. I know from our previous conversations she worries about him all the time. How could she not? His job has him in war-torn countries where he's exposed to constant risk. "If it were up to me . . ." She catches herself, saying on a more upbeat note, "But I'm not one of *those* mothers. Heaven forbid."

She looks perfectly put-together as usual in fitted charcoal trousers and a pale pink silk blouse that show off her trim figure, a pair of pearl earrings, and matching pearl necklace. If I had to choose one word to describe Joan's style, it would be timeless. In her mid-fifties, she's one of those women who's comfortable looking her age and dresses accordingly, in beautifully cut clothes that show off her figure without flaunting it. Her layered, chin-length hair is silver-blond, its natural color, and she hasn't had any face work as far as I can tell. Not that she needs it with her classic bone structure.

"It was nice to finally meet him." I feel my cheeks warm as I recall the circumstances.

"Yes, he mentioned you'd stopped by."

"Yeah, about that, I sort of barged in on him." I have no way of knowing how much he's told her, so I decide to play it safe. "I wasn't aware he'd gotten in a day early so I didn't think to knock."

"Oh dear." She makes a wry face. "Well, no harm done."

My mind flies immediately to the broken vase. Clearly she hasn't yet become aware of it. Not that I don't intend to come clean; I'm only waiting until I can find a suitable replacement, which is proving to be a bit of a challenge—it seems the vase was vintage Waterford. "Nope. It's all good." I must look like a bobble-head doll as I stand there nodding my head and grinning like a fool.

"Are you all right? You look a little flushed." Before I can answer, she's pulling me off to the side away from the crush of other guests. "It's that ghastly business with your mother, isn't it?" We haven't spoken since the news broke, though she left a message on my voicemail expressing her condolences. "And here you are putting on a brave face for the sake of your friend." She gives me a motherly pat on the arm, holding my gaze in a look of wordless sympathy.

"Actually, it's good for me to get out. It takes my mind off all that other stuff."

"We must carry on, mustn't we?" she says with grim resignation, her expression clouding over. No doubt she's thinking of her own adverse circumstances. In addition to her legal woes, she's had to endure the gossip that comes with a high-profile couple's private life being made public. The most recent development was the announcement of Douglas Trousdale's engagement to the twenty-five-year-old actress/model he's shacked up with. But Joan is too ladylike to air her dirty linen, so composes herself and says with a smile, "If there's anything I can do, you have only to ask."

"Actually . . ." Before I can broach the subject of the gala, her eyes dart past me and her face lights up.

"There you are!" she cries in delight. I turn to see Bradley walking toward us. On his arm is a tall, stunning brunette, wearing a teal, silk wrap dress that accentuates her slender curves, and who's a dead ringer for Kate Middleton: dark-lashed hazel eyes, flawless features in a peaches-and-cream complexioned face, and mink-brown hair that falls in loose curls over her shoulders.

"Sorry we're late. My flight was delayed—I only just got in," she apologizes to Joan. She doesn't just look like Kate Middleton. She sounds like Kate Middleton with her plummy British accent that brings to mind tea at Buckingham Palace and riding the hounds at Balmoral.

Bradley makes the introductions. "Tish, this is Genevieve. Genevieve, this is Tish." I'm grateful when he doesn't mention that I work for his parents. Bad enough I look like a commoner in the presence of royalty, wearing my flowered sundress held together with a safety pin in back—one of the straps broke on my way here—and high heels from five seasons ago; I don't need to be seen as the hired help. "Genevieve's visiting from New York." Ah, yes, the girlfriend.

"Lovely to meet you, Tish. Bradley's told me all about you," she says as we shake hands. Her manner is warm and relaxed, giving no hint she knows the circumstances in which Bradley and I became acquainted. Or that he almost received multiple lacerations courtesy of yours truly.

I soon learn she's smart and accomplished in addition to being drop-dead gorgeous, an orthopedic surgeon with a private practice in Manhattan who also volunteers for Doctors Without Borders. She and Bradley met at a hospital in Fallujah, where she was operating on bomb victims and he was covering a story. I wish I could say she was stuck-up because then I'd have a legitimate reason to dislike her, but in fact it's Joan who does the bragging while Genevieve blushes modestly.

"Your girlfriend's nice," I feel compelled to remark to Bradley as we head for the bar a few minutes later, me to refresh my Diet Coke, him to get drinks for the other ladies, who were engrossed in conversation when we left them. Then, because it's too obvious to ignore, "Gorgeous, too."

He doesn't comment. Out of consideration for my squashed ego, I realize with his next words. "You're looking very fetching yourself," he says, smiling as his gaze travels lightly over me.

My cheeks warm. But I'm quick to deflect the gentlemanly compliment. "I clean up good." It's not that I don't think I'm attractive, but I'm not in the same league as Genevieve. When men look at me, all they see at first glance is blond hair and big boobs. Which is why I used to get hit on a lot in bars.

"I didn't say anything to her, in case you were wondering."

"You mean about the fact I saw her boyfriend naked, or that I assaulted you when you were coming out of the shower?" I respond unthinkingly, assuming the "her" in question was Genevieve.

He chuckles. "I was talking about my mom."

"Oh." Great. Now he knows I was picturing him naked. "Right. The vase."

"She didn't even notice it was missing."

"She will. But hopefully not before I've found a replacement." We get in line at the bar.

"Either way, I meant it when I said I'd take the fall, so have no fears. I'm a man of my word." He tips me a wink that goes through me like a shot of whiskey. He's even better-looking than I remembered, wearing jeans that hug him in all the right places and a crisp, white button-down shirt with a fitted dark-gray blazer. He smells of the outdoors and, faintly, of Genevieve's perfume.

"I'm not as worried about the vase as I am about her finding out I almost nailed you with it," I tell him.

He leans in close, the light brush of his lips against my ear and husky intimacy of his voice sending a jolt of electricity straight down through the pit of my stomach as he murmurs, "It'll be our secret, then." When we're headed back to Joan and Genevieve with our drinks, he says, "I was going to phone to see how you were doing, but Daniel said you weren't taking any calls."

I'm warmed by the show of concern, and at the same time annoyed at Daniel, although I know he was only being protective. "That's not entirely true. I was only screening my calls. Because I was sick of dealing with the press. Present company excluded," I remember to add. "Thankfully that seems to have died down." Interest in my story had faded with the news of another celebrity death. The husband of actress Delilah Ward, whose twin-engine Cessna, which he was piloting at the time, went down in the ocean off Catalina Island.

"That's a relief. One less thing to stress about."

Right. Now I only have to worry about nabbing my mom's killer. "You can say that again. Now I know what it's like to be famous. The not-so-fun part, anyway. You can't walk out of your house without blow-drying your hair or putting on makeup. Believe me, no woman in her thirties looks good on her own at six in the morning. At least not on camera. Except maybe Kate Middleton," I blurt.

He chuckles. "I'm just glad to see you looking so well."

"Getting there. I'm behaving myself, at least, which must mean something. Thanks for giving me the benefit of the doubt, by the way. You know, for not assuming I was a madwoman."

"Maybe I did at first," he admits, smiling as he moves closer to let a heavyset woman squeeze past. "But I've seen it before, with soldiers just off the battlefield—they'll fire at anything that moves, their nerves are so shot—so I knew what I was looking at. Lucky for me you weren't armed."

"Lucky for us both. Then your mom really would kill me."

He chuckles again, then his expression turns serious. "Have there been any breaks in the case?"

"None that I know of. But I'm not on the warmest of terms with the lead detective, so he's not giving me much. He and I went to school together," I explain when Bradley arches his eyebrow at me in a questioning look. "Long story. And no, we were never romantically involved."

"So he's not secretly carrying a torch?"

"Hardly. Though a torch was involved." He gives me another quizzical look, at which I explain, "I set fire to his car in high school." No sooner are the words out than I want to snatch them back. God. What's wrong with me? What is it about him that makes me want to pour out my innermost self?

He gives a low whistle. "Whoa. You don't mess around, do you?"

"It wasn't my finest hour." I feel my cheeks warm at the memory.

"He must have done something pretty bad to piss you off that much."

"It wasn't so much what he did but that he wasn't very gentlemanly about it afterwards."

"Ah. I see." Bradley nods in understanding.

"The trouble with getting even is," I reflect aloud, "that it doesn't make things better. If I had to do it over again . . ." I shrug, my voice trailing off. "You want to know why I don't drink anymore? That's why. It tends to cloud your judgment. Though it took me years to figure that out."

"Better late than never."

"*Too* late as far as Spence Breedlove is concerned. What happens in high school doesn't stay in high school when you've lived in the same community your entire life. It comes back to haunt you. Or bite you in the—" I break off when I'm bumped by someone from behind. Thrown off balance, I grab onto Bradley's arm to steady myself, mindless of the fact that he's holding a glass of wine in each hand. Next thing I know, I'm looking at a red wine stain splashed across the front of his white shirt. I stare at it in horror. *Oh no. Not again.* He must think I'm a walking disaster zone.

"God, I'm so sorry!"

"Not your fault," he's quick to assure me, casting a reproachful glance at the retreating back of the offender, a stocky man in a plaid sports coat who appears oblivious.

I feel awful nonetheless. "Once is an accident, twice is cursed."

"It's no big deal, really."

"Come with me." I motion for him to follow as I head for the restroom. If there's one thing I'm good at it's getting out stains.

"We have to stop meeting like this," he intones theatrically when we're closeted in the restroom.

I play along, placing my hand over my heart. "It's no use fighting it, my darling. It's bigger than the both us."

We burst into peals of laughter. Then our eyes lock as the laughter drains away. The restroom is built to accommodate only one person, so it has us standing practically toe-to-toe. For a crazy moment I have the feeling he's about to kiss me. I catch the mingled scents of his minty breath and the wine on his shirt. For a second I forget to breathe. Only when we break eye contact, as he moves to take off his blazer, is the spell broken. He unbuttons his shirt and hands it to me.

I try not to stare at him when he stands before me bare-chested. The last time I saw him in a semi-naked state, I was too freaked out to fully appreciate it. Now I find myself studying him out of the corner of my eye as I get to work on the stain with my handy Tide To-Go pen. When you live in a beach community, buff bodies are part of the scenery, but Bradley's is unlike that of the surfer dudes or volleyball players I'm used to seeing. He's like a panther sighted in the wild, a marvel of symmetry, the wicked scar on his shoulder testament to the dangers he faces in his line of work. With another man I might have worried he'd try to take advantage of me, but with Bradley I worry about what I'd like to do to him, which is to tear off the rest of his clothes.

I avert my gaze to focus on the stain, attacking it with a vigor I normally use in stripping paint from woodwork. "There you go. Good as new," I say, handing his shirt back when I'm done.

"Amazing. How did you do that? It's like a magic trick." He admires my handiwork, but I notice he's in no hurry to put his shirt back on. Maybe because the front is soaking wet. I guess I was a little too assiduous in applying cold water to get the stain out. I grimace and grab a handful of paper towels. "We might do better with that." He points toward the electric hand-dryer on the wall next to the towel dispenser, then punches it on, holding the wet part of his shirt in the airstream until it's dry. "Next time I'll remember to bring a change of clothes," he teases.

I groan. "I'm cursed, I'm telling you."

He turns so we're face-to-face, placing his hands on my shoulders, his eyes crinkled in amusement as he looks into mine. My heart stutters in my chest and once again I forget to breathe. "Accident-prone maybe, not cursed. Just promise not to go off on me if I ever make you mad."

"I don't see that happening," I reply with a shaky laugh.

We emerge from the restroom to find that a line has formed. The guy at the head of the line, a skinny blond hipster with a pierced eyebrow, gives me a knowing smirk as I pass by. I respond with a withering look, the effect of which is kind of spoiled by the fact that my cheeks are on fire.

Joan and Genevieve are still deep in conversation when we rejoin them after another trip to the bar. I perk up when I overhear them talking about the upcoming gala. Until I learn the price of admission is $500 a plate and, even if I could afford to pay that kind of money, seating is at maximum capacity. My heart sinks. When Bradley says to me, "You and Daniel should come," I could have sworn he'd read my mind. He turns to his mother to ask, "You can comp them, can't you?"

She looks momentarily taken aback but quickly recovers her manners. She smiles indulgently at him. "Afraid you'll be bored to death by all the old people? I don't blame you one bit." To me she says, "I'm sure that can be arranged, my dear. There are always last-minute cancellations, so finding seats shouldn't be a problem. That is, if you and Daniel don't have other plans."

Normally I go out of my way to avoid large social gatherings, black-tie affairs in particular. There are few things in life more torturous than having to make small talk with strangers while standing for hours in high heels sucking in one's gut (I've never known evening wear that didn't call for serious flexing of stomach muscles). I used to enjoy parties when they were an excuse to drink, but nowadays I don't see the point unless it's for a good cause like tonight's. But I'll gladly strap on my pantyhose, in lieu of a holster, for a chance to do some detective work.

"We'd love to come," I tell her.

CHAPTER SEVEN

The Saturday evening of the gala I pull into the parking lot at the Fontana at the appointed hour. I feel like the poor relation at a Mafia funeral in my dusty Ford Explorer amidst all the shiny, late-model luxury vehicles. I'm nervous and excited all at once. I take a moment to drink in the view after I've climbed out. The best thing about the Fontana is its spectacular setting, perched on a wind-swept bluff overlooking the sea, surrounded by open land awash in coastal scrub and dotted with Monterey cypress. I gaze out at the ocean, watching the sun set fire to the horizon in a blaze of crimson and gold. Seagulls soar overhead and pelicans skim the swells.

"Never gets old, does it?" Ivy steps up alongside me. She's my plus-one for tonight. I'd forgotten Daniel had a prior engagement when I accepted for him: He's attending an oceanographic convention in Monterey at which Professor Gruen is the keynote speaker. Ivy looks like a fairy princess with her raven curls piled atop her head, secured with mother-of-pearl inlaid combs. She's wearing vintage Balenciaga made of rose silk chiffon, the same gown worn by Grandmother Ladeaux at the debutantes ball in New Orleans the year she came out. My own gown is a designer knockoff, silk crepe in a shimmery gold with a low-cut neck-line that highlights my best assets. In my high heels I tower over Ivy—Malibu Barbie meets Madame Alexander.

"It makes me think of the kingdom in Hamlet," I observe.

Ivy slips her arm through mine. "Let's hope there are no ghosts."

We start down the path that leads through the lushly landscaped grounds to the main building below, built hacienda-style around an inner courtyard. A sand-colored stucco façade splashed in bougainvillea leads to a tiled reception area where we're greeted by an attractive blonde wearing a black silk *cheongsam* embroidered with the Fontana crest. She consults the guest list before waving us on through. We step through an archway into a tiled passageway, which takes us to the courtyard, thronged with party guests. Elegant-looking men and ladies in tuxedos and evening wear stand chatting with one another, bathed in the glow from the foot lights and sconces that ring the perimeter and fairy lights strung along the trellises at either end. The shimmer of satin, the sparkle of jewels—everywhere I look I see something to dazzle the eye.

This year's fundraiser is for Smile Train. I noticed the poster in the reception area on my way in, with its before-and-after photos of underprivileged children whose disfigured faces had been transformed by the surgeons affiliated with the charity, but here in the inner sanctum there's nothing to remind one of life's harsher realities. Servers circulate among the guests with trays of canapés and flutes of champagne. A string quartet plays by the signature mosaic fountain at the center of the courtyard and, poised at either end, are tonight's host and hostess, Douglas and Joan Trousdale. She looks regal in a high-necked lilac chiffon gown; he's the silver fox from Central Casting with his salt-and-pepper hair, athletic build, and golfer's tan. If this were a world map, she'd be in Antarctica and he the Arctic Circle, an apt metaphor given the sub-zero atmosphere between the two. I give them credit for putting on a good face, though. At next year's gala it'll be a new Mrs. Trousdale co-hosting the event, but until then the current Mrs. Trousdale stands proud.

I spot Ivy's boss, Parker Lane, accompanied by his long-time partner, Desmond, and he waves to us. He's dressed as though for a nineteenth-century ball, wearing a morning coat that has him looking like an extra from *Downton Abbey*. Parker is a frustrated costume designer at heart, I'm convinced. Ivy goes over to say hello while I make my way across the courtyard to greet our host.

"Tish, good of you to come." Douglas treats me to his executive handshake while nearly blinding me with his porcelain veneers. I'm surprised he even remembered my name. When I worked at Trousdale Realty, I was just another cog in the wheel; since I became his property manager all my dealings have been with Joan. "Have you met my fiancée, Tiffany?" He turns to the twenty-something blonde at his side, who dutifully offers her hand like a dog performing a trick.

"Delighted," she murmurs.

She could be a model straight out of a Victoria's Secret catalogue, only not as scantily clad. Though the backless and semi-transparent turquoise crepe de chine gown she's wearing, with its neckline that plunges practically to her navel, could certainly qualify as lingerie. Lush, buttery locks tumble over bronzed shoulders and her baby blues are as big and bright as the rock on her finger. I lean in to admire the ring. "Congratulations on your engagement. Have you set a date?"

Her smile falters and she looks to Douglas, who answers for her, "Not yet, but soon." *Soon as I'm done mopping the floor with the current Mrs. Trousdale,* I mentally fill in. Then his gaze moves past me as he greets the couple coming up behind me. "John, Nancy, good of you to come."

I head over to greet Joan, helping myself to a glass of bubbly—sparkling water, that is—along the way. She gives me a smile as genuine as her husband's was false, informing me that she had arranged for Ivy and me to be seated at Bradley's and Genevieve's table at the banquet that's to follow. I don't know whether to be pleased or worried, given how unsettled I feel whenever

I'm around Bradley. I thank her nonetheless, and she says, "They insisted on it. Knowing my son, he'd have found an excuse not to come otherwise. He loathes these affairs. His idea of a party is beer with his buddies." She shakes her head in fond exasperation, while I think, *My kind of guy.*

We chat for a few minutes more before I head off in search of Ivy. I spot her by the fountain chatting with a tall, dark-haired, and saffron-skinned man handsome enough to be a Bollywood star. True to form, she has him captivated; he can't take his eyes off of her. Ivy's irresistible to men. Even when she's not trying to be. Especially then. I leave him to bask in her unadulterated glow while I mingle. I buttonhole several, longtime Fontana employees, who I'd recognized from the website, before I hit pay dirt with an older woman named Seraphina, the colonic irrigation therapist at the wellness center, who's worked there since the seventies when it was a funky Esalen-style retreat owned by Douglas's father, Leon. Better yet, she remembers my mom.

"You're Ava's daughter? Yes, I see the resemblance, now you mention it." She peers at me through the dim glow from the recessed lights in the brick walls of the courtyard, then shakes her head. "She was a lovely woman."

"Did you know her well?"

"Well enough. It was quite a shock when I read about her in the paper. I just assumed . . . well, she was always talking about exotic places she'd like to visit. I'd pictured her living in a foreign country. South America perhaps."

"Why South America?"

"No reason. But if anyone would move there, it was your mom."

"What else do you remember about her?"

"She was very outgoing." Seraphina is the polar opposite: drab and plain. A plainness emphasized by the shapeless gown she's wearing and her unadorned face framed by a coronet of braids. "Everyone liked her. I never heard anyone say a bad word about her, even after—" She breaks off, her cheeks reddening. She seems grateful for the distraction when a server appears with a tray of canapés. She helps herself to a puff pastry. "Have you tried these? They're delicious."

"I know about her lover. It's okay to talk about it," I assure her.

Seraphina makes a rueful face. "I'm sorry. I shouldn't have mentioned it."

"In the larger scheme of things, the fact that she cheated on my dad is the least of it."

"Yes, I suppose." Her eyes dart past me as if in search of a familiar face, someone who will give her an excuse to ditch me and what's shaping up to be an uncomfortable conversation.

"I don't know much about him, though, except that he was on the construction crew that was working here at the time. I was wondering if there was anything you could tell me about him."

"Not really, no. I only knew him to say hello to. There wasn't much socializing between the staff and crew."

"Except with him and my mom."

The color in her cheeks deepens. "Well, yes, there was that. He was very handsome. A lot of the ladies had crushes on him."

Something about the way she said it makes me ask, "But not you?"

"Goodness, no," she says with a laugh. "I'm in a committed relationship."

"So was my mom."

"With my partner, Monica."

"Oh."

"He reminded me of that actor. I can't think which one . . ."

"Clint Eastwood?"

She brightens. "Yes, that's him."

We're interrupted just then by the muffled trilling of my ringtone. I extract my phone from my beaded clutch to see Arthur's bespectacled image on the screen. I'm tempted to let it go to voicemail, but what if it was an emergency? I'd never forgive myself. I excuse myself to take the call.

"This had better be good," I growl into the phone after I've ascertained it's not an emergency.

"Tish, this is *huge!*" he cries excitedly.

"What's huge is that I'm going to be hugely pissed off if this is because you ran out of milk for your cereal or you can't tune in to Showtime. Because I already explained to you why I had to cancel your premium channels. You can't afford it. It was putting you over your monthly budget."

"It's not about that," he replies impatiently. "That's not why I'm calling."

"What, then?"

"I discovered the answer. The key to it all!"

"Arthur, what are you talking about?" An alarm pings in my head.

"It's too complicated to give you a detailed explanation. Think of it as the *psi* of all things computer-related. I stumbled on it by accident when Ray and I were writing the code for our video game."

"Who knew the answers to the universe could be found in gaming?" I remark dryly.

"Tish, this could alter the face of the entire computer industry!"

"Arthur." The alarm in my head is shrilling now. "Did you take your meds today?"

"Yes, I'm sure I did. Don't I always?" he answers distractedly.

"No, you don't. What about yesterday?" I hadn't had time to stop by on my way home from work to check up on him—a broken pipe at the Belknaps' had kept me working late into the evening. "You know what happens when you forget to take your meds." *This is what happens.*

"You're not listening," he says irritably. "This is *important.*"

"I don't doubt it, but can it wait until tomorrow? I'll take you to breakfast and you can tell me all about it then. In the meantime do me a favor and check to make sure you took your meds." I keep them sorted in a pill organizer so, if he skips a day, I'll know.

He blows out an exasperated breath. "All right, if you insist."

"Also, get some sleep."

"Sleep?" His voice rises. "Did Einstein sleep after he discovered $E=MC^2$?"

"Einstein wasn't mentally ill. Plus he was, you know. Einstein."

Seraphina has vanished into the crowd by the time I hang up. I'm wandering around in search of her when I catch sight of Bradley and Genevieve. They might have been walking in on a red carpet; I see heads turning in their direction, eyes tracking their movements. He looks like James Bond fresh from the casinos of Monte Carlo in his tuxedo; she, the princess to whom she bears a striking resemblance, wearing a pearl gray gown shot with silver threads that shimmer around her like spring rain. My green-eyed monster rears its ugly head, and I struggle to contain it. It's not her fault I feel inadequate next to her. Also, what if my leg was about to be amputated, after some terrible accident, and she was the only one who could save it? She'd be a godsend, then.

She spots me and breaks into a grin as she hurries over. "Where's Daniel?" she asks after we've exchanged greetings. I explain that he had a prior engagement and couldn't make it. "What a shame. But I must say, I'm terribly glad *you're* here. I don't know a single other soul." She tucks her arm through mine—my new BFF—but I swiftly extricate myself under the pretext of admiring her dress.

"What are you wearing?" I borrow a red-carpet term. "It's gorgeous."

"Oh, just something I picked up at Harvey Nichols." She casually names an exclusive London department store before complimenting me on my knock-off. "*You* look absolutely smashing."

"Smashing," echoes Bradley, coming up behind her. He tips me an impudent wink, and I flip him the bird when his girlfriend's attention is diverted by the call to supper. "Shall we?" he says, offering us each an arm when the other guests begin making their way toward the tent on the lawn.

Ivy is already seated when we get to our table, conveniently, or more likely through a last-minute shuffling of place cards, next to her new admirer. His name is Rajeev Jaswinder and he's a Stanford-educated computer analyst for IBM, I learn as we chat over the first course—a salad of Meyer-lemon infused crab, baby lettuce, and heirloom tomatoes. If he and Ivy end up getting married, my brother will have someone, besides Ray, who speaks his language. I'm not holding my breath, however. Ivy has rejected more marriage proposals than I have the indecent kind.

I'm conscious of Bradley seated across from me, and it has me feeling the heat that isn't just from three hundred warm bodies inside a tent. I catch his eye at one point, and he gives me a look that seems to say, *I'd rather it was just us, but we have to make nice to these other people because we're well-mannered adults.* The Spanx I'm wearing under my gown suddenly grow that much tighter.

Meanwhile, I'm keeping a bead on Seraphina, seated at another table, the one closest to the entrance. I'm eager to pick up where we left off, but that will have to wait until I can catch her alone.

After supper come the speeches. Joan introduces the director of the charity, a dynamic Jamaican woman in her forties who speaks of the work her organization does. She's followed by a silver-haired surgeon who tells stories of the young people, like the ten-year-old Indian boy, born with a harelip, he'd recently operated on, whose lives have been transformed by Smile Train. Douglas Trousdale makes the closing remarks and thanks everyone for "giving so generously." You'd never know he was being anything but generous toward the wife he'd discarded.

When I glance again at Seraphina's table, I see that her seat is empty. She must have slipped away during the last speech. I excuse myself to go in search of her. That's when I notice Joan and Douglas's chairs (at separate tables naturally), are sitting empty as well. Probably a coincidence. I can't think of a reason why those two would meet in private unless it was to rip each other's heads off. Which is precisely what they're doing—verbally if not physically—when

I encounter them a few minutes later as I'm crossing the lawn on my way to the restrooms. They're in the Zen garden, described on the Fontana website as "a place for quiet reflection," engaged in a heated argument. Low, angry voices ripple through the night air like the currents out at sea.

". . . not one cent more. That was my final offer."

"You think thirty-five years counts for nothing? We'll see what the judge has to say about that!"

"You're forgetting the pre-nup."

"The only reason there's a pre-nup was because your lawyer insisted on it. As I recall, you were against it."

"It's a signed contract. That's all that counts."

"There are ways around it. And it's going to cost you a fortune."

"You greedy bitch. You'd be nothing if it weren't for me," Douglas snarls.

"I should be grateful, is that what you're saying? Oh, that's rich! After all I did for *you*. I was the perfect company wife. All those dinner parties, the functions I organized, the weekends away with your cronies. And the women. Let's not forget that. For her sake I hope your little tramp wises up before it's too late. She'll soon realize she's not the first and she won't be the last."

"You want to know why I cheated on you? Look in the mirror."

"You bastard! How dare you suggest *I'm* to blame?"

"Keep it down!" he hisses. "Christ. Haven't you made enough of a spectacle of yourself? You should have been an actress. You're so good at playing the victim. The loyal, unsuspecting wife, kicked to the curb by her heartless husband. If only our friends knew what you were really like."

Joan gives a shrill laugh. "'Our' friends? They're not your friends. They laugh at you behind your back. You're a walking cliché. You and your trophy wife-to-be. Tiffany." She spits out the name.

I hurry off before I get caught eavesdropping, their angry words ringing in my ears. That's it, I'm never getting married if this is what it can lead to. I'm sure those two were in love at one time like most newlyweds, filled with dreams for the future. And look what's become of them.

Seraphina isn't in the ladies room. Thinking she might have gone for a stroll to get some fresh air, I take a quick tour of the grounds before heading down the footpath that winds along the cliff. The night is cool and clear, the thickly-clustered stars overhead like a lace curtain drawn across the sky. The only the sound is the booming of the surf. I follow the path all the way to where it ends in a scenic overlook and I'm doubling back when I hear a woman's voice cry out. I hurry in the direction from which it seems to be coming, imagining the worst when I spy a scrap of torn fabric caught, fluttering, on a branch of the stunted conifer by the edge of the cliff a few feet away.

"Help!" the voice warbles, louder.

"I'm coming!" I call, my heart pounding.

I squat down and peer over the edge, holding onto a branch of the conifer to keep from falling over. In the moonlight I can make out a female figure in a pale chiffon gown that floats around her like a downed parachute, blown by the ocean wind, huddled on a narrow rock ledge about ten feet below—the only thing preventing her from plunging to certain death. Joan Trousdale.

CHAPTER EIGHT

During my hard-partying days I once took a tumble into a swimming pool. It wouldn't have been a big deal except the pool had been drained; as a result, I ended up in the ER with a broken wrist and two cracked ribs. So the first thought that goes through my head is that Joan must have tripped and fallen after one too many. Not until after she's pulled to safety by the fire department's rescue squad—a necessity of life in a seaside community where tourists are forever getting stranded by high tides or hiking where they shouldn't—do I learn otherwise. I don't smell liquor on her breath and she's not slurring her words when she whispers in my ear, "It wasn't an accident."

She asserts as much to the cops who take her statement at the hospital, then later to me and Bradley. When she insists, "Your father tried to kill me," I know it's not the pain medication talking.

Bradley looks as if he'd sooner be in Syria with mortars exploding around him. His voice is gentle, however. "Mom, you're confused is all. However you feel about Dad, this wasn't his doing."

She remains firm in her conviction. "You weren't there. You don't know. Ask Tish. She'll tell you." She gestures toward me. She'd asked me to come along as a witness, and I could hardly refuse.

"I didn't see anything." I repeat what I told the cops, reminding her I wasn't an eyewitness while taking care not to dismiss her, admittedly biased, account. "It was over by the time I got there."

We're in a suite in the VIP wing, which is nearly as well-appointed as a luxury hotel's: one of the perks of being a major donor of the hospital it would appear. Although Joan's injuries are minor—scrapes and bruises, a sprained wrist—she's being kept overnight for observation. She lies propped in her hospital bed, hooked to an I.V. with her other arm in a sling. I'm seated in the leather recliner. Bradley stands by the window, which looks out on an ornamental walled garden.

"You didn't see his face," Bradley reminds his mom.

"I didn't have to. We'd been arguing not five minutes before. He must have followed me." She told the cops she'd gone for a walk to calm down. "If I hadn't caught that ledge on my way down . . ."

I feel sick to my stomach. I know Douglas Trousdale to be a ruthless businessman, but is he that coldblooded? Maybe, but I find it hard to believe he'd be reckless enough to push his wife over a cliff with a black-tie affair taking place not more than two hundred yards from the scene. Anyone might've come along. As I did. More likely, Joan accidentally tripped in the dark and lost her footing. It must have felt like a push as she was propelled forward by her own momentum.

Bradley sighs. "Mom, you don't know for a fact—"

"He hates me!" she cries tearfully. "*That's* a fact."

"Dad doesn't hate you," he says in a weary voice. "I know you're angry at each other, but once the divorce is final, you can both move on with your lives."

"That won't happen if I'm dead! Mark my words, he'll try again." She turns to me. "Tish, you heard what he said. How beastly he was toward me." I regret now having reported that I'd overhead them arguing.

"I didn't actually say he was . . ." I trail off, aware of the awkward position I'm in. I can't discount Joan's version without making her look like a liar, or worse, a nutcase. But to go along with her would only cause further distress to Bradley. It seems I can't even make a 911 call without putting my ass in the wringer. "Um. Well, whatever, it sounded like you were both pretty upset."

"Of course he wasn't foolish enough to threaten me outright. That's not his style. How often have you heard him say the way to outwit your opponent is to catch him unawares?" she reminds Bradley.

"Business tactics are one thing. That's not the same as attempted murder. And, frankly, I've heard enough." There's a new sharpness to Bradley's voice. "We'll discuss it when you're feeling calmer." He and I exchange a glance. "I'm sure Tish would like to get home. And you should get some rest."

He walks me to the elevator. As we make our way along the corridor, which is deserted at this hour, I'm struck by the peacefulness of the VIP wing compared to the constant swirl of activity on the other floors. "Hospitals are no place for sick people," my grandma used to say, which makes sense only if you've ever tried to get a decent night's sleep in one. When my dad was dying of cancer, in a semi-private room two floors down, his roommate's TV had never stopped blaring and there had been hospital personnel and visitors coming and going at all hours. Here there's only the sighing of respirators and beeping of monitors, and the murmuring voices from the nurses' station.

"She's been under a lot of stress lately," Bradley says after we've walked in silence for a minute.

"Because of the divorce, you mean?"

He nods. "She's taken it hard."

"Divorce is never easy."

"Especially when you're in the middle of one. The only reason I'm here and not in New York is because I knew Mom needed me." He appears to regret that decision. "My dad can be a real prick."

I pause in mid-step, my eyes searching his face. "You don't think—?"

"No," he answers with an emphatic shake of his head. "He may go too far sometimes, but—no. The only thing he ever killed was my respect for him. I'd have forgiven him for walking out on my mom. But he didn't have to humiliate her or try to screw her over in the divorce."

I put myself in her shoes. "I don't know which would be worse, a nasty court battle or finding out my husband was engaged to be married before we were even divorced. Though I have a feeling he'll live to regret it." At the quizzical look he gives me, I clarify, "I met his fiancée."

"Exactly," he says, grim-faced, as if I'd expressed my opinion aloud. "Knowing my dad, she'll end up regretting it even more than him. He likes them young, so if she sticks it out long enough to get crow's feet . . ." He trails off with a shrug, and I cringe at the image of Douglas as an old coot bedding a woman young enough to be his granddaughter. Hugh Hefner redux. Thankfully, I'm too old for him, at thirty-six. Not that he's ever shown any interest in me. I must not be his type.

Bradley lingers when we get to the elevators. "You're sure you don't need me to drive you home?" He's probably worried I'll get into an accident, with good reason given my recent history with him and current state of exhaustion. I'm warmed by his concern. What he doesn't know is that I could've driven the route blind-folded. I'd practically lived here when Dad was dying.

"I'm sure." I touch his arm. "Go back to your mom."

He exhales and pushes a hand through his hair. "Something tells me it's going to be a long night."

I'm tempted to stick around so he won't have to stand watch alone, but it might send the wrong message, so instead I say, "I'm sure Genevieve would love to keep you company." She'd wanted to come with us to the hospital—as had Ivy before I'd persuaded her to have Rajeev take her home instead—and seemed a bit hurt at being rebuffed, however gently. "You should give her a call."

"You're right. I should."

From his tone I can tell he has no intention of doing so. And because I'm me and can't leave well enough alone, I have to weigh in. "Look, it's none of my business, but if you're worried about disturbing her this late, you should be more worried about how mad she'll be if you don't."

"Believe me, it's for her own good," he says.

"Why is that?"

"She'll realize soon enough how fucked up my family is. No sense bursting her bubble."

When the elevator door opens on the main floor, I almost run smack into the man who's stepping in as I'm stepping out. As he lifts his arm to stop me from plowing into him, I catch a glimpse of the black nylon holster strapped to his chest under his navy windbreaker. Then my gaze travels up and I find myself staring into the face of Spence Breedlove. Which probably shouldn't come as a surprise with everything else that's happened tonight—it's merely the coup de grace.

I glare at him. "What, so now you're stalking me?"

"I could ask you the same thing. You seem to have a habit of showing up at crime scenes."

"I didn't realize that's what this was."

"That has yet to be determined. Which is why I'm here."

"Well then, don't let me keep you." I start to move past him, but he seizes my arm, preventing me from going any further, his firm grip at odds with his mild tone.

"Matter of fact, you're just the person I wanted to see."

I yank my arm free, scowling at the blond behemoth towering over me. From the puffiness around his eyes and pillow crease on his cheek, it appears he was pulled from his nice, warm bed, which means he's not in the mood to be messed with. Normally he wouldn't be called in on such a matter, but this wasn't just any domestic dispute; it involved two of the town's most prominent citizens. "What do you want? I already gave my statement to the officers who were here earlier."

"Good," he says. "Then this shouldn't take long."

"This is police harassment," I grumble.

"No, this is me asking nicely." His steely blue eyes hold my gaze.

"This is a total waste of time. You should be talking to Mr. and Mrs. Trousdale. All I did was make the 911 call. That's the extent of my involvement." I rub my arms to quell the goose bumps that erupt from the blast of chilly air as the automated doors at the lobby exit swoosh open. The dress coat I'm wearing over my gown is more for show than warmth.

"And yet," he observes, "I find it curious, your being connected with two separate incidents. Makes me wonder if they might be related in some way."

A minute ago, I was flat-out exhausted. Now suddenly I'm wide awake, my blood buzzing in my veins. "Seriously? Are you suggesting I had something to do with Mr. Trousdale allegedly pushing Mrs. Trousdale over a cliff? Because if you are, then I'll *know* you have it in for me."

"Right. I forgot. You were just the Good Samaritan," he replies in a flat voice.

I narrow my eyes at him. "What, you think I'm lying?"

"I didn't say that. But, see, this is what happens when you interfere with a police investigation. It tends to undermine your credibility." I feel my face redden, at which he goes on, "Yes, that's right, I know about the visit you paid Mr. Cruikshank." I hear the undercurrent of anger in his voice.

"Oh, that." I adopt a nonchalant air. "There's a perfectly good explanation."

"I'm sure there is, and I'm dying to hear it."

"Well, unless you have a warrant for my arrest, it'll have to wait until tomorrow. It's been a long night and I'm tired. I'm going home to bed." I pull my coat around me as I move past him.

The staccato clacking of my high heels against the tiled floor of the atrium lobby is loud in my ears as I hasten toward the exit. Out of the corner of my eye I notice a beefy security guard walking toward me with his two-way in hand and an alert look on his face. All he sees is a woman in distress with a big, scary-looking dude chasing after her. He's closing in on us when Spence flashes his badge and calls, "Police business!" loud enough to have heads turning our way.

God, could this get any more excruciating?

The guard melts away and Spence falls into step with me, saying in a low voice, "We can do this the easy way or the hard way. Your choice. But if you think I'm getting some sadistic pleasure out of this, you're mistaken. I'd love nothing more than for you to be someone else's problem."

I come to a halt as I'm closing in on the glass doors at the exit. Two more steps and my body would trigger the magic eye that would have them sliding open. From there it's a ten-minute drive to my place and the bed that awaits me, where if I'm lucky, I'll catch a few hours of shut-eye before it's time to rise and shine and greet the new day. A day that will have me embroiled in a cold case involving a suspicious death, an attempted murder (if Joan Trousdale is to be believed), and the latest craziness with brother. But I don't take those steps. Because I know what it would cost me.

"Fine. You win."

Spence gives an unsmiling nod. "Come on, I'll buy you a cup of coffee." He holds his hand lightly against the small of my back as we move forward, the doors whooshing open as if at his command.

The nearest place to get coffee is the Denny's on the freeway access road. Normally I wouldn't go there; I avoided all-night eateries even in my drinking days when they were the only places that were open after the bars had closed. Aside from the fact that they're depressing as hell, I've read one too many news accounts of robberies that occur in the wee hours. But I'm with a cop, so I don't have to worry that on top of everything else I've had to endure these past weeks, I'll be kissing the linoleum while some crackhead relieves me of my purse. It's a small consolation.

"Jesus. What happened to you?" Spence stares at me after he's helped me off with my coat, his gaze taking in my evening gown that's torn at the hem and smudged with dirt. I hadn't given much thought to my appearance, but suddenly I'm self-conscious. I flash back to my senior prom and see myself stumbling up the front walk to my house after being dropped off by my date, thoroughly trashed and disheveled. The only thing missing now is the crushed corsage.

I quickly slide into the booth, keeping my coat draped over my shoulders. "This is the price you pay for wearing a knockoff."

I thought it was pretty funny, but he's not smiling as he slides in opposite me. Our waitress, a platinum-haired Marilyn Monroe look-a-like—that is, if Marilyn were still alive today and a senior citizen slinging joe for minimum wage plus tips—materializes to fill the coffee mugs on the table. He says to me, after she's shuffled off, "I think we can both agree the sooner we get this over with, the better, so why don't we make this easy? I'll ask the questions and you answer."

"Fair enough," I concede.

"Okay, so tell me. What has you looking like you were dragged a mile roped to someone's rear bumper?"

I explain about my coming to Joan's aid, how I'd waited with her until the rescue squad arrived, lying flat on my belly at the edge of the cliff to maintain eye contact, when she'd been on the verge of losing it, while reassuring her that help was on the way. I also tell him about the argument I overheard prior and Joan's allegation after the fact. "For what it's worth, I don't think she was lying."

"So you believe her story?" He seems surprised.

"I believe *she* believes it."

"Even though she didn't see him push her?"

"You know the expression: If you see bear tracks in the snow, do you need to see the bear to know it was there?"

He nods and sips his coffee. "I take your point. That still doesn't prove anything."

"No, but if she *was* pushed, Douglas Trousdale would be my number one suspect. He has the motive. With her dead he'd get to keep all the money and he wouldn't have to wait to take his next trip down the aisle. Also, from what I heard of it, their argument was pretty heated."

Spence nods thoughtfully. His next question takes me by surprise. "Do you think he did it?"

I pause as I'm tearing open a sugar packet, looking up at him. "Excuse me? Did you just ask for my opinion?"

His mouth slants in a wry smile. "Off the record."

I dump the sugar in my coffee and stir it in. "Okay, here's what I think: While I don't doubt Mr. Trousdale would love nothing more than to have Mrs. Trousdale conveniently die of natural causes, I can't quite see him pushing her over a cliff in a fit of rage, no."

"Why not?"

"He's not the type. We're talking about a guy who color-coordinates the shirts in his closet."

"Sounds like you know him pretty well."

"Not at all. But you get to know a lot about a person when you look after their home. The guy is anal is all I'm saying. I'm not exaggerating about the shirts. He even has his underwear ironed."

He lifts an eyebrow at me. "You make a habit of going through your clients' underwear drawers?"

I give him a withering look. "No. Their housekeeper mentioned it is all."

"I've known murderers who were fastidious. This one guy? He poisons his wife but saves the receipt from the hardware store where he bought the poison. He was an accountant and accountants don't toss receipts. Though I imagine an IRS audit is the least of his worries now that he's doing life."

"Yeah, but he's not stupid—Mr. Trousdale, I mean. If he was

looking to murder his wife, he'd hire a hit man. That's what rich people do. They outsource."

"That doesn't always apply with crimes of passion."

I'm reminded of Stan, and wonder again if that was how it went down with him and my mom. His prior for assault and battery shows he has a quick temper. Unlike Douglas, who's all business and no heat. "I still don't see it. He's a cold fish underneath his smiling salesman persona."

"You never know what someone is capable of," Spence remarks. "If I've learned one thing in my line of work, it's that human nature is like the ocean: We can only know a small part of it."

"What about you? Have you ever been mad enough to hit someone?" *Me, for instance, after I set fire to your car.*

"No, but I've made my wife mad enough to hit me on more than one occasion," he says with a rueful smile. "In all fairness to Donna, she's had to put up with a lot through the years. When I was a rookie working nights and weekends, I told her things would be different once I made detective. Now I'm on call twenty-four-seven and she's a single parent to our kids, the way she sees it."

"How old are your kids?" I hadn't known until now that he had any. Strange, that I know so little about the guy who affected my life and occupied so much of my thoughts when we were younger.

His expression softens. "Ryan's four; Katie's six. They take turns playing the holy terror, but they're the best thing that ever happened to me. It kills me that I don't get to see enough of them." He's quiet for a moment as he sips his coffee, then he asks, "What about you? You never got the itch?"

"You mean did I ever want to get married or have kids? No on both counts. I have my hands full with my brother."

"Or maybe you never met the right guy."

"You know something," I pause to look up at him as I tear open another sugar packet, "I believe this is the first actual conversation we've ever had. Let's not spoil it by getting too personal."

He shrugs, and gestures toward my coffee as I'm pouring in the sugar. "Would you like a Danish with that?"

"I take my coffee sweet. What of it?" I snap.

"Tish." He looks me in the eye. "Sometimes a Danish is just a Danish."

Not until we're getting ready to leave does he broach the subject we've been avoiding so far. "So," he says, leveling his gaze at me across the table. "Stan Cruikshank."

I'm careful to speak in an even voice. "I was curious about him, so I went to see him, yeah."

"You were interfering in a police investigation."

"I didn't know he was a suspect."

"He's not. Yet. We're still looking into it."

"Is he even a person of interest, or are you just blowing smoke?"

He reaches into his wallet and throws a couple of bills on the table. "It's not as cut and dried as you think."

"Why don't you explain it to me, then? I'm all ears."

He drops his voice, though it's unlikely anyone is eavesdropping. We're the only patrons at this hour and our waitress is nowhere to be seen—I'm beginning to wonder if our Marilyn Monroe look-a-like was just another dead-celebrity sighting. "Look, the DA is up for re-election in the fall and he's not going to prosecute any cases he can't win. Even if I were to launch a full investigation, there simply isn't enough evidence to get a conviction. I'm sorry. That's just how it is."

"Isn't it your job to find evidence? Stan knows something he's not telling, I'm sure of it."

"I need more than your gut feeling to go on."

"So I'm supposed to just wait around until he either confesses or some random witness materializes?"

"I didn't say I wasn't working on it. You just have to trust me."

I snort. "When have you ever given me a reason to trust you?"

I see a flash of emotion in his Tidy-Bowl blue eyes. "Let's leave aside our personal differences," he replies in a tight voice. "I'm asking—no, *telling*—you to back off. Let me do my job."

"Do what you have to do." I slide from the booth. "But I'm telling *you* I won't rest until I find out who killed my mom."

CHAPTER NINE

First thing Monday morning I call to schedule an appointment with Seraphina at the Fontana Wellness Center. She's my only lead at this point, but she'd find it odd if I were to ask her to meet me for coffee, so I have no choice but to put my ass on the line. And I don't mean that figuratively. Woodward and Bernstein had Deep Throat. I'll simply be utilizing a different orifice.

I'm informed by the woman who takes my call that the colonic irrigation therapist had a last-minute cancellation and can squeeze me in that afternoon at two o'clock. I've never felt so unlucky to catch a lucky break. By the time I arrive at the wellness center, I'm a nervous wreck, my palms sweaty and my stomach in an uproar. This is so far out of my comfort zone it's in another galaxy. But I didn't come this far to wimp out, so I bite the bullet and fill out the form I'm given.

At least the setting is pleasant. The walls, the color of a sandy beach, are hung with landscapes painted by local artists. The furniture is Pottery Barn and colorful area rugs soften the effect of the commercial carpeting. The gentle sounds of Native American flute music waft from the speaker system. Within minutes of my arrival I'm ushered down a carpeted hallway to a treatment room with pale peach walls and a framed museum poster of Monet's *Water Lilies*. It holds a chair with a hospital gown folded over it and a padded table covered in a white sheet. An interior door leads to a small bathroom. I do my best to ignore the machine mounted to the wall by the table.

No sooner have I disrobed and donned the hospital gown than Seraphina enters. She greets me warmly. "Tish, hello. I didn't expect to see you again so soon. Now, no need to be nervous." She gives my hand a reassuring squeeze. I must be ten shades of pale. "I promise you'll be glad you came. We have a saying here: Be kind to your body and it will repay the favor."

"Um. I'll take your word for it." I manage a smile.

"Good. Shall we get started, then?" She looks even plainer than she had the other night, wearing matching drawstring trousers and a tunic top, both equally shapeless, that look to be made of dye-free hemp. Her gray hair hangs in a braid down her back. A pair of Dr. Scholl's complete the vegan-chic look. "You may feel some discomfort," she says when I'm lying down, "but it's better if you try to relax. Be sure and let me know if at any point it gets to be too . . . intense, and we can take a break."

I grit my teeth as she goes to work. Good God. I can't believe people do this for the so-called health benefits. Because there can't be anything healthy about whatever is going on down there that has my intestines gurgling like a backed-up drain. "Kind" to my body? More like punishment for the abuse to which I subjected it in the past. I must have the makings of a sleuth if I'm willing to go to such an extreme. Either that or my brother isn't the only crazy one in our family.

We don't get a chance to talk until she's done and I can speak without moaning. "Well, that was certainly an experience," I remark when she returns after leaving me to get dressed. "I can't say I enjoyed it, but hopefully I'll see some benefits when I stop feeling like I'm going to pass out."

"That's the toxins leaving your body," she explains. "You should feel fine in a little while."

"I think I just need to sit down for a minute." When I lower myself into the chair, it's not just a ploy—I really am feeling a bit faint. "By the way, I've been thinking about what you said. You know, when we were talking at the party."

"Oh? I'm sorry you'll have to refresh my memory." I can't tell if she's being evasive or not.

"We were talking about my mom's boyfriend. Stan Cruikshank. I was wondering what else you could tell me about him."

"I told you what I know," she replies guardedly as she's bundling the used linens. She adds, with a note of gentle reproach, "And frankly, I don't see what good could possibly come of dredging up all that old stuff. If you want my advice, you'll let it go. Let the dead rest in peace."

"Stan isn't dead," I remind her.

"No, but that's all in the past."

"There's no statute of limitation on murder."

She gasps and brings a hand to her throat. "Oh, dear." She looks at me with wide eyes. "I had no idea he was a suspect."

"Think about it. She left home to be with him, then they both disappeared. We assumed they'd run off together, but we now know that wasn't the case. What I think is that they got into a fight and he killed her in a fit of rage. That explains why he was on the run until recently. His own brother hadn't heard from him in years." McGee had done some investigating of his own with the help of his seemingly inexhaustible supply of relatives in law enforcement. He'd obtained a copy of Stan's birth certificate. From there it had been easy to locate Stan's only living relative, a brother in his hometown of Lubbock, Texas. "I'm sure the only reason he moved back here was because he figured enough time had passed. He'd have gotten away with it too, if her body hadn't turned up."

"Have the police questioned him?"

"Yeah, but he claims he's innocent and they can't prove

otherwise. Which is where I come in. I'm doing some investigating of my own."

"I see. Well. If there's any way I can be of help . . ." she offers weakly.

"Do you know if he had any friends here at the Fontana? Besides my mom, I mean."

"We didn't socialize, so I wouldn't know. He got along with the men he worked with, as I recall." She smiles thinly. "My dad was a contractor, so I spent a lot of time around construction crews when I was growing up. There's not a lot of subtlety; you're either one of the guys or you're not. Stan was one of the guys."

"Ever see him lose his temper?"

She frowns. "No, I can't say that I did."

"Anything else you remember? No detail too small."

She ponders this, chewing on her lower lip. "There is one thing, but it's not related. I didn't think of it at the time because I didn't know she was dead, but after I learned what had happened to her, it occurred to me your mom must have died around the same time as those other people."

"What other people?" The tiny hairs on the back of my neck stand up.

"They worked here at the Fontana. Martina was one of our massage therapists. Hector was the groundskeeper. Freak accidents in both cases. She was in a car accident and he fell from a ladder. Broke his neck."

A chill goes through me.

"It was especially tragic because they were both so young. But these things happen," she says sadly.

"Do you know for a fact they were accidental deaths?" I'm not so much asking as thinking aloud. I can't take anything at face value after what happened with Joan the other night.

Seraphina becomes flustered. "No, no, no . . . I wasn't suggesting . . . Really, I shouldn't have mentioned it. It was just one of those random thoughts." Before I can question her further, I'm being ushered out the door; she has another client due any minute, she regretfully informs me.

My mind is spinning as I make my exit. *Mom died of a broken neck.*

Coincidence? Maybe. Maybe not.

My last property of the day is the Trousdales' La Mar estate. I stop at the Albertsons' along the way to buy the grocery items Joan asked me to pick up. (She's recuperating at home and must be feeling better if she's concerning herself with mundane matters like paper towels and peanut butter.) Genevieve answers my knock. If I needed further proof of the unfairness of life, it's the sight of her in her bikini. Her body is as flawless as the Photoshopped images of celebrities in magazines. Her legs go on for miles, her waist is Disney-princess proportions, her breasts round and firm and clearly not fake, and there's not a cellulite dimple in sight.

She seems delighted to see me rather than annoyed at the intrusion. Maybe that's because Bradley isn't around. "He went into town to run some errands," she informs me. "Here, let me help with that." She relieves me of the shopping bags that are weighing me down in addition to the ten pounds I gained just looking at her. I go back for the rest. After everything's been stowed in the cupboards, she insists I stay for some iced tea. "I can fix you a sandwich to go with it, if you like."

"I'll pass on the sandwich, but iced tea sounds good." My gut still feels a little rocky. In fact, I may never eat again. Which wouldn't be a bad thing if it means looking as svelte as Genevieve.

"Poor Joan. What a frightful ordeal!" she exclaims when we're sitting outside sipping our iced teas in the shade of the cabana that overlooks the infinity pool. Clearly she knows all about it; there had been no keeping a lid on something so huge. "It's easy to see how she became confused."

"Because she thinks her husband tried to kill her, you mean?"

"Well, yes. I mean, really." She directs her troubled gaze to where the pool meets the sky at the seaward end of the patio in an unbroken line of blue. "Clearly her mind was playing tricks."

"Or it happened the way she said it did. I'm just saying," I add, as she twists around to face me with a horrified gasp.

"You don't really think that, do you?"

"No. But I don't know that we can dismiss it out of hand."

"I refuse to believe it," she says firmly.

Fearing I may have gone too far, I stick to what is factually true. "I guess you know their divorce is pretty acrimonious."

"Yes, and he's been positively beastly about it all." She sounds like Mary Poppins speaking of a naughty child. "But he's not a violent man. Quite the contrary. He's always perfectly lovely with me."

I wouldn't describe Douglas as "lovely," but whatever. "There's a lot of money at stake."

"Masses," she says with the nonchalance of someone born to the manor, as they say in jolly old England. Clearly she comes from wealth—another reason to hate her besides the fact that she's beautiful and accomplished and has a body that belongs on the cover of a *Sports Illustrated* swimsuit edition. Oh yeah, and she's practically engaged to the man on whom I have a crush.

That is, if it were possible to hate someone so nice.

"People have been known to kill for less," I point out.

Even with the big sunglasses she's wearing it's not hard to read her expression. She's clearly aghast. "He'd have to be mad!" She doesn't mean mad as in angry, either. Though there is that.

"It's usually the husband," I remind her.

I have murder on the brain. After my chat with Seraphina, I drove over to the public library downtown, where I combed through old editions of *The Sentinel* on microfilm, in search of news accounts of the two deaths she'd mentioned. They were easy enough to find because they'd both occurred within the same year, the most recent one only a few months before my mom's disappearance. Twenty-six-year-old Martina Vuković had perished in an automobile accident. Thirty-two-year-old Hector Martinez had suffered a fatal fall from an extension ladder. No witnesses in either case: Martina had been driving on an isolated stretch of road late at night and no other vehicle was involved; Hector had been home alone, trimming a tree in his backyard. One thing I was struck by, aside from the obvious Fontana connection, was that they were both immigrants. Martina originated from Bosnia and Hector from Mexico. Coincidence or contributing factor? I was leaning toward the latter. Two foreigners who'd become friends, possibly lovers, out of a shared sense of alienation, and who then stumbled onto something that got them killed.

Douglas Trousdale had been around at the time. It was during the ten-year period, after he'd graduated college and before he went into business for himself, that he'd worked for his father. What if Hector or Martina had caught him embezzling and threatened to expose him? Or he'd been paying them to keep quiet? Whichever, he'd have wanted them gone. Before, I wouldn't have believed him capable of murder, but ever since Joan's misadventure, I've been questioning whether I'm on the right track with Stan. Maybe I should be focusing on Douglas instead.

"There's no doubt in my mind." Genevieve's voice breaks into my reverie. "It's nothing more than a case of someone jumping to the wrong conclusion. I don't blame Joan. It was dark, and she was distraught. But the sooner we can put this behind us the better. Before it gets any uglier."

"Assuming he doesn't try again." I recall Joan's chilling words.

I watch the color drain from Genevieve's face. She sets her iced tea down on the glass Brown Jordan patio table, hard enough to set the ice to rattling. Clearly it hadn't occurred to her until now that the incident in question might, in fact, have been an attempt on Joan's life, and not the last one, either. "Perish the thought," she murmurs, then winces at her unfortunate word choice.

I hear the distant roar of the tractor mower, a reminder that Daniel doesn't have classes to teach on Monday afternoons; he devotes those hours to his maintenance chores around here. I finish my tea and get up to leave. "I should go see what my boyfriend is up to. Thanks for the tea."

She walks me to the back gate. Whatever was worrying her before she seems to have put it behind her. There are no frown lines creasing her unblemished brow and her Kate Middleton smile is back in place. "By the way, I asked Daniel if you two were free for supper on Thursday and he said I should check with you. You don't have any other plans, do you?" She eyes me hopefully.

Great. I'm boxed in. It's not like I can make up an excuse, not with my boyfriend in residence; one slip of the tongue and she'd know I was a liar. She'd be hurt, and though I may not be the nicest person, I'm not cruel. "No. That sounds nice. Can I bring anything? I'm not much of a cook, but I can do a salad. Or we could eat out. I wouldn't want you to go to any trouble."

"Oh, it's not trouble. I love to cook," she assures me. "Actually, it's rather a passion of mine."

"Don't tell me. You studied at the Cordon Bleu," I reply in jest.

"I did, actually," she replies modestly. "The summer before medical school."

Of course. Is there anything this woman isn't good at?

I find Daniel over by the tennis court cutting the grass with the tractor mower. He's shirtless, wearing shorts and sandals, and the stripe of red skin on his nose tells me he's forgotten to put on sun block again. Typical absentminded professor. He waves to me and cuts the engine, climbing down to greet me. "I'm not going to hug you. I'm all sweaty," he says as he walks toward me.

"I'll take that as a sign of affection." I give him a peck on the cheek, then step back to admire the fruits of his labor—grass mowed, hedges clipped, flowerbeds pungent with a fresh application of fertilizer. "Nice work." I don't know how he juggles it with all of the other demands on his time.

He grins at me and pushes his sunglasses onto his head. He looks boyish with his sunburned nose and sandy hair standing up in damp tufts where he's raked his fingers through it in wiping the sweat from his brow. "You done for the day?" I nod, and he says, "Give me another half hour and I'm all yours."

"I may not be able to wait that long."

"Why, what's the hurry?"

"Come with me and you'll find out," I say in my most seductive voice. I give him another kiss, this one on the lips, and turn and head down the path to his place, hips swaying. He needs no further enticement.

A quick shower and he's all over me like maple syrup on French toast. "Wow. You were on fire," I say when we're lying in bed afterwards, naked and sweaty, enjoying the cool breeze from the ceiling fan revolving slowly overhead. "Was it me or seeing Genevieve in her bikini?" I tease him.

"You know I have eyes only for you, Tish." He nuzzles my neck. I know he means it but, truthfully, it's been a while since sparks have flown in the bedroom, so whatever the reason, it's all good.

"You're forgiven, in that case."

"What for?" He draws back to look at me.

"Painting me into a corner when she invited us to supper."

"Oh, that. I did nothing of the kind. I told her I'd have to check with you."

"After you told her we didn't have plans."

"I thought you liked her and Bradley."

"I do. That's beside the point." He looks so taken aback, his eyes clear and blameless as a baby's that I take pity on him. "Never mind. I'm sure it'll be a nice evening. Now tell me about your day."

He does, and I tell him about mine, which I have to say was way more interesting than a contaminated lobster tank and a student flunking out. "Two Fontana employees—three if you count my mom—die within months of each other, both from fatal injuries. You think there could be a connection?"

"I think," he says, lying on his back with his hands laced behind his head, "you may be reading too much into it."

"No, seriously, what are the odds?"

"I don't have the statistics, but my guess is, roughly one in ten thousand." I should have known better than to ask a scientist. "In other words, unlikely but not beyond the realm of possibility."

"Still. I have a funny feeling about it."

He turns his head to look at me. "You suspect foul play?"

"Maybe. I don't know. What if Douglas was behind it? He worked at the Fontana back then."

"And now his wife is claiming he tried to murder her. If this were a movie, the spooky soundtrack would be playing and I'd be yelling, 'Don't go in the basement.'" He deepens his voice as he utters the line from a thousand slasher flicks.

"You think this is all in my head?" I pull myself into an upright position, the better to glare at him.

"Yes, I do. That said, I also think it's perfectly natural under the circumstances." He pulls me back into his embrace, but he might as well be hugging his tractor mower, I'm so tense. "First your mom, then Joan, now this. It's enough to have the Dalai Lama looking suspect."

"There's a lot that doesn't add up," I insist.

"Or you're seeing monsters where there are none." He speaks in the same, calming tone I've heard him use with students when they're in hysterics over a failing grade or some other perceived catastrophe. I wrestle free of his embrace and jump out of bed. He rolls onto his side so he's facing me, head propped on his elbow. "Tish. Please. I'm not trying to pick a fight. I'm on your side."

"No, you're not. You're patronizing me." I start pulling on my clothes.

"I'm sorry if it sounded like I was. I didn't mean it that way. I was only trying to help."

I swing around to face him as I'm zipping up my jeans. "How? How is this helping, Daniel?"

"You're asking questions that could get you fired."

"Are you worried about what would happen to you if I do?"

A hurt look comes over his face, and I start to feel bad. Naturally he's concerned about his living situation. He'd be out on his ear along with me, damned by association, if I were to voice my suspicions about Douglas and it got back to him. Even Joan wouldn't be able to protect us. The property is in both their names, at least until the divorce is final, and he pays the bills. I would have relented, then, if Daniel had lost his temper or even sulked. Instead he heaves a long-suffering sigh, which only incenses me further. He sits up, swinging his feet over the edge of the mattress so they're resting on the floor, arms extended in supplication. "Tish. Please. Don't be this way."

"You think I have a choice? That I can snap my fingers and be a different person?" I demand. "Sorry, I only come in one flavor, and it's not vanilla!" I grab my sneakers and march out the door.

I decide to pay a visit to McGee on my way home. He's not in his office, so I climb the stairs to his apartment. He answers my knock, beer in hand, wearing baggy chinos and a wife beater that shows his tattoos: a coiled rattlesnake on one arm, Jesus on the cross on the other—an interesting statement, if that's what it is. I didn't phone ahead, yet he doesn't seem surprised to see me.

"Pardon the mess. It's the maid's day off." He smirks and steps aside to let me in. The place isn't so much untidy as it is tired-looking with its blue shag carpeting and outmoded furnishings: a worn plaid recliner and matching sofa, laminate coffee table with more cigarette burns than a Guantanamo Bay detainee, and a bookcase that holds a handful of paperbacks and a TV set dating back to when *Family Ties* aired in prime time. The kitchen appliances are seventies-era avocado. "Have a seat." He motions toward the sofa. "Get you something to drink?"

"Water. With ice, if you have it."

"Sure, I got ice. Got running water and cable TV, too." Only McGee would get prickly at an innocuous request. He walks over to the fridge and pulls out an ice-cube tray with more frost than ice from the freezer section. He gives it a good whack against the kitchen sink and drops a handful of cubes in a plastic tumbler. He fills it with water from the tap and brings it to me.

"So, how does a cop end up in a place like this?" I ask when he's seated across from me.

He squints at me. "Why, something wrong with it?"

"No, I was just asking."

"If you must know, it was on account of the previous manager being a crackhead. The owner, Red—he's a friend of my cousin Tommy—found out he was cooking the books to feed his drug habit and fired his ass. That was where I came in. He figured he couldn't do wrong with a cop."

"Interesting."

His raptor eyes fix on me. "Your turn. What brings *you* here? Because I have a feeling this ain't no social call."

"As much as I enjoy your scintillating company, no." I offer up a crooked smile. "Something came up that I'd like to run by you. Is this a good time?"

"Good as any." He bids me to continue with an exaggerated, impresario-style sweep of his arm. I tell him about Martina and Hector and my growing suspicion that Douglas Trousdale had something to do with their deaths. McGee listens intently, showing no indication of whether he thinks I'm onto something or as delusional as my brother. He doesn't weigh in with an opinion until I'm done.

"So Trousdale gets caught with his hand in the till or he's

running some scam. Seems unlikely two low-level employees fresh off the boat would've found out about it, but let's say they did. They threaten to expose him. Or they're blackmailing him in exchange for keeping quiet. He's desperate. And unlike my boss, Red, he can't just send them packing. He needs a permanent solution. The kind that requires the services of a professional." He mulls this over. "Interesting theory."

It sounds even more bizarre coming out of his mouth, yet I can't shake the gut feeling that has me so unsettled. "What I can't figure out is where my mom comes in. If she got tangled up in it somehow and was killed because of it, why dispose of the body? Why not make it look like an accident?"

"Maybe because it would've been one accident too many. Three in a row would've raised suspicion."

"Makes sense. But where does Stan come in? Do you think he was involved?"

"I'd need to know more before I could answer that. So far you got nothing on him."

"He sure acted guilty."

McGee shrugs. "I've had guilty men who could talk a good game and come out smelling like a rose, and innocent men who you'd have bet a paycheck had bodies buried in their backyard."

"It's possible I was wrong about him."

"We won't know until we have more information. Let's see what my brother-in-law can dig up."

"Pete?"

"Nah. Patrick. My sister Connie's husband."

"Is there anyone in your family who's *not* in law enforcement?"

McGee pauses to consider this. With his tattoos and slicked-back Donnie Brasco hair he looks more like an undercover cop, disguised as a dealer, than a retired one. "Well, there's my cousin Danny," he says. "But we all think that's on account of he got dropped on his head as a baby."

I wince, picturing it. "Jesus. You mean he's brain damaged?"

"Worse—a lawyer." He chuckles and tips back his beer.

"Funny. So you think Patrick can help us?"

"He's with the Bureau. They have access to shit you wouldn't believe. Anything on those D. B.'s—accident reports, insurance records, coroner prelims, you name it—if it's out there, he'll find it."

CHAPTER TEN

I'm no stranger to detective work. I've found runaway cats and dogs that were given up for lost and the source of mysterious leaks and noxious odors that had professionals baffled, and I can usually tell, without invading anyone's privacy, who in any given household has a stash of weed or is likely to cheat on his or her spouse. Two days later I get a call from a client, eighty-two-year-old Mrs. Belknap, who's frantic over a report from her next-door neighbor that the pool boy has been using the swimming pool at their vacation home for his own recreation. The following morning, which happens to be the day of the Belknaps' regularly scheduled pool maintenance, I drive over to investigate, arriving in time to catch Pool Boy, a lanky redheaded kid named Colton, in the act. Only it's not him, but his pooch, a gray-muzzled Labrador retriever, paddling in the deep end. He's contrite, explaining that his dog, Maverick, has arthritic hips and his veterinarian prescribed swimming as therapy. He pleads with me not to rat him out. He needs the job to pay off his student loan. I let him off with a warning. I'm not about to get a fellow animal lover fired, and it's not a lie exactly when I report back to my client that he hadn't put so much as one toe in the water.

I head over to the Trousdales' afterward to meet with Joan about some work she wants done on the exterior of the house. I'm

winding along Canyon Oaks Road when I hear an ominous pop-
ping sound and the Explorer starts to shake and shimmy; it's a
tense minute before I can wrestle it onto the shoulder, where I skid
to a stop amid a cloud of dust. Cursing, I get out to find I have a flat
tire, as I suspected. Great. Just what I need. I debate whether or not
to call Triple A before deciding to man up and deal. Never mind I
haven't changed a tire since I learned how in driver's ed.

I'm grabbing the jack and tire iron from in back when the quiet
of the country road is shattered by the crack of a gunshot. Dirt
erupts from the ground, two inches from where I'm standing. I
freeze, the air sucked from my lungs. A split-second later I'm on
my hands and knees commando-crawling toward the ditch that
runs alongside the road. I'm scared out of my wits, but I'm also
mad as hell. I figure it's some numbnuts shooting at squirrels and
missing by a mile. I'm about to call out to him when another bullet
whizzes past my head. I drop onto my belly, holding myself flat to
the ground, inhaling as much dust as air with each breath. A cold
hand tightens around my windpipe with the realization: *He's not
shooting at squirrels.* It appears I'm the target.

I struggle to quell my panic, mumbling a mash-up of every
prayer I learned in catechism along with some language the nuns
wouldn't approve of, then I start crawling again as fast as my knees
and elbows can carry me. I dive headlong into the ditch as another
shot rings out, tearing a chunk from the fencepost above my head.
I start to hyperventilate, emitting squeaky hysterical noises with
each breath. Now it's to my higher power I pray. Unlike the heav-
enly father depicted in the illustrated Bible I'd had as a kid, with
His flowing white beard and celestial robes, my HP is more big
brother than father. The brother who taunts you but also protects
and defends you. *Dude, you've gotta be fucking kidding me. I got
sober for this? So I could end up as road kill?*

I quickly realize that if I want to live to see my next birthday,
my only chance is to get the hell out of Dodge. Because I'm a Hail

Mary away from one of those bullets finding its mark. I rise to crouch, bursting forth in a mad sprint, headed for my SUV. The last time I ran this hard was in seventh grade PE doing the fifty-yard dash. Then, I was one of the slowest in my class; now it's as if my heels have sprouted wings. I'm Wonder Woman. My feet barely touch the ground I'm moving so fast.

Pop, pop, pop. A hail of gunfire kicks up the dirt around me. It seems he's not shooting to kill, he's only trying to scare me. He's doing a good job of it: I've never been so scared in my life. The next bullet cuts close enough to shave hairs from my cheek. I stumble and nearly fall but somehow manage to stay on two feet. I hurl myself into the driver's seat with not a moment to spare as a bullet rips into the door. With shaking hands I turn the key in the ignition. The engine roars to life. Keeping my head down, I shift into drive while at the same time stomping on the gas pedal.

Then I'm careening down the road, the Explorer bumping and lurching like a covered wagon drawn by a team of runaway horses. Luckily mine is the only vehicle on the road or I'd have been in danger of a head-on collision with my flat tire causing me to veer into the oncoming lane. My mind spins. Who was shooting at me, and why? Stan Cruikshank owns a rifle. Douglas Trousdale must as well; I recall his mentioning something once about having gone on a hunting trip.

After a few minutes I realize to my intense relief the only sounds I'm hearing are the thumping of rubber and the wind whistling through the open hatch. Still, my foot refuses to ease from the gas pedal even when the village of La Mar comes into view up ahead (more outpost than village, it consists of an Albertson's, Long's Drugs, Radio Shack, and Arco station, all within a one-block radius). The rim of my flat tire is grinding against the pavement as I come tearing into the Arco and brake to a stop. I'm bathed in sweat, rivulets trickling down my forehead into my eyes. My lungs are on fire and I'm shaking all over. I tumble out to find a guy filling his tank at one of the pumps and gaping at me like I was the lone survivor of a zombie apocalypse.

"Don't ask," I croak as I stagger off.

Only when my hands have stopped shaking do I pull out my phone. I'm ensconced in the manager's office next to the service bay with a water from the vending machine and box of Kleenex with which to mop my still-sweating brow. I dial the number for the landline at the La Mar house, and Bradley picks up after the second ring. I explain that I was delayed by a flat tire and ask him to relay the message to Joan. I don't mention I was also the victim of a sniper attack. I can't go there while I'm still struggling to wrap my brain around the possibility that his father was behind it. He offers to come get me. I decline. He insists. "I'll be there in ten," he says, and hangs up.

I'm punching in Spence's number when I'm interrupted by the trilling of my brother's ringtone, Beethoven's Ninth. "I can't talk now. I'll have to call you back," I inform him. I make a conscious effort to regulate my breathing so as not to worry him. It's no use; he senses something is up.

"What's wrong? You sound funny."

Breathe in, breathe out. "I'm fine. Just some car trouble."

"Are you okay?"

"Yeah. I'm hanging up now. I'll call you in a little w—"

Before I can finish the sentence I'm cut off when he says to someone in the background, "Excuse me, Officer? My sister needs roadside assistance." My blood pressure shoots back up.

"Arthur, who were you talking to? What's going on?"

Another voice comes on the line. "Officer James here."

What the hell? "Jordan, it's me. Tish Ballard." I speak in a calm voice. The voice of someone exercising extreme control in the face of absolute chaos. "Would you mind telling me what's going on?"

"We're taking your brother into custody," he informs me.

"Why, what's he done?"

"Nothing, as far as we know."

"Then why are you taking him into custody?" I'm momentarily distracted by the whining of a hydraulic lift. Through the window onto the service bay I watch as my Explorer slowly ascends, beaten but not vanquished. I shudder at the sight of the bullet hole in the driver's side door.

"He requested it. In fact, he insisted."

I groan inwardly. Because I can imagine Arthur doing just that, if only because the voices in his head told him to. But I'm too rattled right now to approach it in a rational manner. I can only demand, "Don't you have anything better to do than go around arresting law-abiding citizens?"

"He's not under arrest. Yet," he adds in an ominous tone.

"*Yet?* What the hell is that supposed to mean?"

"I won't have answers for you until we run a check to see if there are any outstanding warrants."

"I don't suppose you'd take my word for it."

"Not a chance." Jordan hangs up. He must have figured out I was the instigator of his most embarrassing moment in high school. He was always a prick; now he's a prick with a hard-on.

I call Spence. I'm surprised when he answers—I'd expected to get his voicemail—and even more surprised by the wave of relief that washes through me. It's all I can do not to burst into tears. "It's me, Tish. I think someone just tried to kill me. Or . . . or it was a warning . . . I don't know."

"Slow down. You're not making much sense," he says as I burble on in broken sentences.

I take a deep breath and start over, this time managing to give a more or less coherent account. "I'm pretty sure he was only sending a message, or I'd be on my way to the county morgue right now instead of talking to you. If that's what it was, a warning, it came through loud and clear."

"Maybe this time you'll listen," he replies sternly.

"Fuck you." I don't need a scolding on top of everything else I've had to endure.

"You're sure it wasn't just some kid shooting at tin cans?" he asks in a gentler voice.

"Positive. It was . . . like he was toying with me, you know?" I think of my cat having fun with the mice he catches that he doesn't kill right away.

"Where are you now?"

"The Arco station in La Mar Village."

"Do you need a ride?"

"No, I have someone picking me up. I'll stop in at the station on my way back into town." I don't mention my brother. I'll deal with that when the time comes. "I'm just waiting on the mechanic." My SUV needs a steering realignment in addition to a new tire, so it's not an in-and-out job.

He asks where on Canyon Oaks Road the shooting took place, and I give him the precise location. "I'll send one of my men to check it out."

"I'm sure the shooter's long gone by now, but he might have left some bullet casings. Oh, and you should have a word with Stan Cruikshank. I happen to know for a fact he owns a rifle."

"Copy that." I hear traffic noises in the background which tell me he's already en route. Maybe he's not so incompetent after all. Any softening toward him is erased, however, with his next words. "In the meantime, do me a favor and stay out of trouble. You think you can manage that?"

"Are you implying this was my fault?" I demand.

"You don't want me to answer that," he says, and hangs up.

Minutes later Bradley pulls into the station behind the wheel of the black Escalade his parents keep at the house but that's hardly ever driven, except by Daniel when he uses it to pick up gardening supplies. Anyone who didn't know better would think Bradley was the hired help as well, dressed in holey jeans, a maroon polo shirt with a button missing, and a pair of flip-flops. "Must've been some flat tire," he observes when I start to cry, after I've climbed in the passenger side.

"That was the least of it." I fill him in on the rest while he drives.

"Holy Christ." He darts me an alarmed glance. "So you don't think it was random?"

"No. I think it was because I was making someone nervous with all of the questions I've been asking."

"Who have you been talking to?"

"My mom's boyfriend for one."

"You think he was the shooter?"

"I couldn't say for sure—he didn't show his face. All I know is, Stan owns a rifle and he lives near here, out at Four Chimneys Ranch. Detective Breedlove is on his way there now to have a word with him." I don't mention my suspicions about his father. "For his sake, he'd better have an alibi."

"I'll breathe easier when whoever did this is behind bars." Bradley shakes his curly dark head. He's gripping the steering wheel so tightly I can see the whites of his knuckles. "Jesus. First my mom, now this. I saw less action when I was in Zhargun Shar with the 101st infantry division."

"Yeah, and it's even less fun when you're in the line of fire."

He cuts me a glance, his face furrowed with concern. "Thank God you're all right."

"Just some scrapes and bruises. Nothing that won't heal."

He turns onto the private drive to the estate. Trees and manicured lawns soon give way to an ocean view that's easily the most spectacular of any of my properties. It has what we realtors call the "wow factor." But right now what I'm feeling isn't wowed. The sunlight glinting off the water is an assault on my eyes and it almost hurts to behold such beauty after all the ugliness of the past few weeks. He pulls up in front of the house and turns to me as I'm unbuckling my seatbelt. "Tish, listen to me, if that was just a warning, next time it could be for real. Let the cops handle it. For me getting shot is an occupational hazard, but you don't have to put yourself at risk."

I say nothing. I just nod meekly, touched by his show of concern. He's saying the same thing Spence had basically, except coming from him, I'm not tempted to give my middle finger a workout.

Joan is there to greet me when I walk in. You would never know to look at her that she's recovering from an ordeal of her own. She's as perfectly put together as ever, wearing fawn slacks and a cashmere shell that appears to have been woven from a summer cloud. Her silver-blond bob gleams, not a hair out of place. I catch a whiff of her fragrance, Chanel No. 5, when she hugs me. "What a nuisance," she clucks. "But it could've been worse. Better a flat tire than a fender bender."

"Actually it was a bit more involved than that." I wait until we're sitting down to tell her the whole story. A range of emotions plays over her face as she listens: shock followed by horror and finally dark comprehension.

"I should have known," she mutters. Before I can ask what she meant by that, she's turning to Bradley, seated in the easy chair by the fireplace opposite Joan and me, to ask, "When you spoke with your father, did you mention Tish would be stopping by to have a look at those rotten shingles?"

He flashes her a warning look. "Yes, but if you think Dad had anything to do with this, that's cr—"

She doesn't let him finish. "Why wouldn't I think it?" she cries, her voice rising in agitation. "He tried to kill *me*." Her lovely, patrician face pales at the memory. "Now he's after Tish."

"Why me?" I have my own theory—that Seraphina blabbed to him, and it was his way of warning me not to probe any further— but I want to hear Joan's.

She turns to me. "He must think you saw something the other night."

"The fact is, I didn't. Which I'm sure the police conveyed to him."

"Douglas never takes anything at face value. He sees ulterior motives where there are none. He probably thinks you were only withholding information because you planned to blackmail him."

Bradley says sharply, "Mom, no. This has gone far enough."

She jumps to her feet and starts pacing back and forth on the Navajo rug in front of the fireplace, too distraught to listen to reason. Though I, for one, am not dismissing what she has to say. What if she's right? "You don't know him the way I do! You don't know how his mind works!"

"He's my dad. I think I know him pretty well."

"You only know what he allows you to see. I kept the worst of it from you when you were growing up."

"Mom . . ."

"I was married to the man for thirty-five years. You think I don't know what he's capable of? My God, all the times I turned a blind eye. Not just to the other women but the shady dealings, the way he bullied people—*me* most of all." She whirls around to face her son. "I should have divorced him years ago. The only reason I didn't was because of you, my darling." Her hard expression gives way to a tender one. "I wanted you to have a father you could look up to."

He gets up and goes over to her, putting his arm around her shoulders, saying in a gentle voice, "Mom, I know you're upset, but you need to stop this. Dad's not perfect, no, and he hasn't always done the right thing, but he's not a monster. You shouldn't be putting ideas into Tish's head."

"I'm sorry if I upset you, my dear," she says to me when she's regained her composure. "It's just that I would never forgive myself if anything were to happen to you because I hadn't spoken up." Bradley flashes her another warning look. She takes heed this time and rearranges her features in a semblance of a smile. "But let's put all that aside for now. Why don't I make us some tea?"

"Tea would be nice," I tell her.

She excuses herself, and Bradley sinks down next to me on the sofa with an audible exhalation. He closes his eyes for a second, rubbing his eyelids. "I know this isn't easy for you, either," I say.

"It's not just my parents." He looks at me. His eyes deliver the same high-voltage shock of blue, but I notice they're bloodshot. "Genevieve and I broke up. She flew back to New York this morning."

"Really? Wow, that—I'm surprised to hear it. You seemed so close." I put on a sympathetic face because I know it's wrong to feel happy at the expense of someone else's misery.

"I'm not my father's son, if that's what you're thinking," he says, his mouth thinning in a cheerless smile. "I never cheated on her. It's just that she wants to get married and start a family."

"And you don't."

The expression on his face tells me I guessed correctly. "Not now. Maybe someday." He sighs. "She said she was tired of waiting, and I don't blame her. She has a right to want what she wants."

"It goes both ways."

"True, except I still feel like the shit who broke her heart."

"It's not like you pretended to be someone you weren't. You met at a field hospital in Afghanistan, not a singles' mixer. She must've known you weren't a white-picket-fence, soccer-dad kind of guy."

He grimaces in response, and I don't know if it's because of my bald assessment of him or because he finds the notion of living the suburban dream so abhorrent. "Yeah, and she was okay with it at first. But things change. You start out wanting one thing and end up wanting another."

"I get it. I'm not sure I'm cut out for that life, either. I can't see myself with kids." Or marrying Daniel. "It's not that I don't want them or think I wouldn't make a good mom, but I have my hands full just taking care of my brother. Speaking of which, if you'll excuse me, I have to see about keeping him out of jail." I step out onto the deck to make a call after I've explained the situation.

"I'm on my way," Ivy says when I tell her why I'm calling. I don't mention my own scare; that can wait until later. Right now the most important thing is making sure my brother returns home safely. My biggest worry is that he'll end up in the hospital psych ward, the threat of which, unlike that of his going to jail, is very real. Last time he was there on a seventy-two-hour hold—the maximum length of time by state law they can keep someone who isn't deemed a danger to society or himself—he was disoriented and depressed for weeks afterward. "I shouldn't be more than ten minutes."

I breathe a sigh of relief. "Thanks. I owe you."

"Yeah, and I'm already thinking of ways you can repay me."

Last time she bailed me out of a tight spot—literally, in that case; I'd needed her to crawl behind a heavy piece of furniture at a client's house, which was too narrow a space for me, to retrieve a diamond ring its owner had dropped—I had to watch back-to-back episodes of *Hoarders* in repayment. "Okay, but I'm warning you, I'm all stocked up on crazy. Pizza's on me, but can we make it *The Deadliest Catch* instead of *Hoarders*?" I'll take king crabs over cockroaches any day.

"I'll let you know after I've assessed the situation," she says.

I step back inside just as Joan walks in from the kitchen carrying a tea tray. It holds a pot of tea under a quilted cozy and her best china teacups and saucers, sugar bowl and creamer. There's even a plate of shortbread. It's such a thoughtful and motherly gesture, it brings tears to my eyes. My own mom wasn't the tea-tray type—a mug and Lipton teabag was more like it—but it's a reminder of when I had a mom who cared about me.

I'm on my third cup of tea, still waiting for the call from the mechanic at the Arco station, before Ivy gets back to me. I'm relieved when she reports that my brother is neither under arrest nor "under observation." "They said he was free to go, but I didn't think we should leave until you got here."

"Why, what's wrong?" I start to tense up again.

"Nothing. But you might want to talk to Jordan. God knows I'm not getting anything out of Arthur."

I feel another pulse of alarm. "Is he okay?"

"Physically he's fine." *Mentally not so much.* She doesn't have to say it.

Bradley gives me a ride back to the Arco when my Explorer is ready for pick up. "Listen, about my mom," he says when we're alone, "don't let what she said get to you. She's upset and it's affected her judgment. My dad isn't the madman she's painted him to be. He'll make mincemeat of you if you're negotiating a business deal with him, but otherwise he's perfectly harmless."

"Good to know." I keep my voice light. I don't dare reveal my own suspicions regarding his father until I have evidence to back them up. Part of me hopes I won't find any. Because it would only complicate matters. How can I entertain fantasies about a man whose dad is out to kill me?

After he's dropped me off, with a kiss on the cheek and squeeze of the hand, I unconsciously bring my hand to my mouth as I'm walking away. I can smell his scent on my fingers, buttery with a hint of vanilla. A second later I jerk my hand away, embarrassed to realize it's not from him but the shortbread I ate. *Get a grip.* I'm acting like a schoolgirl with a crush. Next I'll be saving the wrappers from gum he chewed and doodling the name "Mrs. Bradley Trousdale."

Fifteen minutes later, I'm pulling into the parking lot at the municipal building on Center Street. I walk into the police station to find Ivy and my brother seated in the waiting area, such as it is—it consists of a half dozen beige molded-plastic chairs, the kind you see in hospital cafeterias, set in a row against the wall between the vending machine and bullpen. Arthur only glances up at me before going back to whoever he's texting—his friend, Ray, probably—his shoulders hunched and thumbs moving in a flurry over the keypad on his phone. Ivy gives me a wan smile and points in the direction of the bullpen, from which Jordan James is just now emerging.

I go over to him. "Jordan."

I must have caught him at the end of his shift because he's wearing street clothes: jeans and a black *Iron Man* sweatshirt that doesn't disguise his non-*Ironman* gut. He puts a hand out, traffic-cop style, to stop me before I can say another word. "If you're here to accuse me of police harassment, you can save your breath. He approached us, not the other way around."

"Did he give a reason?" I keep my voice down in case Arthur is listening in.

"All he said was that he'd done 'something.'" Jordan makes air quotes with his fingers. "He didn't seem too clear on what exactly it was. We ran a background check. No outstanding warrants."

"I could have told you that. It's just that he sometimes gets . . . confused. Was there anything going on at the time? You know, like an accident or altercation he might have witnessed."

"Nope. Me and Angie, we were coming out of the Mickey D's over on Ocean when he came up to us. At first I thought he was just another tourist. They're always asking directions, to the Boardwalk or aquarium or what have you, like we're the freaking chamber of commerce. But your brother? Shit, that was a new one for me." He shakes his head, smiling to himself, then leans in to add, "I'd get him checked out if I was you. He ain't playing with a full deck, if you know what I mean."

I feel myself stiffen. I've heard every slang word and phrase there is. "Wacko," "a brick shy of a full load," "a screw loose," "bats in the belfry," to name a few. People who wouldn't dream of using the n-word feel no such constraints in making slurs about the mentally ill. I stare at Jordan for a couple of beats before saying, "Do me a favor. If it happens again, give me a call before you take him in. Even if he tells you he mugged an old lady or robbed a 7-Eleven." I hand him my business card.

"Sure. If the little green men from Mars don't get to him first." Jordan snickers at his own joke.

I glance past him into the bullpen, where I notice his female partner, Officer Ruiz, eyeing him with a look of contempt. She doesn't have to be within earshot to know he's being offensive. I'm sure she's been the recipient on more than one occasion. "It might interest you to know my brother has a genius IQ," I inform him, in a frosty voice. "That stands for 'intelligence quotient.' Look it up."

Pretty weak compared to my epic putdowns of yore—like the time I told this creep who'd followed me out of a bar and then pulled out his thing that he'd have to show me more than that if he wanted me to scream, as opposed to howl with laughter—but it has the desired effect. Jordan narrows his eyes at me, his pitted cheeks reddening. He may be dumb, but he knows when he's been insulted.

I'm utterly spent, my head spinning and gait unsteady as I make my way back to Arthur and Ivy. I've had more drama in the past few weeks than most people experience in a lifetime, and it's not over yet. I still have to get my brother sorted out. Then find out who wants me dead and why.

CHAPTER ELEVEN

The following morning I get a call from McGee. He has something he wants to show me, he says. I suggest we meet at the Starbucks in Harborview Plaza. Minutes later I arrive to find him waiting for me, sipping a coffee at one of the tables in back. It's ten o'clock, between the morning rush hour and when the first class at the Pilates studio next door lets out, so we're the only customers.

"What have you got?" I pull up a chair after I've grabbed a latte.

"Good morning to you, too," he says grumpily. He recently quit smoking (his third attempt), so he's even crankier than usual. In keeping with his mood he looks like a bad acid flashback wearing an ill-fitting plaid sports coat over a faded orange T-shirt from the 1999 Burning Man festival and khakis that have seen better days. He tears open a sugar packet, stirs its contents into his coffee, and repeats the process, before finally reaching into the shopping bag on the floor next to him. He pulls out a manila envelope, sliding it across the table toward me. "It's all there—police reports, coroner prelims, insurance claims for both the Vuković girl and Mr. Martinez."

I feel my pulse quicken. "Anything jump out at you?"

"Nothing that would have warranted an investigation. Tox results were clean. Seems neither was a habitual drug user. And there's nothing in the coroner prelims to suggest foul play—as in no injuries that were inconsistent with the official cause of death."

I stir my latte until the foam starts to deflate. "What about a chronic health problem? Something that could've caused an accident. You know, like epilepsy. Or alcoholism," I add on a dry note.

"Nothing that showed up."

"So, in other words, the autopsies are a dead end." I wince at my unfortunate word choice. "What about the police reports? Were there any eyewitnesses?" I ask, hoping the newspaper articles I'd read had gotten it wrong.

He shakes his head. "No one who came forward, at any rate. Cops questioned Martinez's next-door neighbor, a Mrs. Ida Garvey. She said she didn't see or hear anything unusual."

"Doesn't that strike you as odd?"

"That an eighty-seven-year-old lady who was probably hard of hearing and blind as a bat didn't notice anything strange? No. As for the Vuković girl, it was late at night and she was driving on an isolated stretch of road."

"Did they ever find out what caused the accident?"

"The claims adjuster for the insurance company was only able to determine what *didn't* cause it. It wasn't due to mechanical failure and it didn't appear another vehicle was involved. Based on the skid mark pattern she wasn't exceeding the speed limit, either. It was a heavily wooded area, so the best guess was she swerved to avoid hitting a deer and lost control of her car."

"But you don't think it was that." I note the preoccupied frown he wears.

"There was one thing. The rear fender had some scratches with secondary paint on them."

I feel like I just swallowed something cold on an empty stomach. "Do you think there's anything to it?"

He shrugs. "They could've been old."

"Or she was forced off the road that night."

He nods thoughtfully. "Maybe. I'm getting a bad smell. She had a perfect driving record, not so much as a parking ticket, and even though the car was old, she'd kept it in tiptop condition, routine tune-up every year, got it washed every other week according to her roommate. First car she'd ever owned. It was her baby. If those scratches were from an old fender-bender, seems to me she'd have taken it in for repair." He hands me a color Xerox of a photo showing the damage to the fender on which streaks of blue paint were clearly visible. "And what kind of gardener falls from a ladder? Guy like that, I bet he could climb a ladder, with a chainsaw in one hand and full bucket in the other, in his sleep."

"And no one ever asked questions?"

"Who was around to ask questions? The next of kin, south of the border or in Bosnia? Though Martinez had at least one brother who was living in the States, and he filed a wrongful death suit."

I perk up at this. "Against the Fontana?"

"Nah. The manufacturer of the ladder. It went nowhere because their expert witness couldn't find any evidence the ladder owned by Martinez was defective. No probable cause, no case."

I mull this over as McGee tears open another sugar packet, hands twitching like he's jonesing for a cigarette—or a drink—and two thirty-something women wearing Lululemon workout attire and packing yoga mats enter the shop, followed by a tired-looking young mom pushing an infant in a stroller. Yoga Lady 1 orders a skim latte; Yoga Lady 2 wants hers with soy milk. No-sleep Mommy looks like she could give a crap as long as whatever she's drinking is caffeinated.

"Do you ever miss being a cop?" I inquire of McGee when we're walking across the parking lot a few minutes later, headed for our respective vehicles. "This job must seem tame in comparison."

"You would think," he says pointedly.

"I meant aside from that." I'm sure it's not every day corpses turn up at the White Oaks self-storage facility. But the fact that he's helping me proves he hasn't lost the itch. He's going to do some digging into Douglas Trousdale's background. Meanwhile, I have my own plans for Stan Cruikshank.

McGee rolls his shoulders in one of his patented shrugs. "What's to miss? I got full bennies and none of the aggravation."

He's not going to tell the real reason he retired at such a relatively young age. Which is fine. Maybe he'll get around to it one of these days or maybe he won't. I'm not judging. We've all been there.

"One more thing," I say, pausing when I get to my Explorer.

He narrows his eyes at me, his head thrust forward on his neck, his poor excuse for a ponytail dangling over the collar of his desert camo jacket. His shoulders are bunched around his ears as if against the cold wind that blew in with the storm clouds amassing overhead. "Just one, huh?"

"It's a simple question. I'm not asking any favors this time."

"Nothing with you is ever simple."

"You don't want to help me anymore that's fine. I understand. I appreciate everything you've done so far. I guess I'll just have to find a way to manage on my own." I use the oldest of ploys—appealing to the male ego—but he falls for it.

"Fine. You win," he growls. "Whaddya want to know?"

"What's the maximum penalty for breaking and entering?"

I finish my morning rounds after taking leave of McGee. I change the water filter at the Zakarians.' I exhaust the limits of my high school Spanish in communicating to the Cummings' gardener that he need not be so aggressive with his pruning shears (he didn't get the *Edward Scissorhands* reference, or maybe he never saw the movie). At the Martinsons' I finally find the missing hamster, posthumously, under the clothes dryer. Poor thing looks like what I scraped from the lint trap. I bury him in one of the planter boxes on the condo's deck so little Grady Martinson can place a Popsicle-stick cross on his grave like I had with the hamsters who'd died on me when I was kid. Then I head over to my brother's to pick him up for his appointment with his shrink.

On the drive to Dr. Sandefur's office, in a converted Victorian on Laurel Street, my normally chatty brother is quiet. He seems tense. "What's with you? You beg to be taken into custody and now you're worried about seeing your shrink?" I tease, in an attempt to lighten the mood.

He looks presentable at least. He combed his hair for a change and the clothes he's wearing don't look as if they've been slept in. He cuts me an anxious glance. "You're not mad, are you?"

"That you almost got yourself arrested? No, Arthur, I'm not mad. Believe it or not, I have bigger worries at the moment."

"You mean the fact that someone was shooting at you?"

I had debated whether or not to tell him about it, but in the end I did. His mental illness has taken so much already, and I couldn't bear to have it rob us of the open communication we've always shared. "That and finding out who killed Mom. Though I have a hunch they're connected."

"Don't be so sure," he says darkly.

"What do you mean?"

"They're after me. Now they're after you, too."

I don't ask who "they" are. I don't have to. "Arthur." I try to talk some sense into him. "Whoever was shooting at me, it wasn't CIA operatives. That's all in your head. Just like yesterday when you turned yourself in to the cops."

"I had to." This is the first he's spoken of it. Until now he's been as forthcoming as a piece of furniture. "They were following me." He doesn't mean the cops. "I knew it was the only way I'd be safe."

"You can tell Dr. Sandefur all about it," I say gently, my heart breaking for him. But he's not listening.

"They don't fool around, these people. You should know that by now." His eyes, wide and fearful behind his Clark Kent glasses, drop to the bullet hole in the driver's side door. "Dark forces are at play."

That much is true. Except whoever is after me isn't a figment of my imagination. The sensible thing would be to take Bradley's advice. On the other hand, if I have a target on my back, to do nothing would make me a sitting duck. I have to get to the bottom of this. Starting with Stan. He claimed to have been at work all day yesterday and has witnesses to back up his alibi, but that doesn't mean he isn't guilty of other crimes. And since he isn't talking, I'll have to find another source of information. If I could get my hands on an address book or contact list, it could lead to a former accomplice, if there was one, or a friend in whom he'd confided. It might even have Douglas Trousdale's number. Which means breaking into Stan's cabin when he's not home and conducting a search. Being a property manager, I know the most vulnerable points of entry in most homes and how to access them, and I'm confident I can slip in and out with no one the wiser. So I'm not as worried about getting caught as I am that I'll come up empty-handed.

Dr. Sandefur meets with me privately after his session with Arthur. "I think he should go in for some tests," he advises from behind his scrolled walnut desk in what was once the formal parlor of the Victorian home before it was converted into office space. I'm immediately on guard because I know he's not talking about outpatient tests but an inpatient stay, possibly an extended one, at the PCH, which stands for psychiatric health facility, or "puff" in the vernacular of us veterans. Suffice it to say, I'm on familiar terms with everyone on staff at the "puff" in our community.

"Couldn't you try adjusting his meds and see if that works?"

"I could, yes." Dr. Sandefur speaks in a calm, considered voice. "But I don't have to tell you it's hit or miss." What he means is, there's no set formula when it comes to anti-psychotic cocktails; it's a constant juggling act and differs from one patient to the next. "If he's where he's being monitored round the clock, it'll give us a better picture of what's going on." An older man with curly gray hair and eyes the brown of the leather-bound volumes lining his bookshelves and just as creased, he's nothing if not kindly. "Just for a few days, a week at most. He'd be in good hands."

"Easy for you to say." The staff is for the most part competent and compassionate, but every barrel has its rotten apple, and in this one it's the day supervisor, Myrna Hargrave. She never lets up, with her poking and prodding and barking of orders. After Arthur's last stay, eight months ago, he insisted she'd been out to "get" him. I don't know that it was entirely his imagination.

"It's only a recommendation, of course. But I'm sure Arthur would be amenable if you were to exercise your powers of persuasion." His brown eyes twinkle beneath shaggy gray brows.

I sigh. Really, do I have choice when the alternative is far worse? "Okay," I relent, "but on one condition: no Thorazine. I don't want him turned into a zombie like before. He does better on Haldol."

Dr. Sandefur nods. "I concur." He's a good man and the only shrink who has my respect. The others before him were too full of themselves to admit they didn't know dick-all. Schizophrenia is incurable and unknowable; it's all about damage control. Dr. Sandefur doesn't pretend otherwise.

I don't say anything to Arthur about the "puff" as we're leaving. I decide to wait until he's in a more relaxed mood. Instead I inform him that I'm taking him shopping. "It's Wednesday," he reminds me.

"Not grocery shopping. You need new underwear."

I can't have the nurses at the "puff" seeing him in his not-so-tightie whiteys; I'm sure Arthur couldn't care less, but I have my standards. After a trip to the Cress Avenue Mall where I buy him a six-pack of Hanes briefs, three button-down shirts, and a pair of slacks marked down half price, I treat him to lunch at his favorite eatery, the A&W on the freeway access road. He inhales a Papa burger and large order of fries chased by a root beer float, while I nibble halfheartedly on my chili cheese fries.

"I know what you and Dr. Sandefur talked about. He told me," he says before I can broach the topic.

I attempt to make light of it. "He thought you could use a change of scenery."

His eyes meet mine in a level look. "What do *you* think?"

"I kind of have to agree. But it's up to you."

He stares into space for a minute, then slowly brings his gaze back to me. "All right. I'll do it."

I'm surprised by his ready compliance. "You will? No kicking or screaming?"

He shrugs.

"I thought you hated it at the 'puff.'" I sense there's something he's not telling me.

"I do, but that's not the point, is it?"

"What is?"

"I'll be where they can't get to me."

I let it go this time. I love my brother dearly, which means sometimes making peace with the scary dudes in trench coats who lurk in the shadows of his mind. "Yeah, and at least you got new underwear out of it. Always pays to look your best when you're getting a shot in the butt, right?"

I call Dr. Sandefur, then drive Arthur back to his place where we pack a bag and he arranges for his pet gerbil to be cared for by his next-door neighbor in his absence. An hour later he's being admitted to the "puff." "Watch your back," he whispers urgently in my ear as we hug good-bye.

I stop at the Gilded Lily on my way through town. Ivy is busy waiting on a customer when I walk in, an elderly henna-haired lady who's debating whether or not to purchase the antique cast-iron planter she has her eye on. "My marijuana plant would look nice in it," she says, explaining that it's for medicinal purposes only, for her fibromyalgia. Ivy and I exchange a look.

Only in Cypress Bay.

Ivy persuades her that the planter would be a nice addition to her homegrown ganga operation. After she's paid for it, Ivy and I carry it to her station wagon which is parked out back. We wave good-bye to Farmer Jane, and I bring Ivy up-to-date on Arthur when we're alone in the shop. Business is slow this time of day, before the sun goes down on the beachgoers and dinner hour has customers trickling in from the nearby eateries. She's glad to hear my brother's getting the help he needs. She's skeptical at first when I tell her about my plan to break into Stan's cabin.

"Why, because you didn't get enough of him shooting at you?"

"If it was him. That's what I need to find out." The witnesses who corroborated his alibi could have been covering for him, or he could have slipped away for an hour without anyone noticing. Four Chimneys Ranch covers a large area. "Maybe there's a stash of old letters, or an address book that would lead us to someone who could positively identify him as my mom's murderer."

She looks up from sorting a stack of receipts. "There always is when it's Jessica Fletcher doing the snooping. And she doesn't usually get caught. What if one of his neighbors calls the cops?"

"Trust me, they won't even know I was there."

"*He* will. If you take something of his."

"I'm not going to. Except phone numbers, if he has an address book." I hold up my phone, pretending to snap a photo with it.

She shrugs. "Well, if your mind is made up, don't let me stop you."

I stare at her and sink down on the tufted velvet ottoman next to an Art Deco umbrella stand that holds a collection of vintage walking sticks. Suddenly I'm having doubts. "That's it? You're not going to try to talk me out of it?"

"Who me?" She resembles a gypsy fortune-teller with her raven curls spilling over her shoulders, wearing a peasant blouse and full, canary-yellow skirt, bangles on her wrists. "You must have me confused with someone else. I'm your partner-in-crime, not the friend who talks you out of stuff. God, remember what we were like in high school?" The usual teenage stuff—wild parties, boys, sneaking out at night—plus adventures only Ivy could dream up, like when we hitchhiked to a rock concert in Berkeley, Ivy pretending to be the illegitimate daughter of Keith Richards. "I can't believe we got away with it. Well, except that one time." She grins at the memory.

She's referring to when we went skinny-dipping in her next-door neighbor's swimming pool. She'd assured me the Paulsens would be away for the entire weekend. Unfortunately they arrived home a day early, just in time to catch us bare-ass naked. I was mortified. Of course that was before embarrassing myself became a regular thing, with the worsening of my drinking problem.

"Yeah, but you're not supposed to egg me on. Aren't you worried I'll get caught?"

"You won't, not if you're with me. I'll stand watch while you go in."

I shake my head. "Oh, no. I'm not dragging you into this."

"You're not. I'm volunteering."

"You don't have to do this."

"Of course I do. Who else are you going to get?"

"Well . . ."

With a wave of her hand she brushes aside any remaining hesitation on my part. "When do you need me?"

"He plays poker with his buddies on Wednesday nights." I'd gleaned this tidbit of information from Kelsey Cummings, the office manager at the ranch, who also happens to be the daughter of one of my clients. "I'm thinking the sooner the better, before he decides to skip town."

She frowns. "Tonight? That might be a problem." She explains she has a date with Rajeev. He's taking her out to dinner, to that new restaurant downtown that's been getting rave reviews.

"You should go," I tell her. "He seems like a great guy, and you don't want to blow it. He could be the One."

She appears torn, but only for the moment. "No. It's okay. I'm sure he'll understand when I tell him it's an emergency. We can always make it another night." For her the lure of adventure trumps that of romance. Also, she's my best friend and best friends stick by each other.

I stand up and walk over to her. "You're sure about this?"

"Sure I'm sure." She grins. "It'll be one more thing for us to reminisce about when we're old."

If I live that long, I think.

CHAPTER TWELVE

My last stop of the day is the Kims' sprawling split-level, over by the Paso Verde golf course, which boasts Asian-inspired touches like the curved roof that's traditionally for deflecting evil spirits and moon gate onto the outer courtyard. After doing my routine walk-through, I feed the inhabitants of the koi pond, which are the size of kittens and have the instincts of piranha—a sprinkling of fish food sends them into a frenzy—luckily without losing any fingers.

I text Daniel as I'm leaving. *Meet me 4 dinner*? He texts me right back. *On my way.* The sun is setting in a Technicolor blaze by the time I arrive at our go-to eatery, the Salty Dog. It's by the yacht harbor, which is situated at the deepest point of the bay and is a small community unto itself, populated by boat owners, permanent fixtures, and transients alike, as well as the locals and tourists who come for the lively bar scene. Happy hour is in full swing, the bars and eateries along the esplanade thronged with the mostly young, beer-and-margarita crowd. I recall when it was just that for me—happy—back when I could still exercise self-control. I can't help but look back on those days with nostalgia. If Aladdin were a recovering drunk, I know what his first wish would have been: the ability to drink like a normal person. For us sobriety is never more than bittersweet.

The Salty Dog is a local institution that's been in business since the 1960s. The decor consists mainly of strategically draped fishnets studded with starfish and glass floats. Wooden tables shellacked with marine varnish complete the time warp effect. Needless to say, it's all about the food. I find Daniel waiting at one of the picnic tables on the patio drinking a beer. He's wearing a deconstructed blazer over a collared shirt, faded jeans, and loafers: the uniform of university professors. He looks especially cute with his broad-cheeked face tinted pink from the glow of the setting sun. He breaks into a smile when he sees me, but as I draw nearer I see the worried look in his eyes.

"I had a long talk with Professor Gruen today," he says when we're tucking into our fried seafood platters a short while later. "About you." His eyes lock onto mine in a meaningful look.

I don't say anything. I just look at him.

"Turns out Chief Langley is a close, personal friend of his." He names the chief of police for the CBPD. "He could get you twenty-four-hour police protection. He has only to pick up the phone."

"And have Spence think I'm an even bigger pain in the ass than he already does? No thanks." I shake my head and reach for another shrimp.

"What's more important, your safety or someone else's opinion of you?"

I pop the shrimp in my mouth and wipe my greasy fingers on my napkin. "Look, I appreciate the thought," I say when I'm done chewing, "but I can't have cops following me everywhere, watching my every move. I'd feel like the First Lady with her Secret Service detail."

"Why is that a bad thing?"

"Are you kidding? The First Lady has, like, zero privacy and she can't be seen in public without makeup much less wearing sweats. Can you see me in high heels at the supermarket?"

"I don't think the First Lady does her own grocery shopping," he comments dryly, giving me a level look that says, *You can't wise-crack your way out of this one.*

"Don't worry," I say softly, placing a hand over his. "I'm a big girl. I can take care of myself."

"How can you say that? You were almost killed!"

"That was different. I was caught off guard. Now I'm taking precautions."

"Dare I ask?" He lifts a sandy eyebrow.

"If you must know, I bought a gun." McGee helped me select one, a .38 caliber Smith and Wesson, that was suitable for the purposes of defending myself. It wouldn't do me much good in the event of another sniper attack, but if someone tries breaking into my house at night when I'm home . . .

If I was hoping to assuage his fears, it has the opposite effect. Daniel looks even more worried. "Leaving aside the advisability of owning a gun for the moment, do you even know how to shoot it?"

"I'm learning." McGee is giving me lessons.

"I see." He lapses into brooding silence.

"You said I needed protection."

"I didn't meant that kind. I meant professionals who know what they're doing and are trained in the use of firearms."

"Even if I had twenty-four-seven police protection, someone could still sneak up on me." I'd seen it happen enough times on TV crime dramas. "Whoever was shooting at me, he knew what he was doing. Which suggests he was a trained professional himself."

"And you think he's working for Douglas?" The skepticism in Daniel's voice is thicker than the crunchy coating on my batter-fried shrimp.

"I don't know, but it's a definite possibility, wouldn't you say?"

"That's funny. Because when I spoke with Douglas this morning, he seemed very concerned about you."

"You spoke with him?" I feel a frisson of alarm.

"He was at the house, having breakfast with Bradley. I happened to run into him as I was leaving for work. He asked after you. He wanted to make sure you were all right."

"I'll bet," I mutter. "More like he was checking to see what security measures I was taking. You know, for when he tries again."

Daniel makes an exasperated noise. "Tish. This has got to stop. You're spinning a web of conspiracy out of one woman's hysterical imaginings. Would you have suspected him if not for that?"

"How do we know he didn't try to kill Joan? Is it so hard to believe?"

"Frankly, yes."

"Why, because he's charming and drives a Beemer? Not all sociopaths are misfits who had horrible childhoods."

"May I remind you he's donated millions of dollars to charity?"

"The same is true of Bernie Madoff."

He sighs. "In other words, it doesn't matter what I think."

"Of course it matters. Chances are you're right and I'm wrong." I'm determined to end the evening on a positive note. "He's probably guilty of nothing worse than being a dickwad. I'm just not convinced he's innocent, either. But I'll keep my mouth shut, I promise." *Until I have proof.*

"Thank you." He brings my hand to his mouth and kisses it. "And just so you know, vanilla isn't the only flavor I like."

I'm reminded of why I fell in love with him.

After we've eaten, we stroll along the esplanade on our way to the metered parking lot by the marina where our SUVs are parked. Darkness is falling. In the harbor tall masts stand out against the twilight sky. At the bars and eateries happy hour has given way to the hard-drinking crowd, people spilling onto the sidewalk, clutching beers, and talking too loudly, smoking cigarettes.

"Why don't I stay over at your place until this whole thing blows over?" Daniel offers as we're saying our good-byes in the parking lot. "I'd sleep easier if I was there to look out for you."

I hesitate. This places me in an awkward position. I don't want to hurt his feelings, nor do I wish for him to be privy to my extra-curricular activities. "As tempting as that is, you know perfectly well you couldn't possibly keep up with three jobs if you had to make the extra trip every day."

"You have a point," he says with a sigh.

"I'll call at the first hint of trouble, I promise."

I say nothing of the trouble I'm creating for myself.

Rain is falling in a steady drizzle as Ivy and I set out for Four Chimneys Ranch. I feel guilty about her cancelling her date with Mr. Bollywood. I should have insisted she keep it, but Ivy seems cool with it. Instead of evening finery she's wearing what she calls "Black Ops chic": a dark-gray track suit with a neoprene rain jacket over it and her L.L. Bean duck boots.

When we get to the ranch, I pull in behind the darkened stables, a safe distance from the cabins. We climb out. It's quiet except for the pattering of the rain and faint sounds of horses rustling in their stalls. "Hi-ho, Silver," murmurs Ivy when one of them whinnies.

I look at her. "Does that make me the Lone Ranger?"

"Not if it makes me Tonto." Ivy is second banana to no one.

The air smells of damp earth and horse manure. We head down the road toward the cabins, splashing through puddles, the hoods of our waterproof jackets pulled over our heads. I'm carrying my messenger bag with the tools of my trade: flashlight, set of pocket-size screwdrivers, Swiss Army knife, and a baggie of Purina liver treats with which to distract any dogs that might mistake me for an intruder. I'm hopped up on adrenaline, heart racing and nerves humming.

The staff living quarters consists of eight, identical clapboard cabins, each painted brown with green trim, built in a semi-circle around a communal yard. Stan's is the only one that doesn't appear to be occupied at the moment; the windows are dark. My footsteps slow as we draw near. Because I'm starting to think this might be a bad idea. What if Stan isn't at his poker game and only stepped out for a short while? What if he catches us? I'm remembering the look on the Paulsens' faces when they found me and Ivy naked in their swimming pool. They were both Mormons, he a retired dentist and she a former school librarian. I think they were more embarrassed than we were. In the end they were nice about it, after Ivy apologized and promised it wouldn't happen again. Stan, on the other hand, would likely shoot first and ask questions later.

"It's not too late to turn back," Ivy whispers as if sensing my hesitation.

"No, I'm good," I whisper back, hoping she didn't hear the slight tremor in my voice.

"Don't worry. I've got your back."

I reach for her hand and give it a squeeze. "Thanks."

"You can thank me later, after I've saved your bacon."

"Pray it doesn't come to that."

I hear the muttering of TV sets and sounds of music played low from inside the occupied cabins. The cabins are packed so closely together you could bum a smoke from your next-door neighbor without setting foot off your porch. Hardly ideal conditions for a break-in. I'll need the stealth tactics of a ninja to pull this off. The inclement weather is working in our favor, at least. No one is likely to be stepping out for a stroll or to take in the night air from his porch.

When we get to Stan's cabin, Ivy takes up position by the door, in the shadow of the overhang, while I head for the window in front. Windows are generally the most vulnerable point of entry of any home. At the properties I manage I occasionally get locked out, due to a frozen lock or the wind having blown a door. Once because the owners changed the locks then neglected to give me the new key before I was summoned to deal with a household emergency, so I'm quite adept in such matters for someone who's never committed a home robbery. The window I'm looking at is a seventies-era aluminum-frame slider. Piece of cake. I use my screwdriver to pop the screen, then as I'm lowering it to the ground, I hear a dog whining in the cabin next door. I freeze, my heart pounding. I pray the dog's owner doesn't decide to poke his head out to investigate.

"*Tish!*" Ivy hisses.

The sound of her voice jerks me back into motion. I'm relieved to find the window unlocked; it slides open easily at my touch. Then I'm clambering through into the cabin. The interior is as I remembered it, spare to the point of Spartan: the bed neatly made with a white chenille spread and none of the usual clutter of a bachelor pad, no empties or fast food wrappers, no overflowing ashtray. No personal items, either, not so much as a framed photo. This is a man who travels light.

I conduct a quick search by flashlight but don't find a stash of old love letters like Jessica Fletcher would have, just some crumpled receipts and an unpaid bill. No address book either. The dresser drawers hold only neatly folded clothes, and the closet, more clothes on hangers, along with two pairs of cowboy boots and a pair of loafers. I have better luck with his laptop. It's outdated, antediluvian by my brother's standards, but it has what I need. I copy his Outlook address book onto the flash drive I brought with me and scroll through his browser's search history. I see a link for the White Oaks website and my pulse quickens. I click on it and up pops a map of the facility. Not exactly hard evidence, but it suggests Stan was lying when he claimed to have had no prior knowledge of where my mom was buried. *Gotcha, you son of a bitch.*

Outside the rain has gone from drizzle to downpour. A clap of thunder causes me to jump and sets the dog next door howling. A face pops up at the window, peering specter-like from the hood pulled over its head, and I almost let out a scream. But it's only Ivy.

"Hurry," she whispers. "Someone's coming!"

I hear the sound of a car engine and glance past her to see

headlights in the distance. I panic. Instead of taking the easy route, through the door, I climb back out the window. I'm straddling the sill, one leg in and one out, when a pickup truck materializes out of the rainy darkness. I catch a glimpse of a cowboy-hatted figure at the wheel as it rounds the corner to the parking area. I don't have to see his face to know it's Stan. I break out in a cold sweat. My heart is hammering so hard it feels like someone performing CPR on me. If we're not gone in two seconds, we're toast.

The hem of my parka snags on a loose screw in the window frame as I'm hauling my left leg over the sill. Muttering curses, I struggle to pull it free while Ivy tugs on my sleeve, hissing, "Come *on.*"

"Go!" I whisper-shriek at the sound of a truck door slamming followed by footsteps crunching over gravel. "I'll catch up with you!" I give her a kick with my free leg when she doesn't obey.

She lets out a muffled yelp. "Ow! That hurt."

"Go!" I order, more forcefully. No sense in us both getting caught.

She hesitates a second longer, wearing an expression I never expected to see on her face: sheer panic. This from someone who gets her kicks from skydiving and who never met a road she didn't yearn to race down. I've always wondered if there was anything in this world Ivy feared. Now I know: She's scared of something bad happening to me. I'm awash with love for her in that moment.

"I'll be back," she whispers, then grabs my messenger bag and vanishes into the darkness.

Thunder cracks. Lightning flashes. The crunching of footsteps grows louder. With a final tug, accompanied by the sound of ripping fabric, I free my jacket from whatever it was caught on and swing my other leg over the sill. I let out a sob with relief when I have both feet on the ground. But before I can take so much as a single step, a man's deep voice booms, "Stop, or I'll shoot!"

CHAPTER THIRTEEN

I may not have shown much respect for the law lately, but I have more than enough for the superior strength of the man standing before me and the rifle aimed at my chest, so I obey his command. "Evening, Stan." I strike a relaxed tone. A dog won't bite if you don't show fear, and he's Big Dog. "Home so soon? Guess tonight wasn't your lucky night, huh?" *Or mine, for that matter.*

He ignores the reference to his poker game. "What the hell do you think you're doing?" With two long-legged strides he closes the gap between us. He towers over me: an Ionic column of a man, all hard-packed muscle and blazing eyes. Rainwater dribbles from the brim of his cowboy hat where it forms a natural spout. Dark, wet patches stand out on the suede jacket he's wearing.

"I was in the neighborhood and thought I'd stop by."

"Cute." He's not smiling.

The neighbor's dog is barking like crazy now. Stan darts a glance in that direction, looking nervous all of a sudden. He produces a set of keys and in one swift motion unlocks the door to his cabin. He grabs me roughly by the arm and pulls me inside with him, shutting the door behind him. He doesn't turn on any lights. There's only the dim glow from the porch fixture. It's a moment before my eyes adjust to the darkness and the room's shadowy contours take shape.

"Sit down!" he barks.

I never knew one's knees could knock from fright—I'd always thought it was a figure of speech—but mine are doing just that. I sink down on the bed, not taking my eyes off him. "Go ahead. Shoot me. But you won't get away with it. Not like with that stunt you pulled the other day."

"What makes you think I did it?"

"Gee, I don't know. You seemed pretty jumpy that day I came to see you, and the next thing I know, I'm the target of a one-man turkey shoot. Now you're pointing a rifle at me. What am I supposed to think?"

"I was at work all day. Like I told Detective Breedlove."

"So you said."

"I got witnesses to back me up."

"How do I know they weren't just covering for you?"

"Jesus. What is it with you?" Standing against the window with his face in shadow, he looks like an anonymous source in a *Sixty Minutes* interview. "If anyone has a beef, it's me. You've been nothing but a pain in the ass since the day we met. Now I catch you breaking into my place."

"You lied about not knowing my mom was dead. I wanted to know what else you were lying about."

"What did you expect to find? A diary? Or maybe I have the missing eighteen minutes of the Nixon tapes squirreled away somewhere." I hear the disdain in his voice but also a note of fear.

"I'm not naïve," I snap. "But I did find one thing. I noticed the link for the White Oaks website when I was scrolling through your search history." I glance at his computer. "Which I found interesting, considering you claimed not to have known where Mom was or how she got there."

I see him stiffen. "No crime against surfing the Web."

"No, but it is to kill someone and dispose of the body."

"I don't know nothing about that. Like I told you, Ava and me, we parted ways. End of story." I notice his Texas twang has grown thicker, like he's hiding behind his good-ole-boy persona.

I ignore his protestations. "You want to know my theory? I think it was a lover's quarrel that got out of hand." I don't mention my other theory, the one involving Douglas Trousdale. "You lashed out at her. I'm sure you didn't mean to kill her—you didn't know your own strength, or she fell and hit her head—but you'd have done time even if it was involuntary manslaughter. So you disposed of the body and left town to make it look like you and she had run off together."

He shakes his head. "You watch too much TV."

"*You're* Starfish Enterprises, aren't you?" I press on. "You leased the unit in the name of a dummy corporation so it couldn't be traced back to you. Except you weren't in it alone. You had a buddy help dispose of the body. How do I know this? Because it wasn't by accident that it turned up after all these years. You two must've had a falling out. He must've been out to get you when he fixed it so the shit would hit the fan." To use Ivy's expression. "He had to have known the trail would lead back to you. What, did you cheat him out of some money, sleep with his wife?"

"You're blowing smoke," Stan growls.

"Where there's smoke, there's fire."

"You got nothing on me."

"No, but Detective Breedlove might be interested to know what's on your computer."

In a sudden move that takes me by surprise, he seizes the computer, yanking the cord from the electrical outlet into which it's plugged, and tosses it out the open window like it's a Frisbee. I hear the muffled crash of electronics meeting concrete amid the drumming of the rain. "'Bout time I got myself a new one, anyway," he says mildly, turning back to me. "Now, where were we?"

I point a shaky finger at him. "You can't run forever. The truth will come out eventually."

"The truth?" He steps from the shadows, and I see his features are contorted in a mask of anguish. The man standing before me is not the callous-seeming figure of my first visit. "You have no idea."

"Tell me, then." I switch tactics, adopting a cajoling tone. "I can see it's eating at you. You'd feel better if you got it off your chest. What've you got to lose? I can't use it against you if I'm dead."

"Dead?" He gives a harsh laugh. "Quit being so dramatic."

"So you're not going to kill me?" I feel my body go slack with relief.

"Hell no. You ain't worth going to prison for."

"You could've fooled me." I gesture toward the rifle.

"I was apprehending an intruder," he reminds me.

"Yeah, okay, but I didn't take anything, and the only thing that got broken was the computer you smashed."

"Tell it to the cops," he growls and then whips out his cell phone and places a 911 call. "Hello? This is Stan Cruikshank out at Four Chimneys Ranch. I'd like to report a break-in . . ."

On second thought, I might've been better off if he'd pulled the trigger.

"This is getting old."

Spence looks anything but amused as he says this. We're standing in the rain, a short distance from where a patrol car sits with its engine idling and bubble light flashing. I'm soaking wet in my flimsy rain gear while he's fully weatherproofed, wearing a heavy-duty slicker and rubber boots and holding an umbrella over his head. He hasn't offered to share the umbrella with me.

"I can explain," I tell him.

"I don't doubt it. And you'll have all the time in the world where you're going."

"Why do you have to be such an asshole?" I burst out, close to the breaking point.

"Funny, that's not how I see it," he says coldly. "What I see is a guy who was relaxing at home, just settling in with the wife to watch some TV after getting the kids off to bed, when he gets called to *yet another crime scene* starring the one and only Tish Ballard. Now, you tell me, which one of us is the asshole in that scenario?" I haven't seen him this angry since I torched his car.

He has a point. I have been turning up at a lot of crime scenes lately. Though in all fairness, this is the first one from which I've been escorted in handcuffs. What's ironic is that the cops were already en route when Stan made his 911 call. Ivy beat him to it, having decided she'd rather visit me in jail than attend my funeral. "I didn't do anything those other times." I defend myself.

"Really. Because I'm starting to see a pattern here."

"Like what?"

"I don't know yet. I haven't figured it out yet. All I know is, you're the common denominator."

"If you hadn't flunked math, you'd know that's the key to the solution, not the problem." I couldn't resist reminding him of his weak spot. It had been the talk of the campus at the time. He'd almost lost a college scholarship because of it and had to go to summer school to take the class again.

I know the barb hits its mark when he flushes, his already tight lips disappearing into his square-jawed face. Then he rocks back on his heels as if to better take in the sorry sight I make in my soggy clothes with my wet hair plastered to my head, and his expression softens slightly. He must feel sorry for me, if only a little, because his grip, when he takes my arm to guide me to the cruiser, is surprisingly gentle. The thing that pisses me off the most about Spence Breedlove is that I can't get a fix on him. Just when I think he's a total asshole, he displays a shred of humanity.

As I'm assisted into the backseat, the driver, Jordan James, turns around to address me. On the proverbial shoe that fits, he's the gum stuck to the sole. "Well, well, what have we got here?" He's smiling, but his eyes are cold. Yeah, he definitely knows it was me who pulled that dirty trick on him at our junior prom. "I don't know which one of you is crazier, you or your brother."

I glare at him. "Fuck you."

"Be my guest." A not so subtle reference to my reputation in high school as a slut. Which is when I realize what else handcuffs are good for: They prevent you from making rude hand gestures.

His partner, Officer Ruiz, doesn't so much as look at me. I wonder if she regrets being nice to me before, now that I'm a known felon. Jordan starts the engine. I see the ranch owner, Mr. Valparaiso, a stocky figure in a rain poncho, standing outside Stan's cabin conversing with him. Shadowy figures watch from the other doorways as the cruiser swings around, headed for the road.

Spence is there, ahead of me, when I arrive at the station. He personally takes me through the booking process. The only nice thing I can say about him is that, unlike Jordan James, he doesn't appear to be taking pleasure in my misery. He's all business. "Stan's the one you should be talking to," I tell him, appealing to his better nature, as he's escorting me to the holding cell.

"So I'm not the only asshole," he comments dryly.

"I'm sorry I called you that." I won't get anywhere with him if I don't play nice. "But I was right about Stan. I found something on his computer." I say nothing about what's on the flash drive that was confiscated along with my personal items. I'm in enough hot water as it is.

"Really. And what might that be?"

"The link for the White Oaks website in his search history. I made the mistake of mentioning it, and he freaked. That's why he smashed his computer. It proves he's hiding something."

"Well, why didn't you say so in the first place? I can get a warrant issued with evidence like that. The DA can coast to victory in the election on the conviction. I should be thanking you instead of locking you up."

"Go ahead, mock me. I'm telling you he's guilty."

"Your word against his."

I hug myself, shivering. I haven't stopped shivering since I got here, despite the desk sergeant, Bill Hadley, having been kind enough to loan me his fleece jacket. I know him from when I brokered the deal on an acre lot he and his wife had bought. In a weird way I find Spence's presence comforting. He's a familiar face and relatively safe haven in the midst of all the madness.

"Don't you see? He was lying when he told me he didn't know my mom was dead. He knew all along. Because he killed her. He hid the body where no one would find it. *He's* Starfish Enterprises."

He appears unmoved as he walks at my side, a firm grip on my elbow. "Oh, I see, all right. I see that you obtained unlawful entry to Mr. Cruikshank's residence and it almost got you killed." He cuts me a glance, and I catch the flash of anger in his eyes, eyes the blue of the porcelain god to whom I once prayed on nights like this (my one consolation in all this is that it wasn't booze that brought me down) and he mutters to himself, "As if I don't have enough to worry about."

I manage a feeble smile. "You were worried? Gee, I didn't know you cared."

He snorts in disgust. He's wearing his civvies—jeans and a USC sweatshirt from his college days—his detective's badge on a lanyard around his neck. I picture him at home with his wife, his arm around her shoulders as they sit in front of the TV, and feel a stab of longing, wishing that same strong arm were around me right now. I give myself a mental shake. I must be losing it.

"Can I get you anything?" he asks, not unkindly, as he's locking me in the holding cell.

"Yeah. A lawyer." When I spoke with Ivy earlier, she assured me she had someone lined up, a woman who she said was one of the top criminal defense attorneys in the county. But I don't know what time she'll be here, or if she's coming at all. She might not get here until tomorrow.

"I meant coffee or a blanket," he says. "Your lawyer's on his way."

I look at him in confusion. "You mean 'she,' don't you?"

"No, the man I spoke with was definitely a 'he.'"

"This lawyer . . . you spoke with him?" Now I'm even more confused.

Spence nods. "He's with the firm that's handling Mr. Trousdale's divorce. He called to let us know you weren't to be questioned without him present."

I stare at him, dumfounded. "Wait. Are you saying Douglas— Mr. Trousdale sent him?"

"So it would seem."

"But why? I don't get it. Something's fishy." I start pacing in my cell like a lifer gone stir-crazy, never mind I've been locked up for all of sixty seconds.

"Don't look a gift horse in the mouth. You should be thanking the man."

"How did he even know I'd been arrested?"

"Seems he was there when your boyfriend got the call." I had asked Ivy to give Daniel the heads-up, knowing he'd never forgive me if he had to read about it in the newspaper. "And you thought he was a cold-hearted son of a bitch. Goes to show how wrong you can be about someone," he says, fixing me with a pointed look before he turns and walks away, leaving me to my own thoughts.

I sit on the cot in the holding cell, which thankfully I have all to myself, my shoulders hunched and my arms crossed over my stomach in a vain attempt to keep from shivering. Douglas Trousdale scares me even more than Stan. I can't quite put my finger on what it is about him I find so creepy. It's not just the seed of suspicion planted by Joan. I didn't trust him even when I worked at Trousdale Realty. Smarmy I can handle; it's easy to spot and easy to avoid. But he's smooth. He'll charm you into thinking you're his new best friend, then stab you in the back after he's gotten what he wanted. I don't know that he's evil enough to commit murder, but if even half of what Joan says about him is true, I have no wish to become personally acquainted with his dark side.

I don't know how much time has passed before I'm roused from a light doze by a male voice. "Ms. Ballard?" I blink and sit up straight, peering out at a trim, middle-aged man with salt-and-pepper hair and twinkly gray-green eyes, dressed in gray slacks and a yellow golf sweater over a crisp oxford shirt. "Grant Weathers," he introduces himself. "Mr. Trousdale sent me. He thought you might need an attorney." I'm instantly put at ease by his relaxed, confident manner.

"One question. Can you get me out of here?"

"Let's see what I can do." He smiles as if to say *piece of cake.*

Things move swiftly after that. I'm formally questioned with Grant on hand to advise and deflect, then whisked down the hall to a conference room for the bail hearing, presided over by a judge via Skype (seems Grant has ties to the legal community here, even though his firm is based in San Francisco, and he pulled some strings to get it expedited). Bail is set at $50,000. I'm thinking I may yet have to spend the night in jail, since even a percentage of that would be a stretch and neither Ivy nor Daniel has that kind of money, when I learn that Mr. Trousdale posted bond. I don't know whether to be relieved or nervous. He spared no expense in getting me sprung. But why? What does he want in exchange? There are no free rides with a man like Douglas Trousdale.

Is he hoping to win my trust or get me alone—to where he can dump my body after he's done away with me? I'm as jittery as the bride of an arranged marriage on her wedding day when Grant and I are buzzed through to the reception area where Douglas awaits. The two men confer with each other briefly before Grant takes his leave. Finally, Douglas turns to me, almost blinding me with the glare of his piercing gaze and porcelain veneers. His charm may be false but it's not inconsiderable. "Shall we?" He escorts me out to where his Beemer is parked, his hand lightly resting against the small of my back in a gesture that's oddly familiar for someone I barely know.

He's dressed casually, if you define "casual" as the sort of leisurewear you'd expect to see on a prince of Qatar, in designer jeans, V-neck sweater in burgundy cashmere, and custom-made calfskin loafers (he has all his footwear made in Hong Kong, according to Joan), a gold Rolex on his wrist. His blue eyes, complemented by his expertly-cut silver hair, remind me of the glass tiles on the backsplash of the kitchen at the La Mar House that go so nicely with the brushed-stainless appliances, with all of the warmth.

He opens the door on the passenger side of his silver BMW 620i convertible. Another person would be on their knees thanking him, but I'm filled with trepidation instead as I sink into the cognac leather seat. He's the stranger with a pocketful of candy I was warned against as a kid.

"That went well, I think." He turns the key in the ignition and the engine purrs to life. He sounds as pleased as if speaking of a successful open house and not an incarceration.

"Yes. Um, thank you," I remember to add.

"You're most welcome." He adjusts a control on the dashboard, and after a minute I'm treated to radiant heat toasting my butt in addition to the warm air blowing from the vents. "If you're still cold, you can put my coat over you." He indicates the overcoat lying across the backseat.

"I'm fine, thanks," I say, hugging myself to keep from shivering.

Another of the Beemer's nifty features, besides heated seats, is the built-in Bluetooth. At the touch of a button I'm listening to Bradley's voice on speakerphone. It's like sinking into a hot bath; my tension eases. He seems equally relieved, glad that I'm none the worse for wear after being locked up. The concern he's expressing suggests Ivy did some heavy spinning in telling the story, because you would have thought I was the victim and not the perpetrator.

"Don't worry, you're in good hands," he says. I don't know if he means Grant Weathers' or his father's.

"He wanted to be here, but felt it would be awkward," Douglas informs me after he's hung up.

"Because of my boyfriend, you mean? Well, as you can see, he wouldn't have been stepping on anyone's toes," I note bitterly. I'm sure Daniel's mad at me, and while I know he has every right— I shouldn't have led him to believe I'd be staying in last night— I'm still hurt that he didn't show. Also, he's well aware I don't trust Douglas. How could he have thrown me in the lion's den?

"Daniel was pretty . . . worked up. I persuaded him it would be in your best interests to sit this one out. No need to amp up the drama quotient, right?" He tips me a collegial wink, one savvy salesperson to another. I can't picture Daniel "worked up," but even a patient man has his limits.

"Well, when you put it that way . . ."

He makes the turn onto Ocean. We cruise through the darkened streets of the business district where the storefronts, except the all-night drugstore, are shuttered at this hour. The heavy downpour of earlier has given way to a light drizzle. The only sounds are the hum of the engine and sizzle of tires on wet pavement. "You two will laugh about this someday when you're old and gray."

"Tell him that. He doesn't see me living to a ripe old age. Not since I almost got plugged in a one-man turkey shoot."

He grimaces at the reminder. "Shocking to think something like that could happen in our community. Do the police have any leads?" I study his face, but it's like looking in a one-way mirror: I can't see what's behind it.

"Not yet. They're working on it." I make it sound like an active investigation, though with no eyewitness and not even a bullet casing recovered from the scene, it's anything but. Whoever the shooter was, he was careful to leave no trace. Careful like a man who has his boxers ironed.

"I gather it wasn't a random shooting. Any idea why you were targeted?"

"No, but I have my suspicions." I let that sit for a moment, hanging in the air like a question mark in a comic-strip bubble. But the expression on his face is pensive rather than furtive.

"Does it have anything to do with the reason you broke into Mr. Cruikshank's place? I heard he was a person of interest in your mother's death."

"Stan was one of the last people to see her alive." I stick to the facts rather than voice my suspicion that my mom's death is linked to those other fatalities, which Douglas may or may not have had something to do with.

"So, what do you think happened? Another tale of misbegotten love gone wrong?"

"I don't know. That's what I'm trying to find out," I answer cautiously. We've left the business district behind and are cruising through the tree-lined residential streets on the outskirts of town.

"Well, if there's anything I can do . . ."

"Thanks, you've done more than enough already." He cuts me a startled glance at the sharp edge in my voice. I didn't mean to sound bitchy, but I'm too wiped out to keep a lid on my emotions.

But I have no wish to become a dead body dumped by the side of the road, so I'm relieved when he doesn't take offense. "I apologize if I overstepped," he says. "It comes from being a boss." He gives a wry chuckle. "You get in the habit of telling people what to do rather than asking."

"No. It's just . . . I don't get it," I burst out. "You pay me to look after your property, and I'm caught breaking into someone's else's? That's reason to fire me, not go all Daddy Warbucks on me."

"Let's just say it's my way of showing my appreciation."

"It wasn't necessary. You always give me a nice tip at Christmas."

"Don't be so modest. You defended me against my wife's vicious accusation."

So that's what this is about. "I didn't . . . I mean, I simply told the truth."

"You could just as easily have cast doubt."

I shift in my seat, my unease growing. What's really going on here? Is he angling to find out what I might have witnessed that I didn't tell the cops? Does he think I'm looking to get money out of him in exchange for keeping quiet? "I'm not going to lie and say I saw something I didn't. I *did* hear you arguing, though." I throw that out there to see how he'll react, but he only sighs.

"A man can only be pushed so far." Interesting he used the word "pushed." A Freudian slip? I reserve judgment for the moment. I want to hear his side of it. "Regardless of what you heard or whatever she might have told you, I don't wish her any ill. I only want to get on with my life."

"It might help if you were to call off the dogs." I can't resist putting in my two cents.

This elicits another deep sigh. "Believe me, I'd love nothing more. It wasn't my decision to drag out the divorce. I'm not going to let her run roughshod over me, but I'm not greedy. Nor am I vindictive. She refuses to believe that, of course. She sees dark motives where there are none. And just when I thought it couldn't get any nastier . . ." He shakes his head, wearing a look of distress.

"It's embarrassing, to say the least," he goes on, "not to mention potentially damaging to my career. But what pains me most is to watch someone I once cared for, the mother of my son, unravel before my eyes." He shakes his head. "And she wonders why I was unhappy in our marriage."

"So that's why you left? Because you thought she'd gone crazy?"

"It's not always because of another woman," he says, responding to the skepticism in my voice. "I know what people are saying, that Tiffany was the reason for the split, but she merely happened to come along at a time when I was feeling . . . open to other possibilities, shall we say."

One of which was getting in her pants. "You and Joan must have been happy at one time." I probe a little deeper.

"Very much so. When we were first together." He falls silent, lost in some memory, and there's just the purring of the engine. His Beemer is like a Lippizaner stallion compared to my workhorse of an SUV; it's such a smooth ride I'm barely aware we're moving as we fly through the darkened streets. "She was quite beautiful. I was so dazzled that I couldn't see if she had the qualities I was looking for in a wife. Not that I was in the market for a wife. I was young, just out of college."

"Why get married then?"

"I was in love. And my dad adored her. She was the daughter he never had. My mother died when I was five and he never remarried." He reflects on this, adding, "I don't think they were very happy together, my parents. Dad could be . . ." He trails off, asking, "Did you know him?"

"I met him once." My dad was picking my mom up from work that day and he'd sent me in to fetch her. She was with Leon at the time; they were going over inventory for the gift shop. "He made quite an impression. I remember thinking he looked like Jesus, or at least the way I'd imagined Jesus to look." I picture him in my mind: a tall, striking figure with wavy golden hair to his shoulders and piercing blue eyes. He wore loose-fitting garb and thick "Jesus" sandals. What seemed god-like to me then I now know to be charisma. Leon had charisma to burn, like his son.

"It was an image he cultivated." I hear a slight edge in his voice, but he says nothing more on the subject. Their relationship was clearly complicated. "As for Joan, I feel it's only fair to warn you, if you haven't figured it out for yourself, you're dealing with a disturbed individual."

I squirm in my comfy, heated, leather seat. "I don't know about that. I mean, you *did* leave her for another woman, so of course she's upset. But 'disturbed'? That's kind of harsh, don't you think?"

"She accused me of trying to kill her!" he cries.

I don't answer. I'm not convinced Joan was imagining things.

"Did you know she was seeing a psychiatrist?" he goes on.

"She and a lot of other people. That doesn't mean she's crazy." My thoughts turn to my brother. I wonder how he's faring at the "puff." I don't see how he could be any worse off than I am right now.

"Don't mistake me. I think psychiatry is a fine thing. But I worry it may not be enough in her case."

I narrow my eyes at him. "Are you saying she should be institutionalized?" It's a sore subject. In the not too distant past, before the laws were changed in the 1980s, mentally ill people like my brother were routinely locked away in institutions without their consent. They didn't even have to be mentally ill. A husband whose wife had become inconvenient, for whatever reason, had only to enlist one or two sympathetic "witnesses" to testify in court as to her "mental instability" to get her committed. The good old days, as far as Douglas is concerned. But like the seasoned salesperson he is, he's quick to change strategy at seeing that I'm not buying his pitch.

"No, of course not. I just want you to understand where I'm coming from."

"I'm not sure I do."

"People take sides in a divorce. And Joan can be very persuasive. I'd hate to see you get sucked in."

"I don't believe everything I'm told. I make up my own mind."

What I want to say is, *You don't fool me.* I can see through his ploy. He thinks that by painting Joan as a lunatic, he can avert suspicion from himself. I recall what Spence said about me being the "common denominator." The same is true of Douglas. Based on proximity alone he was the common denominator in three seemingly unrelated deaths. He was employed at the Fontana the year Martina and Hector died and my mom went missing. And that's not all. McGee discovered, when he looked into Douglas' background, that while he was a student at UC Santa Barbara, a female classmate of his was brutally slain on campus. He wasn't named in connection to the murder—the killer was never caught—but it has me wondering: Is the man sitting next to me just another husband making excuses for trading in his old wife for a newer model . . . or a serial killer?

"Here we are." I'm roused from my dark reverie at the sound of Douglas' voice.

I look out the window, relieved to see we've arrived at my house. Only then does it occur to me I was so preoccupied I'd neglected to give him my address. "How do you know where I live?"

He doesn't answer. He only says, smiling his patented smile, "Good night, Tish. Sleep tight."

I'm hurrying up the front walk when I hear a familiar voice call my name. I lurch to a halt, my eyes darting to my porch where a shadowy figure is seated on the wooden chest that holds my gardening supplies and that doubles as a bench. A fresh surge of adrenaline has me wide awake where a moment ago I was so wiped out I couldn't have walked a straight line in a field sobriety test.

"What the hell are *you* doing here?" I cry.

CHAPTER FOURTEEN

Stan rises and steps down from the porch, walking to meet me, the clicking of his boot heels like a movie sound effect—the part in an old Western when the sheriff and outlaw face off against each other. High noon at the OK Corral. Except it's the dead of night and neither of us is armed. He doesn't even look particularly threatening, unlike earlier tonight when he was channeling Dirty Harry. He looks old and tired, the lines bracketing his mouth deep as fissures in a rock face.

He stops a few feet from me, raising his hand in the universal I-come-in-peace gesture. "We need to talk." His voice rumbles from his chest.

I stare at him as if we were standing eye-to-eye even though he's a half foot taller. "Let me get this straight. First you threaten me, then have me thrown in jail—which, by the way, totally could've been avoided if you'd been straight with me to begin with instead of forcing me to go to extremes—and now here you are on my doorstep. Wanting to talk. At one-freaking-thirty in the morning."

He sighs wearily. "I can explain."

"By all means. This I got to hear." I remain rooted to the spot, arms crossed over my chest.

"Not out here. Can we talk inside?" He gestures toward the house.

"Right. So you can strangle me after you almost shot me dead. Twice."

"If I wanted you dead, I wouldn't be wasting my breath talking to you. I could take you out with one shot." I hear the exasperation in his voice, but it quickly gives way to a conciliatory tone. "What I said before, I wasn't lying. It wasn't me shooting at you the other day."

"Why should I believe you?"

"You can decide for yourself after you've heard me out."

I don't know if it's the heaviness in his voice or remembering the look on his face earlier tonight when we were talking about my mom, but I sense he means no harm. Also, I'm curious. I've come too far and risked too much to pass up the opportunity to hear what he has to say. I incline my head in a nod of acquiescence and he falls in behind me as I move past him to climb the porch steps. I unlock the door and he follows me inside. My cat materializes from the shadows, meowing piteously. Stan scoops him up, cradling him in the crook of his arm and rubbing him behind his ears where he likes to be scratched. "Nice kitty. Big fella, aren't you? Hercules closes his eyes and starts to purr, kneading the front of Stan's jacket with his paws.

"Traitor," I mutter under my breath. To Stan I say, "Do you want some coffee?"

"If it's no trouble," he says, shyly almost. He lowers my cat to the floor and politely removes his cowboy hat as he straightens. "Nice place you got here," he remarks, glancing around him.

"Thanks." Of all the bizarre twists and turns of tonight, this is the most bizarre: my exchanging pleasantries with a guy who, hours ago, was pointing a rifle at me. "Make yourself at home. Be with you in a minute." I totter down the hall to my bedroom. I can't spend another minute in my damp clothes even if it means leaving Stan to ransack my house or come after me with an ax.

I return, wearing sweats and my Ugg slippers, to find him seated at the kitchen table, the coffeemaker gurgling and two mugs set out. He's even fed my cat. He nods towards Hercules, who has his head buried in his food bowl, explaining, "He was meowing. Figured he was hungry."

"He's always hungry." I slide into the chair across from Stan, fixing him with my steeliest gaze. "Okay, so tell me. Why are you here? What's so important all of a sudden it couldn't wait, after you put me through the seven circles of Hell trying to pry information out of you?"

He releases a breath. "It's a long story and not a pretty one, so bear with me. But I swear everything you're about to hear is the God's honest truth." He raises his right hand as though his left hand were resting on a bible. "You were right about one thing: Your mom's death was no accident."

His words have the effect of several hundred volts of electricity slamming through my body. I'd known all along, in my gut, but it's still a shock hearing it from his lips. "You . . . you killed her?"

He shakes his head, grim-faced. "I never laid a hand on her. I wasn't lying about that, either."

"Then who did?"

"I'll get to that in a minute. First, you should know I loved her. We were going to make a life together. I'm sorry if that's tough to hear, on account of your dad and all, but that's just how it was. I'm not saying she didn't love him, too—she did in her own way. I had a devil of a time convincing her to leave him. She worried about her kids most of all. But I promised her we'd work it out." His face constricts momentarily with some inner torment. "I had a job and a nice three-bedroom lined up in Bakersfield. The plan was to come back for you and your brother once we were settled."

"Except she never did," I say in a dull voice.

"No," he says softly, looking down at his fists, curled loosely on the table, before dragging his bloodshot eyes up to meet mine. "She would have, though. Don't ever doubt that." My throat grows tight. It's as if all the tears I held in through the years are backed up, pressing behind my eyes like a dam about to burst. A torrent of questions roils in my mind as I listen to him go on. "That morning, I dropped her off at my place after I'd come to fetch her. She was gonna pack up the rest of my things so we could head out for Bakersfield soon as I got home from work. I'd have kept on driving, left everything I owned behind—I wish to God I had—but I was owed a week's pay and we needed the money. When I got home that afternoon . . ." His voice cracks and he pauses to collect himself. "I found her in the basement, lying at the bottom of the stairs."

"Dead?" I force the word past numb lips. I can't bear to think of her suffering at the end while the life drained out of her.

"Yeah." Again, that flash of agony on his face. "And like I said, it weren't no accident."

"Are you sure she couldn't have tripped and fallen?"

"Sure as I am that a rattler bites when you step on it. She wasn't the first. He'd killed two others."

A chill travels down my spine. "You said 'he.' Do you mean Douglas Trousdale?"

He gives me a baffled look, then shakes his head. "Him? Nah. Maybe he knew about it, or was involved in some way, but he took orders from his old man. Leon was the one running the show."

I stare at him, aghast. "Are you saying it was *Leon*? That's impossible."

"Believe it."

"No way," I insist. "You must be mistaken. He . . . he was a vegetarian. He wouldn't kill a chicken much less another human being." It's a lame defense, I realize as I'm voicing it. That's when it dawns on me: I didn't know the man. I only know his reputation, as a guru who preached the gospel of mind-body awareness. What if the Christ-like figure I recall from childhood wasn't so saintly after all?

Stan nods, wearing a look of disgust. "Yeah, he had everyone fooled with that hippie-dippy act of his. Everyone except your mom, and even she bought into it at first. Until she found out he was a wolf in sheep's clothing. He had her killed because she'd found out about the others."

"Hector and Martina." I breathe their names.

He looks surprised. "You know about them?"

I nod my head. "Someone mentioned Mom had disappeared around the same time they died, so I did some research. People get killed in freak accidents, sure. But two people from the same place of business? Both dying in freak accidents within three months of each other? That raised a red flag."

"You're your mother's daughter all right." His mouth slants in a mirthless smile.

"What I don't get is *why.*"

"She wondered the same thing after she'd stumbled on a letter from the insurance company. It was something to do with a payout on a life policy for Hector Martinez. She couldn't understand why Leon was the beneficiary, and not the dead guy's family. When she looked into it, she learned something that knocked her for a loop: he had *all* his employees insured. They were worth more dead than alive—two hundred thousand apiece, twice that if it was an accidental death, on account of the double indemnity clause. He'd already collected on the Vuković girl."

"Wait. Are you serious? I've never heard of such a thing."

"You'd be surprised. Lots of companies do it. Big corporations, too. What I call 'stealing pennies off a dead man's eyes' they call 'standard practice,'" he says, his voice thick with contempt.

"You're saying they were killed for the money?"

"Sure looks that way. Seems Leon got in over his head building the new wing. It was nowhere near done and cost overruns were through the roof. The bank wouldn't extend his loan and he was having trouble meeting the payments. So he figures why not cash in on a couple of those policies."

"My God. That's . . . that's diabolical."

"That was the exact word she used. The tip-off for her was when I told her about the cost overruns on the new wing. She did some more digging and the other pieces fell into place. It was that more than anything that finally convinced her to quit her job and leave town. She was scared of what would happen if Leon were to find out she was on to him."

"Why didn't she go to the police?"

"He was a powerful man, and all she had was circumstantial evidence. She knew they'd never go after him. He'd come after her instead. She didn't want you and your brother growing up without a mom." Sadly, that had come to pass, but I can't dwell on that now. I have to focus on the here and now. If that was Douglas, or his hired gun, who was sending me a message warning me to back off, it means he'll stop at nothing to keep his father's secrets from becoming a public scandal. I hug myself, shivering, at the thought. "But the son of a bitch got her in the end. He wasn't taking any chances. I'd have been next—I knew too much—if I hadn't taken a powder."

"You ran because you were scared for your life?"

He stiffens, clearly affronted at the suggestion that he hadn't been man enough to go head to head with Leon. "It wasn't *me* I was worried about. I couldn't let him take the one thing she had left to give."

I feel the blood drain from my face as comprehension dawns. "The insurance money."

He nods. "It was the icing on the cake," he says grimly.

"So you got rid of the body to make it look like she'd run away with you." Thus condemning her family—me and my brother, and our dad until he'd passed away—to a lifetime of never knowing. I'm angry about that, but at the same time I have to admit it was a courageous move.

"Also because I knew the cops would try to pin it on me."

"You had an alibi. You were at work all day."

"Yeah, except I didn't come straight home. I'd stopped to see about a job this fella had called about—a light fixture he needed to have installed. I figured I could knock it out in an hour and pick up some extra cash for the trip. I waited for him, but he never showed. I know now it was set up."

He rises to fetch the coffee—not because he wants any, I sense, but only because it's something to do—and I notice his hand is trembling as he fills the mugs he'd set out. "They coulda thrown me in jail. Hell, shot me dead on the spot. I was so broke up, I didn't care what happened to me." His Texas drawl has become more pronounced with each passing minute. "But I guess my will to survive was stronger than my wish to die," he says, regretfully almost, as he hands me my mug.

"Did someone help you dispose of the body?" My cat starts to meow at my feet, winding in and out between my ankles as if he senses my agitation. I scoop him up, hugging him to my chest. I must have been holding him a little too tightly because he leaps from my arms back onto the floor.

Stan looks startled by the question. "No. What makes you think that?"

"If no one else knew about it, or even knew she was dead, who arranged for me to find her?"

He grimaces. "That would be me. And don't think I haven't regretted it."

"*You?*" I stare at him. "I don't get it. Why put yourself at risk? And why now, after all these years?"

For the longest time he doesn't answer. He just sits staring into middle space while he sips his coffee. Then he slowly brings his gaze back to me. "It all started when I moved back here. I figured enough time had passed. The old man was gone and the rest was history—or so I thought." He looks to the window, his pale reflection staring back from the darkened glass. "I don't believe in ghosts or any of that mumbo jumbo about communicating with spirits, but I could *feel* her. Everywhere I went, she was right there beside me. It was like she was sending me a message, only I didn't know what it was. Then one day it hit me: She wanted me to make it right with you and your brother. Let you know she hadn't run out on you. I didn't know if I'd be doing you any favors, but I figured a hard truth was better than unanswered questions." He makes a wry face. "I didn't count on you being so doggone persistent. You were s'posed to let the cops handle it."

I ignore the look of mild reproach he gives me. "You weren't worried the trail would lead back to you?"

He shrugs. "No DA in his right mind would try a case on evidence thin as that."

"Turns out you were right." I recall my dispiriting conversation with Spence.

"Except you wouldn't let go. I did everything I could to shake you, but you were on me like a tick on a hound." I detect a note of grudging admiration. "Ever thought about taking up bull riding?"

I smile thinly. "Something to consider if I decide to give up sleuthing," I reply in jest.

The crinkle of amusement fades from around his eyes. "You'd be better off. With bulls, it ain't personal."

I wrap my fingers around my steaming mug to warm them. I can't seem to shake the chill that had set in earlier, despite the coziness of my kitchen and dry clothes I'd changed into. Not because I'm still afraid of Stan but because I fear he was telling the truth. "You think my life is in danger?"

"I do. The old man may be dead, but it looks like his son is carrying on the family tradition. Either he got wind of the fact that you were asking questions or somebody tipped him off." I wonder if it was Daniel. Had he unwittingly placed me in the crosshairs? "That's why I'm here. When I heard he drove you home after posting bond, I figured it was my duty to warn you before it was too late."

"Who told you he posted bond?"

"Desk sergeant at the station."

I lift an eyebrow at him. "What, you called to make sure I was locked up and no longer a menace to society?"

"I wish." He rolls his eyes. "I told 'em I was dropping the charges against you."

"Gee, I'm touched."

"Well, I don't mind telling you I was mighty glad to see you coming up that walk." A reluctant smile edges onto his weather-beaten face. "If you're smart, you'll steer clear of Trousdale. Don't make the same mistake as your mom. Let sleeping dogs lie—the mean ones bite."

"Her only mistake was in thinking she could escape. She should have gone to the press. They're always looking for a juicy story, even if the cops would've blown her off." I should know; I'd had reporters snapping at my heels after the story broke about my discovering my mother's remains. "If Leon had been under public scrutiny, he wouldn't have dared lay a finger on her."

"Maybe." Stan ponders this, his expression darkening.

"Did she make copies of everything she'd found? You know, bank statements, loan documents, correspondence with the insurance company, that kind of thing?"

He gives a lackluster nod. "She had a whole file. It was in a safe deposit box at the bank, but she'd gotten it out to take with us. When I went to look for it after she . . . after." He blinks and clears his throat. "It was gone. He must've found it. And destroyed it along with the original documents."

"I don't doubt it, but from your description it sounds like it was quite the paper trail, so maybe there are still traces of it. Stuff that was overlooked or misfiled, copies he didn't know existed." I'd worked in a busy office where papers regularly and mysteriously went missing—like all the socks that get "eaten" by clothes dryers—and we're talking about an era when paperless wasn't an option.

"Wouldn't it have been chucked at some point?"

"Not necessarily. I'll bet there's boxes of old files in storage at the

Fontana." Even companies that have gone paperless keep archives of everything that gets filed away in case of an IRS audit and then forgotten about. "Think of it as an archeological dig, a bone here, a potsherd there, and little by little a picture forms. I only need enough of a picture to raise questions. The tabloids aren't scrupulous about fact-checking, you may have noticed. Unless you believe Jennifer Aniston has been pregnant more times than is humanly possible. They'd eat it up. The billionaire who allegedly tried to kill his wife implicated in several other murders? Throw in interviews with the victims' grieving family members and you've got the makings of a media frenzy. Douglas wouldn't dare come near me. The police might even be pressured into opening an investigation."

Stan remains skeptical. "Even if you're right, you can't just waltz in and start poking around."

"True," I agree. "But it just so happens I know someone who has access. Someone who I'm reasonably certain would be only too willing to assist me in getting the goods on Mr. Trousdale."

"And who would that be?"

"Mrs. Trousdale."

I tumble into bed after seeing Stan out, only to be rudely awakened a mere five hours later by the alarm clock I only vaguely recall having set before I fell asleep, out of an even more dimly remembered sense of duty. I could easily sleep another eight hours, but I have work to do. I shuffle into the kitchen, where I nuke the dregs from the coffee pot and sit down to make some calls.

The first one is to McGee. We were supposed to meet at the firing range at eight-thirty for another lesson, but in my current, sleep-deprived state I'd probably miss if I were to shoot at a barn door while standing right in front of it. "Sorry it's last minute," I apologize about having to cancel.

"Your funeral," he rasps.

I groan. "Don't. Not even in jest. You have no idea what I went through last night." I tell him the whole, hairy tale, starting with my bungled burglary attempt and subsequent arrest and ending with Stan's shocking revelation. "I'm still trying to wrap my brain around it. Leon Trousdale a serial killer? My God. He was the Deepak Chopra of his day around here. I remember my mom telling me he used to get these huge turnouts whenever he'd give a lecture, complete with groupies. He was like a cross between a rock star and a televangelist."

"Like Jim Jones. Till his followers drank the Kool-Aid," McGee intones darkly.

"Leon was every bit as evil, just not on a mass scale. And from what I can see, the apple didn't fall far from the tree with his son. Talk about the father-son duo from hell."

"Reminds me of when I was a rookie working vice. This one time? We picked up a guy for soliciting along with his sixteen-year-old son. Turned out it was a regular thing with them; every Saturday night they'd go trawling for prostitutes. Heart-warming to see such family togetherness."

"Ugh. That's disgusting."

"You were lucky you got home in one piece." His voice gruff with concern, he asks, "You okay?"

"Yes . . . no. I'm not, actually, unless you define 'okay' as having a pulse." I close my eyes and rub with two fingers where a vein is throbbing in my right temple. "I didn't get to sleep until three in the morning."

"What are doing up so early?"

"Early bird gets the worm. Except I don't know if I'm the bird or the worm."

"Well, if you need me, you know where to reach me." This is the closest we've come to a Disney Family Channel moment. "Meanwhile I'll do some poking around, see what else I can dig up." Seems I awoke a sleeping bear in enlisting McGee. Once a cop always a cop. And knowing him, I have no doubt he's got something up his sleeve. I just hope it's an ace and not his Glock 9 mm revolver.

I'm hanging up when I hear the soft thump of the cat door. Hercules returning from his pre-dawn prowls. He pads over to me and sinks onto his haunches, tail twitching, looking up at me expectantly. His Royal Highness doesn't like to be kept waiting. "No luck finding any mice, huh?" I give him a scratch behind the ears before getting up to replenish his food and water bowls. He usually has something to show for his hunting expeditions, though I can't say I'm not grateful to be spared the sight of a bloody corpse, if only the small, feathered or furry kind.

My next call is to Ivy. I know it's bad when she doesn't advocate going all vigilante on Douglas but advises caution instead, after I've brought her up to date. "I don't know, Tish. Maybe you should take a step back. For God's sake, the man's a sociopath! And you know what's more dangerous than a sociopath? A stinking rich sociopath. He can afford to hire a hit man. And not just any hit man. I'm talking shady-foreign-government-ex-military."

"You sound like my brother." I laugh, but it's a nervous laugh.

Then she says something that scares me even more: "You should call Daniel."

She must *really* be worried if she'd have me invoking the wrath of my boyfriend, whom she doesn't even like.

"You're right. I should. And I will." I'm a bad person and even worse girlfriend for waiting this long to return the five, increasingly frantic messages he's left on my voicemail. It's just that I don't need a lecture. Which is exactly what I get when I finally get around to phoning him.

"Jesus, Tish, what were you thinking? You could've been killed! You're lucky you were only arrested."

"Yes, I'm fine, thank you for asking," I reply testily.

"Oh, no. You're not putting this on me." I've never heard him sound so angry. "I have every right to be upset. If you'd listened to me in the first place . . ."

"I was desperate, okay? I needed answers and I wasn't getting any from Spence."

"And look where it got you."

"Fine, I admit it wasn't the smartest move. But would you please hold off on the lecture at least until I've fully woken up and my head stops throbbing?" I rub my temple where it's still pulsing.

"This isn't just about you, you know," he says in a voice thick with hurt and disappointment. "I was worried sick! You could have had the decency to return my phone calls at the very least. Where I come from, that's not how you treat someone you care about."

"If you cared about *me*, you wouldn't have thrown me in the lion's den," I snap. "You knew I didn't trust Douglas. How could you?" I no longer think it was Daniel who, unwittingly, placed me in the crosshairs—more likely it was Genevieve, currying favor with the man she'd hoped to one day call father-in-law—but that doesn't change the fact that he put me at risk. "Look, we were both wrong," I say in a gentler voice. "And I'm sorry I worried you."

"It wasn't only that. You lied to me."

"I didn't. I just . . ."

"Omitted the truth. Same thing."

He's right, and I feel bad for hurting him. Besides the fact that I *do* care about him, he's a good guy. He's dedicated his life to cleaning up the ocean and making the world a better place. Whereas all I seem to be doing is making a mess of things. "I'm sorry. I should have told you. I wasn't thinking."

"No, you weren't," he agrees. "You weren't thinking about me at all."

I have nothing to say to that. Because it would only lead to a conversation about our general unsuitability as a couple, which I'm not ready to have. I can only repeat once more that I'm sorry.

My final phone call of the morning is to the "puff," where I speak with the assistant day supervisor, Candace Arnold. Like the holiday-themed clothing she favors at Christmastime, the registered nurse and grandmother of four is nothing if not cheerful. She assures me my brother is adjusting well and on his best behavior. "Good as gold, bless his heart." I'm less than reassured. Last time those words were used to describe him, it was only because they had him so doped up, he was a virtual zombie. But I can't think about that right now; I have too much else to worry about.

No sooner do I hang up on Candace than the phone rings. A glance at my caller ID has me smiling when a minute ago I was frowning. The sound of Bradley's voice acts on me like a tonic, reviving my pulse and stirring my bludgeoned senses back to life. "Morning. Did I wake you?"

"Not a chance. A pot of coffee and I'm still dragging."

"Well, at least you're still in the land of the living."

"If my vital signs are any indication."

"That bad, huh?"

"I've had worse nights, but none that didn't involve my getting shitfaced."

"How about I buy you breakfast and you can tell me all about it?"

"Sounds tempting, but I'm afraid I wouldn't make very good company. I didn't get much sleep last night."

"All the more reason. You could probably do with some nourishment."

"Another eight hours of sleep is more like it."

"Is that an option?"

"I wish. Unfortunately, duty calls." My properties are like household pets. Leave them unattended for any length of time and you'll be looking at puddles on the floor and other nasty surprises.

"We can grab a bite before work, in that case. I won't take no for an answer."

I hesitate only a beat. "Meet me at the Bluejay in an hour." I'm helpless to resist, even as the little voice in my head I've been ignoring lately whispers, *You'll regret this.* How can I look him in the eye, knowing what I know?

I arrive to find the restaurant packed with a line stretching out the door—reminiscent of a Vermont country kitchen with wooden farm tables and white wainscoting, Hoosier cabinets and walls hung with photos of the owner's grandparents' chicken farm, the Bluejay is a cozy alternative to the breezier beach-themed eateries in this town, popular with locals and tourists alike—yet I'm not surprised to see Bradley seated, at one of the window tables no less. He's not the kind of man to cool his heels wherever there's a female to be dazzled into giving him preference, like the cute brunette hostess whose face fell when I walked past her headed for Bradley.

"Hey." His face lights up, and he stands to greet me.

"Hey." My heart is pounding. He's more tempting than what's on the menu, savory and sweet rolled into one delicious package, with his bedroom eyes and aura of tangled sheets and passion-filled nights. He's wearing a gray hoodie over a Swiss Army T-shirt, black with the brand logo in red, and jeans that caress him the way I'd like to. His dark curls are still damp from the shower, a reminder of our first, fateful meeting, which, it occurs to me, was a foreshadowing of what was to come. His quick reflexes saved him from being injured when I'd hurled that vase at him, but he won't be able to protect himself from the bombshell about his grandfather when I go public with it.

I slide into the ladder-back chair opposite him. The window next to where we're sitting looks out on the patio that comprises the outdoor seating area, where morning fog lingers and the only creature stirring is a squirrel nibbling an acorn. When I bring my gaze back to Bradley, I find him studying me. "You don't look like someone who's running on empty," he remarks, smiling.

"If I dig down deep, I might find a compliment buried in there somewhere."

"That was my clumsy way of saying you look good."

"Emphasis on 'clumsy.'" I feel the tension go out of me as we banter.

"In my defense, I'm out of practice. In Muslim countries it's generally considered unwise to pay a compliment to a woman who isn't your wife or sister. God help me if I were to tell a woman I wasn't related to, who happened to be sitting across from me in a restaurant, she looked lovely." He makes a gun with his thumb and forefinger and holds it to his head as he clicks his tongue.

"In that case, you're forgiven." I keep my voice light, though his pantomime sends a shudder through me, as if I'd swallowed an ice cube whole. The compliment isn't lost on me, however. I'm glad I took the time to blow out my hair and put on makeup. I'm wearing the nicest clothes I could find in my closet that wouldn't have me looking like I'd purposely dressed up: slim-fitting black jeans and a fuchsia jersey top with a scoop neck. I don't normally wear jewelry to work, not since a parrot belonging to one of my clients nearly tore off my earlobe along with one of my hoop earrings when it flew onto my shoulder as I was cleaning its cage. But today I'm sporting silver studs in my ears and a moonstone pendant, one of Ivy's creations, on a chain around my neck.

Bradley signals to our waiter, a college-age kid with shaggy blond hair who looks vaguely familiar. As he's walking toward us I remember where I know him from—we met at a university function; he's one of Daniel's grad students. I duck my head, pretending to study the menu even though I know it by heart from all the times I've eaten here. It's a knee-jerk reaction and totally juvenile. I'm acting like a high school girl who's worried her boyfriend will get jealous if it gets back to him she was seen with another guy, not a grown woman who's free to have male friends. I'm relieved nonetheless when the grad student/waiter takes our orders without showing so much as a flicker of recognition.

When our food comes—the buckwheat-pecan waffle for me, and green chili breakfast burrito for Bradley—and I'm attacking what's on my plate (I didn't realize how hungry I was until I inhaled the delicious smells wafting toward me), Bradley observes, with a wry chuckle, "Nothing like criminal activity for working up an appetite. Good thing you didn't spend the night in jail."

"Why is that, aside from the obvious?"

"The food isn't nearly as good."

"And you know this because . . ." I twirl my fork at him in a let's-hear-it gesture.

"I spent a night in jail once when I was sixteen."

"DUI?" It's the first thing that comes to mind, having been pulled over on more than one occasion during my drinking days.

"No, but close. I was at a party that got raided. Me and a bunch of other kids were charged with underage drinking. I also got possession—I had a couple joints on me. I was a first-time offender so I'd have had it easy except that Dad decided to teach me a lesson—over my mom's strong objection, I might add. He didn't bail me out until the next day. Which was how I ended up overnighting in the drunk tank at County with a couple of homeless winos named, I kid you not, Hank and Frank." He places a hand over his heart, eyes twinkling. "I promise you I'm a reformed man."

"Reformed my ass," I tease him. "You just found a way to get your kicks legally."

He shrugs, flashing me an unrepentant grin. "What about you? What's your excuse?"

I consider how best to phrase it. "I broke the law, okay, but there were mitigating factors."

"Such as?"

"I was looking for information."

"And did you find it?"

"Yes and no." I use my fork to spear a morsel of waffle with which to mop up the syrup on my plate while I studiously avoid his gaze. "Actually, I'm thinking I may have been wrong about Stan."

"Really. What made you change your mind?"

My heart starts to pound again. I want to give him an honest answer, but how do you tell someone you care about that his grandfather was a serial killer and his father might be one, too? "He was there when I got home last night. He wanted me to know he was dropping the charges against me."

Bradley considers this as he refills his coffee cup from the thermos on the table. "I'm glad the charges were dropped, but I'm having trouble with the bit about him showing up unannounced. To me that says 'stalker.' Why drive all the way over to your house in the middle of the night when he could've picked up the phone, or better yet, had your lawyer give you the good news?"

"I guess he felt he owed it to my mom." It sounds lame even as I'm saying it.

"And based solely on that you're prepared to give him a pass?" I can tell his newsman's nose is twitching. He senses there's more to the story. But I'm not going to give it to him. Not just yet.

"I've been known to be wrong from time to time." I strike a casual note, even as the horrid knowledge I bear twists and gnaws inside me. "How's your burrito? Not too spicy, I hope?"

"No, just the way I like it. It's delicious. I haven't tasted anything this good in a while. Not since Genevieve left." He pauses to reflect on this as he chews. "I do miss her cooking, I have to admit."

I refrain from asking, *Is that all you miss?* "Are you two still on speaking terms?" I ask instead.

"Sure. Just because we broke up, it doesn't mean we aren't still friends."

"It's not the same for every couple. Look at your parents."

He makes a face. "Point taken. But that's an extreme example. She and I are . . . I was on the phone with her for an hour last night, as a matter of fact." If I was looking to get a status report on their relationship, he's not giving me much. I have no choice but to take the direct approach.

"Any chance you'll get back together?"

"I don't see how. There's no middle ground." He puts his fork down with a sigh. "Christ. I feel like such a jerk. She's not wrong to want what she wants."

"No, but we don't always get what we want."

"True," he agrees, wearing a look of regret.

"I feel that way about Daniel. We're compatible, but we don't always see eye-to-eye. It's not that we want different things, just that we're very different from each other." I feel a stab of guilt. I shouldn't be discussing my relationship with an outsider. Not just any outsider, a man on whom I have a secret crush. It doesn't seem fair to Daniel. "Maybe that's how it is with most couples. What do I know? I have nothing to compare it to. My parents' marriage was anything but normal."

"My mom and dad put a lot of energy into making theirs seem normal, but I, for one, was never fooled," he says. "You know it's bad when your kid is begging to be sent to boarding school."

"You don't have to be from an unhappy home to want to go to boarding school," I point out.

"I was nine."

"Oh."

He pops a piece of bacon in his mouth and chews. "There should be a patron saint for fucked-up families."

I wince inwardly. If only he knew . . .

Talk turns to his work. You'd think it was all a great adventure, to hear him tell it. He'd traveled the Taliban strongholds along the border between Pakistan and Afghanistan, embedded with an army infantry division; seen action in Iraq and Afghanistan; and, in the past five years alone, witnessed the toppling of the dictatorships in Egypt and then Libya. "Got some killer footage of them storming the presidential palace," he reminisces fondly of the latter, seemingly unaware of my mouth hanging open. I never thought I'd meet someone who was more of an adrenaline junkie than Ivy.

"When do you go back?" I ask, torn between wishing he'd stick around longer and wanting to spare him the worst of the media storm when the truth comes out about his grandfather. That is, if I succeed in creating one. I don't know whether or not Joan will cooperate in that effort. I have a feeling she will, but I can't be sure until I've spoken with her. Just thinking about it causes my stomach to twist, bringing the sour taste of maple syrup mixed with bile.

"Week after next. Just got word from the bureau chief." He studies me when I don't respond right away. "Why the long face? Don't tell me you're going to miss me."

"Maybe just a little." I hold my thumb and forefinger a scant inch apart, at which he breaks out in a grin. "But how can a lone projectile-throwing woman compete with the thrill of the war zone?"

He chuckles. "My life isn't as exciting as yours, apparently."

"That reminds me. I should give your mom a call and explain about last night. You know, so she won't think I'm moonlighting as a cat burglar."

He nods his approval. "I only gave her the bare bones, so she'll want to hear from you. Oh, and throw in a good word for my dad while you're at it." He means the fact that his father came to my rescue. My stomach executes another half gainer as I think about how I'd been alone in a car with a man who'd been complicit, if not actively involved, in at least three murders.

"Believe me, he'll be topic number one."

CHAPTER FIFTEEN

The Trousdales' townhouse in the exclusive district of Pacific Heights is a prime example of turn-of-the-century Second Empire architecture. Easily the most impressive on the block, its three stories boast rounded cornices and classical pediments, a center wing flanked by French windows with ornate wrought-iron balconies. Round *oeil de boeuf* windows peer like old-fashioned monocles from either end of the patterned-slate mansard roof. A small entry porch with a domed portico leads to a hallway that opens onto a formal parlor furnished in period antiques.

"What can I get you to drink?" inquires Joan after I'm settled on the rose-silk settee by the fireplace. An array of non-alcoholic beverages sits on a silver tray on the Sheraton sideboard. I'd confided to her that I was in AA, and clearly she hasn't forgotten. I appreciate her thoughtfulness even though I don't mind when others drink around me. I tell her I'll take a Diet Coke.

As she pours our beverages I take a moment to survey the room, taking in the carved, Italianate marble fireplace, twelve-foot corniced ceiling, and bay window flanked by stained-glass panels. "You have a lovely home," I remark. "The photos don't do it justice." I'm referring to the five-page spread in the book on historic mansions of San Francisco, a copy of which sits on the coffee table at the La Mar house.

She turns to face me, a frosty drink in each hand. "Thank you. Remarkable, isn't it? That she's still standing after two catastrophic earthquakes." She means the 1901 quake that decimated most of the city's buildings and the one in 1989, known as Loma Prieta. "She's a tough old gal," she adds, smiling, and I have a feeling she's referring to more than the house. She crosses the room and hands me my drink, then sits down on the Empire sofa opposite me with her iced tea. The flames flickering in the gas fireplace cast a rosy glow over her face, with its fine patrician features, that's benefited, in my opinion, from not having been nipped or tucked or injected with Botox. "Now then, you said over the phone there was something important you wanted to discuss?"

I take a sip of my Diet Coke. I'm so nervous my hands are sweating, but my throat is parched. Unless I enlist Joan as an ally, my mission is doomed. "First, I should explain about last night . . ."

"I assumed you hadn't come all this way to tell me the pool filter was acting up again," she puts in, arching an eyebrow at me. She looks every inch the lady of the manor dressed in a cream silk blouse and fawn slacks, a rope of pearls around her neck and matching pearl earrings in her ears.

"It is, but we can get to that later. If I still have a job, that is." I give her an ingratiating smile.

"Of course, that goes without saying." She dismisses my concern with a wave of her manicured hand. "I'm sure you have a perfectly good explanation for why you were arrested."

I continue to smile, my lips stretched like a rubber band that might snap from my face and go flying across the room at any moment. "I promise you I'm not in the habit of breaking into other people's homes. I mean, what kind of property manager would I be? How would that look on my resume? 'She waters your houseplants by day and robs you blind at night.' Can you im—" I break off when I realize I sound like a comedian with a bad case of flop sweat playing to a handful of angry drunks in an otherwise deserted night club. Though, in all fairness to Joan, she seems more confused than unsympathetic. "Um. See, the thing is . . . I was conducting an investigation. Into my mom's death. The cops weren't getting anywhere—their hands are tied—but being as I'm a civilian, I figured I could . . . go outside the box. Unfortunately, my plan backfired."

"I see. Yes, I remember your mentioning you were making some inquiries." She puts it politely.

"I was looking to get the dirt on my mom's former boyfriend. But it turned out I'd only scratched the surface with him. There was something much, much bigger and a whole lot nastier underneath." I take another sip of my Diet Coke. My throat is so dry you could strike a match on it.

She regards me with bright interest. "Well? You mustn't keep me in suspense."

"I'll get to that in a minute. First, did you know it was your husband who bailed me out last night?"

"My soon-to-be *ex*-husband," she corrects me. "Yes. How very kind of him." Her voice is thick with sarcasm. "Let me guess. He was hoping to persuade you he's entirely innocent of any allegations against him."

"Something like that. But don't worry, I won't be testifying in his defense."

Mistaking my meaning, she says, with a sigh of resignation, "I appreciate your partisanship, my dear, but I'm afraid there's no chance he'll be charged, much less put on trial, for what he did to me. It was naïve of me to ever think the authorities would take my word over his."

"No doubt you're right about that. But let's say he was guilty of other crimes."

Her eyes widen in alarm. "Did he—?"

"No, he was the perfect gentleman last night. I'm talking about when he was shooting at me."

"So that *was* him? I knew it!" she cries.

"Or someone who was working for him," I say, recalling Ivy's theory about the ex-military hit man.

"Do you have proof?" she asks. I'm feeling better about my chances of enlisting her help. The eagerness in her voice tells me she'd be willing to stick her neck out if it meant putting him behind bars.

"Not yet, but I'm working on it. It's more complicated than you know." I pause for dramatic effect, the brief silence measured by the ticking of the grandfather clock out in the hallway, before I drop my bombshell. "I have reason to believe he was involved in at least three murders."

She gasps, the color draining from her face. "You're saying there were . . . *others*? But how—I don't understand. Where did you come by such information?" I notice she isn't questioning his guilt.

"Let's just say I have it on good authority." I repeat the tale as it was told to me by Stan.

"No!" she cries when I get to the part about Leon. "That's preposterous. Leon wasn't like that. He would never . . . he wasn't a monster. He was a good man." I've never seen her so agitated.

"No, he was good at fooling people."

"It wasn't an act," she insists. "He was a gentle soul."

"He was the mastermind. It all leads back to him."

"The man you're describing . . . that's not the man I knew." She frowns as she stares into middle space, absently playing with the rope of pearls around her neck, looping it around and around her fingers until it resembles a hangman's noose. She has it pulled so taut it's left a red mark on her neck. "We were close. He was like a father to me. I'd have known, or at least suspected . . ."

I realize I need to take a different approach, given the deep bond between she and her father-in-law—Douglas wasn't lying about that—so I say in a gentler voice, "Okay, let's say I'm wrong and he really was the man you describe. You'd want to clear him of suspicion, wouldn't you?"

"W-what do you mean?" She eyes me in confusion.

"Let's suppose Douglas acted alone without his father's knowledge. If we could find a way to prove it, Leon's name wouldn't be dragged through the mud." I pause to let this sink in. "Do you know if the Fontana has records that date back to when my mom worked there?"

For a long minute the only sounds are the ticking of the grandfather clock and hissing of the gas flames in the fireplace. Then Joan answers, "I believe so. When I worked there, we had a system. Everything pertaining to the tax returns for that year went into one file, in case we were audited. There's a storage area in the basement below the offices where all those boxes are kept."

I'm reminded that she worked at the Fontana, as an administrative assistant—secretary, they were called back then—before she was married. It was how she and Douglas met. I imagine her being swept off her feet by the handsome, charismatic son of her employer. It must have seemed a dream come true. Instead it ended up being her worst nightmare. Now she's faced with an impossible choice: bring down her hated husband or let him get away with murder to protect the man she revered.

"Can you get access?" I ask, my pulse racing.

"I can, yes. The question is, will I?" she says sharply. She knows I'm talking about more than a set of keys and the passcode for the alarm system.

"We need to put an end to this," I appeal to her, "before he hurts someone else. Don't forget what he did to you. If you hadn't caught that ledge on the way down . . ."

She releases her death grip on the pearls and abruptly rises to her feet, pacing over to the fireplace. She holds onto the mantel as if to steady herself as she stares at the grouping of family photos that sits on it—Bradley, in his cap and gown on graduation day; a formal portrait of the family taken back when Bradley had braces on his teeth; a candid shot of Joan and her young son at the beach, building a sand castle together—as if to remind herself of the life she once knew. "Forget? How could I ever forget? I can't close my eyes at night without seeing those rocks below . . ." She trails off with a visible shudder, then straightens and turns to face me. "Don't think I don't know what you're asking of me. If what you're saying is true, my husband didn't act alone. He lived for his father's approval. He'd have done anything for him. *Anything.*" Her eyes flash.

"Those other people . . . my mom . . . they didn't deserve to die. You can help me avenge their deaths."

Her mouth contorts in an expression halfway between a mirthless smile and rueful grimace. "Would you think me horribly selfish if I said I was more interested in putting my husband behind bars?"

"No. I'd think you were only human."

She nods and says, with grim resolve: "Then let's do this."

CHAPTER SIXTEEN

If Trousdale's having you tailed," rasps McGee, with his customary cheer, on the drive to the Fontana the following evening, "you can add a bullet in the head to the menu of spa treatments."

I suppress a groan. "Trust you to always look at the bright side."

"He knows you're on to him," Ivy weighs in from the passenger seat. "Mr. Trousdale, I mean. If that was him shooting at you before." We're headed south on Highway 1 in my Explorer, passing through a wooded area. I'm careful to observe the speed limit, mindful of the deer that make this stretch hazardous at night. Though it seems I'm in greater danger of a certain two-legged beast, rather than the four-legged variety, springing out at me.

"He *suspects*. He can't know for a fact," I remind her. "He won't until I bust this thing wide open." Assuming I get lucky tonight. "But if there's a remote chance I'm being tailed, that's what you guys are here for." McGee had insisted he come along as bodyguard and Ivy was not about to miss out on all the "fun." At least this time she hadn't had to cancel a date with Mr. Bollywood, Rajeev, with whom she'd been out twice since and who, from her description, was smitten.

"Don't worry, I got you covered," McGee says in his cop's voice. I catch a glimpse of his Glock 9 mm revolver in the rearview mirror as he pulls it from under the desert camo jacket he's wearing.

"Is that thing loaded?" I ask nervously.

"Can I hold it?" Ivy wants to know. She's like a kid on Christmas wanting to play with another kid's toy.

"No." He tucks it back under his jacket. I don't know if he was responding to my question or Ivy's.

"Look, you guys, I'd be lying if I said I wasn't nervous. But I don't expect any trouble tonight, so let's keep the paranoid talk to a minimum, okay? I get enough of that from my brother."

My thoughts wander to Arthur. Patients at the "puff" aren't allowed visitors or phone calls, so I've had to rely on the staff for status reports. They've been nice about it, all except one. I flash back on my run-in earlier in the day with the day supervisor at the "puff," Myrna Hargrave, a demon disguised as an RN who I'm convinced is the reincarnation of Madame Chiang Kai-shek. Last time, she had Arthur so terrorized he couldn't move his bowels for a week. When she wasn't sticking needles in him or cramming meds down his throat, she was shoving suppositories up his ass. Just my luck, I happened to arrive when she was manning the front desk.

I was greeted with the usual, impatient air reserved for family members. She consulted his chart while I stared at her hair, which she wore in the 'do made popular by Farrah Fawcett in the seventies, dyed-blond and so heavily sprayed it could withstand gale-force winds. I wondered what she saw when she looked in the mirror. It couldn't be what I was looking at, or she wouldn't be seen in public. "Ah yes, there've been some changes in his meds," she said without elaborating.

I felt a dart of anxiety. A change in meds could mean any one of a variety of things: the dosages had been upped or decreased; he was suffering from side effects that required additional drugs; they had him on Thorazine. He could be getting better or worse. I had no way of knowing.

"That's it? There's nothing else you can tell me?" I said after she'd tucked the chart away, in a brisk move clearly meant to be a dismissal. I spoke in an even voice, struggling to keep my anxiety at bay.

"You'll have to speak with Dr. Kennedy." She named the chief psychiatrist on staff.

"I will. As soon as he calls me back. I've left a couple messages on his voicemail."

"He's a very busy man." She sniffed.

"Okay, but in the meantime, how does he seem to you? Arthur, I mean. In general."

She stared down from the few extra inches of height she had on me. Myrna Hargrave was a large woman in every respect, which made her small mouth look disproportionately tiny, especially when pursed. "I'm not authorized to give out information on patients. As you well know, Miss Ballard." The glint in her eye told me she was enjoying this. It was payback for the complaint I registered against her the last time. Why else get me riled up by hinting at trouble in Arthur land?

"I'm not asking for a medical opinion. A simple observation will do." My brother's mind is like a banana republic, ruled by a mercurial dictator who could be overthrown at any time. When he's at the "puff" where I can't keep an eye on him, I require daily reassurance that his tenuous hold hasn't crumbled. Myrna Hargrave was using my one weak spot against me.

"You will have to speak with Dr. Kennedy," she repeated, this time enunciating each word as if I were hard of hearing or had cognitive impairment.

"If there's something the matter with my brother, I want to know. Please, just tell me that much. Because I'm his person. You know, to contact in case of an emergency." I heard the pleading note in my voice, which made me even madder. I hated that she was making me beg.

She remained unmoved. "I'm sorry. I can't help you. It's against the rules."

"Fuck the rules!" I lost it, finally.

She eyed me, narrowly, as if I were an out-of-control patient for whom she was contemplating a course of action—strait-jacket or heavy sedation? Perhaps a round of electro-shock therapy, and if that didn't do the trick, a lobotomy? "There's no need for foul language, Miss Ballard."

"You'd rather I called you a name?" I snapped. "I'll give you a hint. It rhymes with 'witch.'"

"If you keep that up, I'm going to have to ask you to leave."

I didn't wait to be asked. I spun on my heel and stalked out. Only because I didn't want my brother to pay the consequences if I were to slug her, which I was sorely tempted to do.

I glance in my rearview mirror, after I've taken the exit for the Fontana, to make sure we're not being followed, but I see only the red glow of my taillights. This land is owned by the Trousdales and remains undeveloped in keeping with Fontana's image as a true getaway. Normally I enjoy the remote and unspoiled location, but right now all I see are trees forming a dark mass on either side of the road, no glowing windows to indicate the presence of other warm bodies.

Minutes later, I'm winding my way up the hill to the Fontana. At the top I make a right turn into the parking lot where the road ends. The only other vehicles parked there are a white panel truck, presumably the night watchman's, and Joan's midnight-blue Lexus. There's no sign of life. Nothing stirring in the shadows of the surrounding trees or along the path to the buildings below.

"Looks like the coast is clear," I say.

A hand falls heavily on my shoulder as I'm reaching for the door handle and McGee's voice rasps in my ear, "Wait right here." He leaps out, gun drawn, and is swallowed by the darkness.

"Pleasant fellow," Ivy observes mildly.

"He takes some getting used to," I agree. "But I owe him a lot. Don't forget, I never would've connected all the dots if it hadn't been for him." There's no such thing as a functioning alcoholic—it's a myth propagated by drunks looking for an excuse not to get sober—but McGee is as close to one as I've ever seen. I just hope coffee is the only thing in the thermos he's brought with him.

He returns a few minutes later, giving me the all-clear signal.

I climb out, and Ivy springs from the passenger side. "You're sure you don't want me to come with?" She looks like a ninja in her dark clothing with her hair tucked under a black knit cap. She's been hovering over me—as much as a woman who stands five foot two can over someone my size—like a mother hen ever since the night of my arrest. Knowing her, I am fully aware she's also loath to miss the action.

"I wish. I could use the extra pair of hands. But the night watchman might get suspicious." Joan's cover story is that the Internet is down at her house and she needs to use the computers in the office. I'm playing the part of her assistant. Two assistants might look funny, and we don't want the night watchman putting in a call to the boss. "Don't worry. I'm sure everything will be fine."

"Last time you said that, you almost got your head blown off," she reminds me.

"Stan was only bluffing. He's the good guy, remember?" I just didn't know it then.

"Which makes Mr. Trousdale the bad guy. Be sure your phone stays on so I can call if he shows up." Her worried eyes search my face.

"Anyone comes after you, they'll find out what this is for." McGee pats the bulge under his desert camo jacket.

I set off down the path. The grounds are well-lit, due to a network of belowground electrical cables, so I have no trouble seeing where I'm going. At the same time, I'm uncomfortably aware I'd make an easy target for a sniper should one be lurking in the bushes. I tell myself I'm jumpy only because Ivy and McGee spooked me with all their talk. How would Douglas Trousdale know I was here unless he'd followed me? The only other person, besides Ivy and McGee, who knows about tonight's venture—or treasure hunt, as I prefer to think of it—is Joan, and why would she blab to her soon-to-be-ex when the whole purpose is to bring him down?

I'm nearing the main building, steps from the outer court-yard with its decorative clay wine casks and pergola festooned in crimson bougainvillea, when I freeze in my tracks at the sound of something—or someone—rustling in the bushes. A moment later, a small dark shape scuttles from the shadows, a rabbit most likely. Then there's only the sound of distant waves breaking against the shore. That, and the pounding of my hair-trigger heart. Silly me. I'm conjuring up assassins where there are none when I should be concentrating on what's in front of me.

I cut across the courtyard, headed for the side entrance Joan had left unlocked. I step through a gate into a passageway that leads to the inner courtyard, where I pause to get my bearings. The courtyard is paved in Saltillo tiles and enclosed by eight-foot brick walls covered in grapevines. At the center stands the majestic fountain that gives the Fontana its name. ("Fontana" is Spanish for fountain.) I gaze upon it, thinking the photo on the website doesn't do it justice. Water trickles from tiered basins lined with mosaic tiles depicting various aquatic creatures, its gurgling reminiscent of the CDs of soothing nature sounds and Pan flute music sold in the gift shop. Lit from within, it glows, jewel-like, in the darkness. From the shadows along the perimeter of the courtyard peer the pale faces of the orchids that bloom in clay pots. Overhead stars shimmer through a thin cloud cover and the moon is swaddled in a gossamer blanket.

A columned arcade along one side leads to a corridor lined with various treatment rooms, the gift shop, men's and women's locker rooms, saunas, and Japanese communal bath. As I pass the gift shop I catch a heady whiff of the aromatic oils sold there—a mixture of citrus, lavender, and bergamot—scents I associate with my mom, from when she worked there. I experience the familiar ache of loss. What's different is that I feel her presence, stronger than ever. *I won't let you down, Mom.*

The last door on the left stands open partway. I peek into what appears to be a guard station. Not much more than a closet, it holds a built-in desk and chair. On the desk is a computer monitor showing live feeds from various parts of the complex. No sign of the night watchman; he must be taking a bathroom break. It might have seemed overkill—the CC-TV cameras and night watchman—if Joan hadn't explained why it was needed. It seems the Fontana's remote location makes it a magnet for thieves and vandals, and with a response time of twenty minutes or more before the cops can get here, the alarm system is useless. I duck inside to take a closer look at the monitor feeds, where I'm reassured at seeing nothing stirring, before I continue on.

At the end of the corridor a glass door opens onto a covered walkway. I can see the smaller building that houses the offices, where I've arranged to meet Joan. Beyond lies the wellness center, an impressive stone-and-cedar structure built to resemble a Buddhist temple. You can practice the downward dog while looking out over the ocean where it's walled in glass at one end. I've been told there's nothing quite like it. But gazing on it now I feel a deep chill that isn't from the cool night air. The visitors who flock here from all corners of the globe, to cleanse their bodies of toxins and clear their minds, would be horrified to know how it came about.

I hear a mechanical whirring noise as I'm pushing open the door to the office—it sounds like an electric pencil sharpener, only louder. I enter to find cardboard cartons full of files stacked on the floor and files strewn about. Shredded paper spills from an open plastic garbage bag. A tall figure who looks to be male, dressed in navy sweatpants and a gray sweatshirt with the hood pulled over his head, stands with his back to me by the bank of office equipment that stretches along one wall. The source of the whirring noise is the papers he's feeding into an electric shredder. Douglas? A jolt of alarm goes through me. Then the whirring stops and the figure turns around.

"Joan!" I cry in relief. "Oh my God, you scared me. I didn't recognize you at first." Maybe it's because I'm used to seeing her dressed as if for a magazine photo shoot—in designer duds and pearls. The only other time I saw her in sweats, they were Loro Piana cashmere.

She smiles at me, except there's something odd about her smile—it doesn't reach her eyes. They glitter coldly. "Hello, Tish. Right on time as usual," she notes with a glance at her watch. "You're nothing if not reliable. A rare quality in a property manager, I've found. Unsupervised help tends to be lazy help. Which is why it'll be such a shame to lose you." She doesn't even sound like herself. Instead of her normal honeyed tones, she speaks in a sickly sweet voice.

I stare at her in confusion. "W-what are you talking about?"

"You haven't figured it out yet? I guess you're not as smart as I thought."

Had she decided she couldn't go through with it? Was she planning to fire me? "What's all this?" I motion toward the pile of confetti she's made of the documents she's shredded. "What are you doing?"

"Cleaning house. Did you really think I'd let you drag his name through the mud? Have the press make him out to be a monster?"

"He tried to kill you!" I remind her. "You want him to get away with it?"

"I'm not talking about Douglas. He wouldn't have the balls."

"But I thought . . ."

"That was me—I staged it," she says, looking pleased with herself. "I was headed back to the party when I heard you coming—only I didn't know it was you—and decided to . . . improvise."

"What, by jumping off a cliff?"

"Don't be silly. I didn't *jump*. I lowered myself down. It's easy when you're not afraid of heights."

"Oh my God." She's crazy. Just like Douglas said. I take a step back.

"My husband can rot in hell, but I'm not going to let you, or anyone, destroy Leon's legacy. Or my inheritance. All this," she makes a sweeping gesture with her arm, "will soon be mine."

"He murdered innocent people!"

"Yes," she agrees. "He *was* a monster. Not that I loved him any less for it." The hard look on her face gives way to one of tenderness, sending a trickle of ice-water down my spine.

"So you knew what he was like all along?"

"No, at first I knew him only as my kind boss who'd taken an interest in me, then later as my dear father-in-law. It wasn't until Douglas and I had been married for some years that Leon felt I was ready to know the whole truth. Naturally I was . . . disturbed when he first confided in me. But I was also smart enough to realize we'd all go down with the ship if I said anything. Besides, what good would it have done? Those people were dead and gone—nothing was going to bring them back."

"'Those people?'" I echo in disbelief. "One of them was my *mom*."

"Your mother, yes." She puts on a mock sympathetic face. "It was unfortunate she got mixed up in it. Which was why she had to go. He couldn't have her blabbing to anyone who would listen." She pauses to reflect on this before saying gently, "I'm sorry for your loss, my dear. Truly I am. But if it's any consolation, you'll soon be joining her."

"W-what are you talking about?"

"Don't tell me you haven't guessed. Why do you think I had you meet me here at night?"

"I thought you were going to help me."

I take another wobbly step back, bumping into the CD tower behind me. It topples with a loud crash, sending the CDs that get fed into the speaker system during hours of operation—soothing

New Age music to lend to the Fontana's relaxing atmosphere—spilling across the beige carpet. Joan's un-Botoxed brow creases in annoyance, but other than that, my clumsiness barely registers. She's more focused on keeping me in her sights as she pulls a gun from the pocket of her hoodie.

It's the kind McGee referred to as a "Saturday night special" when we were gun shopping at Markey's. He'd dismissed it as a "toy," but, in Joan's hand, it doesn't look like a plaything. It looks frighteningly real. She takes aim, and the bottom drops out of my stomach like the trap door at a hanging.

"It's no use, my dear," she purrs. "You're not going anywhere."

CHAPTER SEVENTEEN

The missing pieces of the puzzle fall into place. It was Joan all along, I realize. *She* was the one shooting at me from the woods. She knew the route I'd be taking, and approximately what time I'd be travelling it, because it was she who'd arranged to meet with me at the La Mar house. When Bradley showed up at the Arco station, I didn't think to ask if his mother had been at the house when I'd phoned, but she couldn't have been. She would've arrived shortly thereafter.

"Not another move," she commands when I edge back a step, "or I'll shoot."

I freeze on the spot, because unlike Stan, she means business. "You won't get away with this. I didn't come alone—my friends are waiting outside." I can't let her see that I'm scared shitless.

She gives a dry chuckle. "Nice try."

"I'm not bluffing. If you kill me, they'll know it was you."

"Really. And what will they know, exactly? They have only your say-so that you arranged to meet with me."

"Oh yeah? And what will you tell the cops when they ask what *you* were doing here?"

"It's quite simple, really. I stopped by to pick this up." She produces an envelope, stamped and postmarked, from her other pocket. "It's addressed to me, but it was sent here by mistake." No mistake about it; obviously she'd set it up so she'd have an excuse to come. "I caught you breaking in, and, believing you to be an armed intruder, shot you. Most unfortunate, of course—tragic, really—but given your recent arrest, I don't think the police will have any reason to doubt my story." She bares her teeth in a smile that sends another trickle of ice-water down my spine.

"I see you've thought of everything." I put on a show of bravado even as my heart sinks. Any hope I had of reasoning with her has gone the way of the shredded contents of the plastic trash bag at my feet. "There's just one thing you failed to factor in."

"Oh, and what would that be?" She looks more amused than worried.

"The fact that you're bat-shit crazy. Your husband knows it, and I'm betting even your friends are wondering by now. How much longer do you think you can pull off your Saint Joan act?"

"I see Douglas has been filling your ear. So much for my counting on your loyalty," she adds with a shake of her head. "But I suppose it was to be expected. He's the one signing the checks."

"I don't need him to tell me what I can see with my own eyes." I gesture toward the gun aimed at me.

"You should ask yourself what's crazier, my wanting to hold on to what's mine—what I've *earned* putting up with that man for years—or your thinking I'd let you ruin everything? That I'd *help* you?"

"So this is just about the money."

"A great deal of money. A fortune."

"Money isn't everything."

"If you'd ever gone hungry or had to let disgusting men paw you for tips, you might feel differently."

"I'm talking about basic human decency. You can't put a price on that!"

I cast a glance up, looking for the closed-circuit camera I noticed outside, above the door, as I was coming in. Because with my hands tied, so to speak, the night watchman is my only hope. But it seems the Fontana management didn't anticipate a threat from, say, a disgruntled worker gone postal—or the boss's deranged wife—when they had the new security system installed. My desperation mounts. I'm trembling all over, my heart knocking like a washing machine spinning out of whack.

"Spare me the sermon." Joan shows no emotion except in her eyes—they glitter with contempt, and something more. Something old and deep and twisted. "You have no idea what it's like to have nothing, to go without. Before I got married, every day of my life was a struggle."

"I didn't have it so easy, either," I remind her.

"You had a home. I didn't even have parents, much less a mom or dad to tuck me in at night. I wish I could say I'd been raised by wolves. Wolves are social creatures, not like the animals who call themselves 'foster parents.' I ran away when I was sixteen. Picked up work here and there. I did whatever I had to in order to survive." Activities best not mentioned in polite company, I'm guessing. "I met Leon through the food bank." She refers to Loaves and Fishes, one of several local charities he'd founded, all part of his disguise, I know now. "I was just another girl down on her luck, but he must have seen something in me, because he offered me a job. He didn't change my life; he *saved* it." Her expression softens briefly. "Marrying Douglas was just the added bonus. And you know the best part? I was in love with him—head over heels." She gives a bitter laugh. "For a time I was even fooled into believing he loved me."

I'm stunned. I had no idea. In the past she'd led me to believe she came from a privileged background. Though, come to think of it, she was always fuzzy on the details—now I know why. But none of it changes the fact that she's crazy. I don't mean "crazy" like my brother, but the kind of crazy that usually ends very badly. As in school shootings. It gives me an idea, though. I realize I'm well-equipped to deal with a crazy person. I've certainly had plenty of practice.

"I'm sure he loved you. He probably still does, deep down." I speak in a soothing voice. "You had a lot of good years together, didn't you? So he had a midlife crisis. It happens. I guarantee he'll be bored with Tiffany before the year is out. Then he'll realize what a fool he was and beg you to take him back."

I catch a glimmer in her eye—a touch of nostalgia perhaps?— then it's gone. "I wouldn't take him back if he came crawling on his hands and knees," she declares with a scornful toss of her head. The hood of her sweatshirt slips back to reveal the velvet headband holding her smooth silver-blond bob in place. Throw in a twinset and pearls and she could be hosting a Junior League tea. I stifle the laughter clawing its way up my throat. "Besides, he's of no further use to me. By the time I'm done with him, I'll have it all. He'll wish our divorce is his worst nightmare."

"What, are you going to kill him, too?"

"No. That would be too quick, too painless. He needs to suffer."

"Torture, you mean."

"In a way, though nothing so mundane as what you're no doubt imagining. I have something more fun in store. Soon he'll make another 'attempt on my life.' And this time I'll make sure there's enough evidence to get him charged. A gun registered in his name, or perhaps a bloody glove—which, unlike O. J.'s, will fit. Lucky for me, I'll have escaped with only superficial wounds."

The smile on her face makes me think of creatures that eat their mates. "Looks like you've got it all figured out."

Her praying-mantis smile gives way to a frown of annoyance. "What I didn't count on was *you*. Sticking your nose where it didn't belong. You were so persistent. You never give up, do you?"

"So I've been told." Stan had accused me of the same thing.

"Even going so far as to pump that clueless idiot, Seraphina, for information."

"Actually, as I recall, she was the one doing the pumping," I say of the colonic irrigation therapist.

Joan ignores my gallows humor. "She may be an idiot, but she's loyal. Did she mention she was my closest friend when I worked here? I send her a Harry and David fruit basket every year at Christmas. Call me sentimental. She told me you'd been to see her, that you were asking questions."

Once wasn't enough for old Seraphina. I'm taking it up the ass again, thanks to her.

"Which is why you have to be terminated." I know she doesn't mean my tenure as her property manager, either. I start to quake in earnest. My blood isn't just running cold. If I were a Sub Zero, like the one at the La Mar house, I'd be spitting ice cubes. "Sadly you've given me no alternative."

She starts toward me, her face expressionless, as though she's wearing a mask that shows only her eyes. Those horrid, glittering eyes. I recoil at the sound when she thumbs the safety on her pistol. I'm about to make my Hail Mary pass, with me as the football, and hurl myself at her in an attempt to knock the gun from her hand, when I catch a lucky break. She steps on one of the jewel cases strewn over the carpet and it slides out from under her, causing her to lose her footing. She wobbles and almost falls, her arms pinwheeling as she attempts to regain her balance.

I don't hesitate. I make a run for it.

Outside I make a beeline for the wellness center. Was it only a few weeks ago I was there freaking over what was nothing, really, compared to the threat of being gunned down by a deranged society matron? Now it's a refuge where I can take cover while I phone for backup. I'm closing in on the entrance when I hear Joan's voice call from behind, echoing along the covered walkway, "It's no use, Tish! You can't escape!" I glance over my shoulder, surprised to see she's gaining on me. Christ. How can a woman her age move so fast? She's in better shape than I am! Must be from all those charity walkathons. I, on the other hand, am rapidly losing steam. I can't catch my breath and the stitch in my side is like a needle lodged between my ribs. I grit my teeth, digging deep into my reserves, and am rewarded by a burst of speed I didn't know I had in me.

I'm no more than six feet from the glass door at the entrance when a shot rings out. The bullet slams into the concrete column to my right. My step falters and I let out a yelp as fragments of concrete fly at my face like shrapnel. I feel a burning sensation in my cheek and blood dribbles down the side of my neck. I ignore it, knowing if I don't keep moving, I'm doomed.

Another gunshot rings out and this time the glass door, bordered in decorative tiles and flanked by potted ferns, explodes in a million pieces. My heart stops, but I don't slow my pace. I dive through the opening, somehow managing to keep from being ripped to shreds by the shards sticking from the doorframe like shark's teeth. My feet crunch over the pebbles of glass in my path. Joan did me a favor in providing instant access, though something tells me that wasn't her intention.

I streak through the reception area and down the corridor beyond, ducking into the first treatment room I come to. Only when the door is locked behind me do I pause to catch my breath, doubled over with my hands on my knees, gasping for air. I gingerly probe my cheek where it's bleeding. A scab is starting to form, so the wound couldn't be too deep. I can hear the muffled drumbeat of Joan's footsteps growing louder. And a locked door isn't going to stop her. Society Matron Joan would knock politely and go away when no one answered, but Rambo Joan won't observe the niceties; she'll bust her way in. My only hope is if my friends get to me before she does.

I thumb the light switch, so I can see what I'm doing, and pull out my phone, only to have it slide from my sweaty grasp and go skittering across the floor. Damn. I retrieve it, but when I go to call Ivy, there's no signal. I must be in one of the dead zones for which this remote area is known. *What now?* I'm freaking out. Full-on panic attack. Black dots swarm at the periphery of my vision as I sway on my feet, about to pass out. I flash back to when I almost drowned in the ocean, when I was six or seven, after I was dragged under by a huge wave. I recall my panic at being caught in the churning surf, unable to breathe, helpless to save myself. Luckily an adult who happened to be swimming nearby came to my rescue. But there's no one to save me now. I'll have to rely on my own wits.

Get a grip, Tish. I draw in a deep breath, then another one. After a moment my head clears.

I glance around me, searching for a means of escape, but there are no doors connecting the room to the ones on either side, and the window is too small to squeeze through. Nor is there a sharp instrument or blunt object that could be used as a weapon, I find after I've clawed through the contents of the drawers and cupboards in the built-in cabinet. There's just a chair, the adjustable kind like you see in dentists' offices, that's bolted to the floor and a machine of some sort, roughly the size and shape of a freestanding ATM—for laser hair removal, I'm guessing from the poster on the wall showing before-and-after photos of female upper lips with and without mustaches. Which wouldn't do me much good. Unwanted hairs are the least of my worries.

I jump at the sound of the door handle rattling, followed by Joan's voice. "You're only making this harder for yourself." Speaking of hairs, I feel the tiny ones on the back of my neck stand up.

"Fuck you!" I yell through the door.

"Now, now, there's no need for foul language," she chides, reminiscent of Myrna Hargrave at the "puff." "Do you know how I rose above my circumstances, Tish? By refusing to sink to the level of those around me, that's how. By never, ever using the f-word."

"What, did you take out your aggression pulling the wings from flies and setting kittens on fire?"

"Don't be ridiculous," she snaps.

"So it's just people you like to torture?"

"I'm not a sadist." She sounds offended by the suggestion. "I only do what needs to be done. What others find . . . distasteful. I won't get any pleasure from killing you, if that's what you're thinking."

"That was you in the woods taking potshots at me, wasn't it?"

"A warning you failed to heed."

I check my phone. Now there's a single bar where before there were none. I feel a flicker of hope. If I can keep her distracted until I get a signal . . . "Where'd you learn to shoot like that? An article in *Martha Stewart Living* on how to bag your own Thanksgiving turkey?"

"One of my foster dads was in the military. He used to take me with him to the shooting range. He taught me everything there is to know about firearms. Only decent thing any of them ever did for me."

"Nothing says father-daughter bonding like a warm gun."

Her voice turns hard. "Enough. No more games. Open up." She starts hammering on the door with the barrel of her gun. *Thunk thunk thunk.* The sound is like an iron spike being driven into my skull.

I frantically rummage through the cupboards in search of a sharp instrument or blunt object. There's nothing but boxes of tissues and surgical gloves, tubes of ointment. I'm doomed. Dread fills my chest like the seawater that had me choking when I was a kid. Then, just when I've about given up hope, some instinct causes me to look up. The ceiling is the acoustical-tile kind, at one end of which is the access panel to a crawlspace: the *deus ex machina* of cheesy movies, a plot device so creaky I'd have been rolling my eyes had I been watching it on TV. Now it's the answer to my prayers.

Better yet, the panel is located above the built-in cabinet, where I'm able to dislodge it after climbing onto the countertop. That's as far as I get—try as I might, I don't possess the upper body strength to hoist myself through the opening. I'm panting with my efforts, cursing myself for not having taken advantage of my gym membership. Meanwhile the infernal hammering has given way to an even scarier silence that tells me Joan is getting ready to make her next move.

What now? I stand frozen atop the counter like a hood ornament on a speeding car headed for disaster. Sweat is pouring from my body in rivulets. My heart is pounding hard enough to crack a rib.

Use your head. I hear the words in my mind as clearly as if she'd spoken them aloud. It was what my mom used to say whenever I whined to her that my homework was too hard. My panic recedes slightly. I look around me, thinking there must be something I could use as a step stool. The question is what? The lone piece of furniture is the chair bolted to the floor. Then it comes to me: the cupboard shelves could serve as a makeshift ladder if I angled my body the right way. I'm pulling off my sneakers so I can make like a monkey when I hear Joan call through the door, in a singsong voice, "Come out, come out, wherever you are." As if this were a game of hide-and-seek.

Come find me, bitch. I knot the shoelaces together and sling them around my neck—I may need my sneakers later on. Hanging on to the open cupboard doors, I climb onto the lowest shelf. I reach up and grab the edge of the opening, as I climb the next "rung," while simultaneously angling my body into position. It's an awkward position, to say the least, and the cupboard hinges groan ominously as the shelf creaks with my weight. I say a little prayer that both will hold a few seconds more, then, with a mighty push, launch myself backwards and up into the crawlspace.

It's so dark I can't see anything at first. The crawlspace is cramped and airless and stinks of dust, mice droppings, and disuse. I feel another panic attack coming on. *No time for that,* I tell myself. I start moving. Even with the flashlight on my phone to guide the way, it's slow going, an obstacle course of crossbeams to duck under and bundles of electrical cables to navigate around.

I estimate I've traveled roughly the length of the room when the stillness is shattered by a round of gunshots. I freeze, then, realizing I have less than a minute before Joan goes from blasting the door open to pumping holes in the ceiling, start scrambling as fast as my hands and knees will carry me. Just when I'm starting to think God has decided my sorry ass might be worth saving after all, despite the fact that it hasn't warmed a church pew in a while, I feel something sharp rip into my flesh below my right knee. I bite down on my lip to keep from crying out. It's more than a scratch, from the hot, painful throbbing in my leg and blood seeping into my jeans, but there's no time to stop and assess the damage. I clench my jaw and keep moving.

"Very clever, my dear! An 'A' for effort! But you won't get far." Joan's voice floats from below.

My panic gives way to anger. Drunks, even sober ones, tend to have a short fuse—put two belligerent drunks together in a bar and you're looking at a fight—and I'm no exception. Right now I'm mad enough to see myself morphing into the Incredible Hulk and crashing through the ceiling onto her head. It's not just that she threatened and bullied me. She tricked me. And there's nothing I hate more than being tricked. It's a reminder of all the years I spent fooling myself.

That candy-ass bitch doesn't know who she's dealing with. I didn't go through hell to get sober so I could die young. I push aside the panicky thoughts crowding my head and think about my brother instead. How would he survive without me, in a world where the mentally ill are only marginally less misunderstood than in the Dark Ages? For his sake, if not my own, I need to make it out alive.

My heart leaps when I spy another access panel just ahead. Presumably it leads to another treatment room. I yank it open and toss my sneakers into the darkness below, then drop down through the opening, bracing myself for a hard landing and praying I won't break a bone. But instead of a hard surface, I land on a solid mass that gives slightly with my weight.

I shine my flashlight, and find myself face-to-face with a dead man.

CHAPTER EIGHTEEN

clap a hand over my mouth to muffle my scream. The body is that of a man in uniform, fortyish, thickset, with a mustache and curly brown hair. The night watchman. Joan must have lured him from his post on some pretext, then . . . No, wait, he's not dead. He's still breathing, thank God. No blood, either, that I can see. Judging from the egg-sized lump on his head he was knocked unconscious. Possibly drugged for extra measure, because he didn't so much as stir when I landed on him (and believe me, I'm no featherweight). Even when he regains consciousness he's not going anywhere. His wrists and ankles are bound with duct tape. I'm sure Joan intended to pin that on me as well. Why not? I couldn't defend myself in court if I were dead.

But I'll attend to him later—if make it out alive—right now there's not a moment to lose. I hobble over to the door in my bare feet, teeth gritted against the lightning bolts of pain shooting up my leg, and open it a crack, peering into the hallway. I was hoping to see my way clear, but instead I see Joan walking slowly in my direction, in no hurry because she knows there's no getting past her.

I know it, too. Gone is the tiny flame of hope I'd nurtured. I ease the door shut and lock it. Now what? I'm trapped, and this time there's no way out. A heavy sense of futility settles over me, and that scares me more than anything. Because to surrender means certain death. I give myself a mental shake. *No fucking way.* If I die, it won't be as a sitting duck. It's not the meek who shall inherit the Earth. It's the stubborn—people like me who never say never, who fight to the end.

I flip the switch for the overhead. The room, with its peach walls and museum poster of Monet's *Water Lilies*, its padded table and chair, looks familiar. I've been here before. I remember when, and start to laugh. I rock in silent laughter, leaning into the door, until tears roll down my cheeks.

Then I get moving.

I search for something I can use to defend myself, but this room is even more spare than the one I was in before. The only built-in is a floating desktop with a couple of drawers, one of which holds the disposable sterile nozzles that get discarded after each use (and that could only be used to inflict pain if Joan were tied down). There's nothing in the small, adjoining bathroom other than a sink and toilet. The one chair, sadly, isn't bulletproof, nor is it heavy enough to use to bludgeon anyone larger than a small child. I'm feeling the walls start to close in when I spy the coat hook on the back of the door. It gives me an idea, not the hook itself but the end that's screwed into the raised panel. It won't make for much of a weapon, but it's bound to be sharp at least.

A bullet tears through the doorjamb as I'm wrestling with the hook, narrowly missing me. This time, Joan didn't bother to knock. I flatten myself against the wall next to the door where I'm out of range, my heart knocking in my chest as she continues to blast away. So much for her cover story that she caught me breaking in and mistook me for a burglar. How is she going to explain the wreckage to the cops when they get here? Clearly she's parted ways with reality altogether.

My eyes frantically scan the room. There's *got* to be some other option. I can't die like a cornered mouse. My gaze falls on the machine mounted to the wall facing the padded table. I remember it all too well from my last visit: the equivalent of water-boarding disguised as alternative medicine. It has hot and cold valves and a flexible hose. Acting purely on instinct, and fueled by adrenaline, I race over to it and crank open one of the valves, while at the same time seizing the hose and directing a blast of water in Joan's face as she comes bursting through the door.

She screams, and only then do I realize the water is scalding hot. She clutches her face, which is red and kind of boiled looking. But she quickly recovers and throws herself at me as I'm making a run for it. She must work out with weights in addition to all those walkathons, because not only is she quick on her feet, she has serious upper body strength. I'm no match for her physically in my weakened state. The one thing I have going for me is that I'm royally pissed.

"You fucking *bitch*!" I deliver a kick to her shin.

She lets out a yelp and reflexively loosens her grip. My next move, which I learned in a self-defense class some years ago and which I haven't had occasion to practice since, surprises me as much as Joan. I break free while simultaneously grabbing her arm and twisting it behind her back. When I have her pinned, I wrest the gun from her hand. I might have even have gotten away with it if she hadn't hip-butted me, sending me staggering backward. I trip over the prone figure of the night watchman and go down, hard, dropping the gun as I fall onto my backside in a sprawl of limbs, my injured knee shrieking in protest. I see a blur of movement out of the corner of my eye as Joan dives to retrieve the gun. And I do mean dive: The puddle of water on the floor causes her to slip, sending her flying through the air before she lands facedown with a wet smack.

Wham. I'm on her before she can lift her head off the floor. I straddle her back, holding her pinned with my weight while I grab a handful of her hair to restrict her movements. Escape is the furthest thing from my mind just then. I want revenge. "You thought you could get rid of me? Think again. You're going down, lady, and

I'll be with you all the way—as the star witness for the prosecution. Oh, and another thing, you know that vase of yours that's missing? It was me that broke it. I was going to replace it, but something tells me you won't need it where you're going."

She bucks and writhes beneath me. She lost her headband in our earlier scuffle and her hair hangs in wet tangles over her face except the handful I'm clutching. "Get. Off. Me," she grinds out.

"Or what, you'll fire me? Don't bother. I quit."

She utters a string of expletives.

I cluck my tongue. "Such language. And I thought you didn't believe in swearing."

This elicits more curse words, ones so vile I wouldn't utter them myself.

"Dear me, what would the other ladies think? Though I don't suppose they'll be visiting you in prison. You'll be hanging with a whole new crowd. Ladies with tattoos and bad haircuts who don't lunch."

I'm pulling out my phone with my free hand when she breaks loose with a violent, twisting motion. In the blink of an eye she slithers across the floor to grab hold of the gun.

Once again I find myself at the wrong end of the barrel.

"Don't come near me! If you touch me again, I'll scream!" she shrieks in the high-pitched voice of a young girl. She's looking at me but not seeing me; she's somewhere else in her mind.

"Joan, no . . ." I make an attempt to get through to her. "It's too late for that. Don't you see? You'd have to kill him, too." I gesture toward the prone figure of the night watchman who's starting to come around—I can hear him moaning and his eyelids are fluttering. "And you're not going to do that. What would be the point? Nobody would believe your story. Not with all this wreckage."

"He's a bad, bad man," she says in her little-girl voice.

"No, he isn't. He didn't do anything. And you don't want to spend the rest of your life in prison for murder. If you let us go, you're only looking at five to ten years max." I don't know whether or not that's true, but that's what they always say on TV crime dramas. "Now, give me the gun . . ."

"You can't make me. I'll tell. This time I *will*, I swear," she whimpers, not hearing me.

My blood turns to ice in my veins. It sounds as if she was sexually abused growing up, possibly by one of her foster dads. Which is horrible, of course, but no surprise given her history. But now she has me or the night watchman, or both of us, confused with whoever hurt her. Which means there's no reasoning with her. It would take years and a team of shrinks, and even then . . . who knows? All I know is, it's over for me and probably the poor guy lying next to me. For his sake I hope she gets it over with before he regains full consciousness. Because it's no fun watching your life flash before your eyes, let me tell you. Especially when yours has been less than exemplary. I burned too many bridges, hurt too many people, including the people I love the most. And it sucks to know I won't live long enough to truly make up for all that. There's a joke in AA that goes, "Poor me, poor me . . . pour me another one." Suddenly it's not so funny. I close my eyes and say a final prayer. *Dear God, look after Arthur when I'm gone.*

"Drop the weapon!"

The sound of McGee's voice cuts through the roaring of blood in my ears. I open my eyes to see him standing in the doorway striking a two-handed cop stance as he takes aim with his Glock 9mm. Rock solid and dead sober. I've never been so happy to see anyone in my entire life. Though I think it's safe to say Joan doesn't share the sentiment. She shoots him a withering glance as though he were a workman who'd tracked mud all over her nice, clean carpet. I don't wait for her to drop the gun—she's incapable of acting rationally—I throw myself at her while she's momentarily distracted. I manage to knock her down, but she maintains her grip on the gun. I see a petite, curly-haired figure dart past McGee as he's closing in, and a child-sized foot in a black Adidas sneaker stomps down on Joan's wrist while I hold her pinned to the floor. I look up to see Ivy poised over us, staring in shock at the woman she belatedly recognized as Joan.

"Mrs. Trousdale?" She turns to me with a look of confusion after I've pried the gun from Joan's cold but far from dead hand and McGee has her subdued. "Tish, what in God's name is going on?"

"Long story," I gasp.

CHAPTER NINETEEN

I t was all that coffee," McGee explains later on, at the hospital, after my leg wound has been stitched up and dressed. "I got out to take a piss, and that's when I heard the shots."

"And to think I worried about what was in that thermos." I'm reclining in my curtained cubicle in the ER, my bandaged leg propped on a pillow. I'm in pretty good shape overall. Other than the stitches in my leg, it's just minor cuts and bruises. I'd be on my way home by now, except we have to wait for Spence. He'll have some questions, and, no doubt, some choice words for me.

McGee adopts an aggrieved look, his hands shoved deep in the pockets of his camo jacket, his ponytail hanging over the collar like something fished from a drain. "I gave you my word."

"I know, and I'm sorry I doubted you. Though I'm still saving you a chair."

"This is the thanks I get." He rolls his eyes up at the ceiling.

"It'll do you good." I reach for his hand and give it a quick squeeze. He's not a touchy-feely kind of guy. A group hug and you'd run the risk of getting shot. "Thank you. If you guys hadn't shown up when you did, I'd be down there," I point toward the morgue on the floor below, "instead of up here enjoying the amenities."

"Don't even." Ivy flashes me a warning look.

Through the curtain around my cubicle where the two ends

don't meet I see another patient being wheeled past on a gurney, a teenage boy with what looks to be multiple injuries. A shudder goes through me, and when Ivy and I exchange a look I know the same goose walked over her grave. The events of tonight have taken their toll on her. Despite two coffees and a pack of Skittles from the vending machine, she looks pale and wan. I do my best to cheer her.

"My point is, I'm still here, so I must be made of strong stuff. Also, I didn't go through hell to get sober so I could be offed by a crazy, society bitch. Think how it would have looked. I'd have been the laughingstock of AA."

Ivy musters a half smile. "I see you haven't lost your sense of humor."

"Never. I'm donating it to science when I die."

"No more talk of death." She swats my arm, and I wince.

"Ouch. Watch it." I ache all over. I used muscles tonight I haven't flexed since the president's fitness test in sixth-grade PE. I seriously need to start working out at the gym.

"Tish?" Daniel steps through the part in the curtains.

He looks, as one might expect, disheveled, distraught, and more than a little bewildered by the news of his girlfriend's near demise at the hands of her erstwhile client and his landlady. He didn't waste time getting here. Ivy phoned him not more than a half hour ago and it's a twenty-five minute drive from La Mar. He's wearing cargo shorts and the holey Iggy Pop T-shirt he uses as a pajama top. His sandy hair is mussed and a pillow crease stands out on his left cheek. I'm torn between feeling happy to see him and wishing he hadn't come. I can't decide which is the predominant emotion, so I opt for a lighthearted remark. "Dude. Seriously?" I point down at his feet. He's wearing sandals with socks, the ultimate fashion crime even in a laidback beach community.

His face grows redder, and not from embarrassment. Seems I missed the mark in aiming for levity. "Are you all right? How bad is it? My God." His gaze travels from my bandaged cheek to my gauze-wrapped leg, resting on my pant leg that was cut open by the resident who attended to me.

I downplay my injuries. "I'm a little banged up, but I'll live."

"Thank God for that. When Ivy told me shots had been fired and you were hurt . . ." He forks his fingers through his hair, holding his head between his hands, in unconscious parody of an actor playing a character in a soap opera who's just received life-altering news, before dropping them to his sides with an audible exhalation. "Frankly, I didn't know what to think."

"Sorry. I couldn't really get it into it over the phone," Ivy apologizes. "There was a lot going on."

Daniel doesn't take his eyes off me. "I'm just glad you're all right."

"I am." *I think.* I won't know for certain until the shock that's currently acting as a buffer—I feel weirdly calm for someone who narrowly escaped death, at the hands of a psychotic society matron no less, and who isn't high on painkillers (class-A narcotics are verboten in AA)—wears off.

McGee steps forward to introduce himself, and the two men shake hands.

"Ivy tells me we have you to thank," Daniel says.

McGee gives a low, guttural laugh. "Nah." He jerks his stubbled chin in my direction. "It was her show. Me and Ms. Ladeaux here, we only got there in time for the closing number."

Thank you, McGee. For throwing me under the bus, that is. Daniel turns to stare at me as if waiting for an explanation. The look on his face tells me it had better be a good one. I give him the short version, though there's no softening the horror of it. He shakes his head, clearly at a loss for words.

"Only you," he says, at last.

"I didn't ask for this!" I defend myself.

"No, but you put yourself at risk. What happened to letting the cops handle it?"

"I never promised."

"That's not how I remember it."

"Look, I admit it wasn't one of my better ideas, but I wasn't breaking any laws and I didn't think I'd be in danger. How was I to know she was a maniac? She wears pearls and twinsets! She sits on the boards of charitable organizations! Though I'm pretty sure she won't be hosting any more fundraisers. She's more likely to stage a prison riot if it's the side of her I saw tonight."

Without warning, I burst into tears. Daniel sits down next to me and gathers me in his arms, making soothing circles on my back with his palm while I sob into the wrinkled face of Iggy Pop. Amid the sounds of my blubbering and the comforting noises Daniel's making, I hear Ivy say, "Um, we'll give you two some privacy." I look up to see her and McGee making their exit.

I pull myself together, blowing my nose into the tissue provided by Daniel. "You want to know what I was like after a few drinks? You're looking at it."

He smiles at me crookedly. "So you were a maudlin drunk?"

"When I wasn't throwing punches."

"At least tonight you have a good excuse."

"Lack of excuses was never my problem." A drunk can always find an excuse to drink. A happy occasion to celebrate. Sorrows to drown. A new beginning. A bad breakup. A stubbed toe.

"I'm glad I didn't know you then."

I fall into the pillows at my back, closing my eyes for a minute and letting the cacophony of the ER wash over me. The calm voices of doctors and nurses blending with the agitated ones of family members, speaking more than one language; the cries and moans of patients in pain; the rattle of gurneys being rolled past; the ceaseless squawking of the PA system. I open my eyes to find Daniel regarding me with an anxious expression. "I'm not sure you know me now," I say to him.

"What do you mean?"

"Remember when you said you liked more than one flavor?"

He nods. "You accused me of only liking vanilla. Incorrectly, I might add."

"It wasn't what you said, it was the *way* you said it. Like you were willing to accept me the way I am even though you wished I was different."

"I never asked you to change." A defensive note creeps into his voice.

"True. But be honest. If we'd met on Match.com, would I have ticked all the boxes? My point is, you love me in spite of who I am, not because of it." I raise a hand to still him when he starts to protest. "No, I get it, I do. And I don't blame you. It goes both ways—I was trying just as hard to fit the square peg in the round hole. When I yelled at you, it was only out of frustration."

"I don't understand. What do you want from me?"

"Nothing."

He blinks at me in confusion. "What?"

"What I want, you can't give me," I say gently. "You would if you could. I know that. You're a good person, Daniel. But we're just too different, and I think it's time we finally admitted it."

"Are you breaking up with me?"

I start to feel woozy. It's all catching up to me. The room is revolving like a merry-go-round winding down and my brain feels like it was spooned into my skull. "Yes . . . no . . . I don't know."

"You're obviously still in shock," he notes, his calm voice at odds with his stricken expression, "so may I suggest we table the discussion until you're feeling better?"

I nod in mute acquiescence, looking down at the soggy tissue in my hand, though I know I won't feel any differently tomorrow.

Spence chooses that moment to appear, stepping through the curtains into the cubicle. "Is this a good time?" His steely gaze travels back and forth between me to Daniel. It's more a hint than a question.

Daniel takes the hint. "I was just leaving." He gives me a peck on the cheek before rising. "Let me know when you're ready to go home."

"No, don't wait. Ivy can take me home." She and McGee drove over in my Explorer after I was brought here by ambulance. "You should get some sleep. You have classes tomorrow."

He looks a little hurt at being dismissed but doesn't say anything.

When we're alone together, Spence says, "I'd ask how you're doing, but it's pretty obvious."

"You should see the other guy."

"I have. I stopped by the station on my way here. She's not talking without her lawyer present, but I gather you've had quite a night. Want to tell me about it? If you're feeling up to it, that is."

"Like I have a choice."

"I promise to go easy on you."

"Gee, thanks. You're all heart."

"Actually, it was your friend Ivy. She threatened to sue me for police brutality if I didn't behave."

"Why, did you come to beat up on me?"

He cocks his blond head to one side. "What have I ever done to give you that impression?"

"Should I make a list?"

"What I'd like," he says slowly, maintaining eye contact, "is to know how we ever got off on the wrong foot to begin with. I realize this may not be the best time, but I would like to set the record straight before we go any further, because it seems to be getting in the way of me doing my job. I wasn't the one who spread those rumors about you when we were in high school."

"No, you just bragged to all your friends that you'd tapped me."

"One friend. Jake Dorfman." He names his closest buddy in high school. "What can I say? He's got a big mouth. One of the reasons I stopped being friends with him. And I never told him I tap—" He breaks off, the ridges of his cheekbones reddening. "As unbelievable as it may seem, I actually liked you. I felt bad about what happened the night of the party because I knew you were wasted. In my defense, I was drunk too. I was also sixteen, alone with a pretty girl who seemed willing. I'm not making excuses—I was wrong to take advantage. I owe you an apology for that."

If don't know which surprises me more, the fact that he's apologizing or that I believe he's sincere. Did I misjudge him, or is it just that he caught me at a vulnerable moment? Probably a mixture of both. I manage a small smile. "Apology accepted. But I've got to say, your timing sucks. Why didn't you say something years ago instead of letting me think the worst?"

"Would you have listened?"

I sigh. "Probably not."

"Also, you did set fire to my Camaro."

"Yeah, well, there's that. I guess I owe you an apology, too. I'm sorry."

"You're forgiven."

"I'll make it up to you by washing your car. I'll even wax it."

"Hell no. I'm not letting you near my car." We both laugh, and he asks, "So are we good?"

I nod, and he breaks into a grin. At the dazzling display of even white teeth showcased by full lips and square jaw, I'm reminded of why half the girls in our class at Harbor High, me included (before we had sex), were in love with him. "Actually, I'm starting to think you must like me. You've been showing up at crime scenes lately. What does this one make? Four, five. I've lost count."

"If you're so pathetic you have to get your ego gratification from playing the big man with crime victims, I'm not going to argue with you." I adopt a bored look, suppressing the smile struggling to break loose. "Now can we please get on with it? As much as I'm enjoying your scintillating company and the comforts of this fine establishment, I'd like to get home to my own bed."

"You and me both. Believe it or not, this wasn't my first trip to the ER tonight. I was here earlier with my dad." He exhales wearily as he produces his notebook.

"Nothing serious, I hope."

"Ruptured disc. He's having surgery in the morning."

I make a sympathetic face. "How did that happen?"

"He was doing the limbo. Seventy-five years old and he still thinks he's a kid." Spence shakes his head in fond exasperation, adding, at the questioning look I give him, "It was the party for my parents' fortieth. They made it a luau, in keeping with their Hawaiian honeymoon."

"Ah, that explains it." I gesture toward the outfit he's wearing: a Hawaiian-print shirt paired with off-white trousers. "Elvis called and he wants his *Blue Hawaii* duds back." He chuckles. I pause to study him. Something else about him is different. "Hey, I just noticed. You're not wearing your contacts." His natural eye color is gray-blue, the color of the ocean on a foggy day.

"Yeah. I lost one in the shower, then decided to hell with it—it wasn't me. I only did it for Donna. She thought it made me look like Brad Pitt," he explains, his face reddening. Before I can reply, he points a finger in my direction and narrows his eyes. "Spare me the smart remarks, okay?"

"Actually, I was going to say it makes you look more—" I break off before I can say the word *human*, finishing instead with, "like yourself."

"Coming from you, I'm not sure I should take that as a compliment."

"I meant it as one. It's a good look for you."

"I'll like it better when the new glasses I ordered are ready." He massages the bridge of his nose as if his eyes are bothering him. Which makes him seem more vulnerable as well as human. This is more than I can handle in my present state, so I make a wisecrack to get back on familiar ground.

"So I guess this is it for you and Thelma, huh? Or is it Louise?

I always get the two mixed up. The movie," I prompt at the blank look he gives me. "Brad Pitt's breakout role?"

"Keep talking and I'll find something to charge you with," he growls.

"I have a better idea. You play nice, in exchange for which I'll put in a good word with the DA."

"What makes you think I need you to put in a good word?"

"Well, you did get shown up by a rank amateur. The fact is, I smelled a rat and you didn't."

"If by that you mean, during the course of my investigation, I found no evidence to substantiate Mrs. Trousdale's allegations against Mr. Trousdale, then yes, that's an accurate statement."

"Well, when you put it that way . . ."

"Also, it seems I wasn't the only one who was misled," he reminds me.

"Okay, so I didn't know she was lying. But he's far from innocent. He knew about those other victims."

Spence's gaze locks onto mine. "Hold on. You're saying there were other victims?"

"Hector and Martina. And my mom." My voice quavers. I'm starting to come down from the shock-induced high I was on, my calm demeanor cracking as I rapidly lose altitude.

"Let's back up and start from the beginning." Spence speaks in the calm voice of air traffic control. I focus on his Hawaiian-print shirt, a bright splash against the beige curtain behind him.

I draw a shaky breath. "You'd better pull up a chair. This may take a while."

It's almost three by the time Ivy turns into the driveway of my Craftsman bungalow after we've dropped off McGee. The moon is on the wane. The other houses on the block are dark and all is quiet. It seems as though an age of mankind has passed since we set out on our expedition. "I'm staying over," Ivy announces as she cuts the engine. "You shouldn't be alone tonight."

"Technically it's morning," I point out. "Go home. You must be exhausted."

"Which means I won't notice I'm sleeping on the world's lumpiest sofa." She fails to appreciate that the sleeper sofa in my living room is a genuine Morris. Whenever I remind her of its value as an antique, she says, "There's a reason they don't make them anymore."

I'm too tired to argue. I'm also glad she insisted. I'd never admit it, but I'm scared to be alone. When I was a kid, I watched this horror movie on TV about aliens who invade Earth by taking human form. I know now there's no such thing, but Joan's morphing from lady of the manor to psycho bitch from hell was close enough to make me fearful of what might be out there. "Fine," I say, "but may I remind you my cat is known to mistake prone figures for scratching posts."

Ivy shrugs. "As long as he doesn't mistake me for a mouse and try to chew off my face." Though she probably wouldn't have noticed that, either. Within minutes of making up the sofa bed (admittedly not the most comfortable to sleep on), she's dead to the world. I can hear her snoring as I limp down the hallway toward my own bed, where, minutes later, I fall asleep almost before my head hits the pillow.

I wake to daylight streaming through the blinds and my cat curled next to me. Hercules slits open his yellow eyes to fix me with his unblinkingly stare, then, after a leisurely stretch, springs onto the floor. He streaks down the hallway as I make my way to the bathroom, where I pee and down a couple aspirin before hobbling into the kitchen. Ivy is seated at the table drinking coffee and reading the morning paper, wearing my blue terry cloth bathrobe that looks like a man's on her.

"The good news is you aren't mentioned by name," she says, gesturing toward the front page spread open on my red Formica-and-chrome table. "You're referred to as the 'alleged victim.'"

I'd asked Spence not to disclose my name to the reporter from the *Sentinel* who'd covered the story of Joan's arrest. I needed at least a day to recover before all hell broke loose. It seems he kept his word. "I won't be anonymous for long. The DA is holding a press conference after I meet with him today." The meeting is scheduled for this afternoon. My stomach twists at the prospect. "Then I'll have to wade through reporters and camera crews to get to work in the mornings."

"Yeah, but you're a hero." She gets up to pop a couple of split bagels in the toaster oven while I pour myself a cup of coffee.

"Tell that to Bradley Trousdale." I can only imagine what he's going through right now. How cruelly ironic that, after the mayhem of the Middle East, he should come home to the equivalent in his personal life. I'm also selfishly thinking about what it will mean for us. Or, to be more accurate, what it *won't* mean. I hoped we could become more than friends, but that's not going to happen.

"He can't blame you. You're the victim," Ivy points out.

"True." I sit down at the table. "But I'm tainted by association."

"It wasn't your fault," she insists.

"He had a bomb dropped on him. And I was the one flying the Enola Gray."

"He won't let that get in the way."

"Of what? Sending me hate mail?"

"I was thinking of something a little more romantic."

"Romantic? Please. I'm a walking reminder of the worst thing that's ever happened to him."

"Give it time. Once the dust settles . . ."

I stare at her. Sometimes I wonder who's weirder, my brother or my best friend. Right now the prize would have to go to Ivy. "Not happening. How can you even think that?"

"I saw the way he was looking at you the night of the gala. I'm pretty sure his girlfriend noticed, too." The toaster pings, and she grabs a couple plates and the tub of cream cheese from the fridge.

"Genevieve? No way."

"Way."

"Why was she being so nice to me then?"

"'Keep your friends close and your enemies closer,'" she quotes.

"She knew I had a boyfriend."

"Who you weren't in love with. Let's face it, your breaking up with Daniel was long overdue."

I sigh at the reminder. "He's still hoping we can work it out."

"What do *you* want?" She holds my gaze.

I sip my coffee, watching while she slathers the toasted bagels with cream cheese. "I think it's time to move on." I feel a dull throb as I say this. Not so much because it's over between us, but because I don't feel as bad about it as I should, which is sadder to me than the breakup itself.

"You made the right decision."

"Of course you would think that."

"I never said I didn't like him. What's not to like? He's kind and smart and environmentally conscious. I'd totally vote for him if he ever decided to run for office. But he isn't for you."

"That doesn't make it suck any less."

"For him no," she agrees. "For you it could be the start of something great."

I consider this as I nibble my bagel. I know Bradley is attracted to me. There's too much heat between us for it to be one-sided. But what could possibly come of it? The obstacles are too great. I'm giving evidence against his mom and pointing a finger at his dad. Needless to say Bradley won't be bringing me home for Thanksgiving anytime soon. Or ever. Also, there's Genevieve, who will undoubtedly resurface to lend support, and show what she has to offer besides beauty, brains, and the culinary chops to compete on *Top Chef*, while I have nothing to offer but headaches.

Not exactly the makings of a storybook romance.

CHAPTER TWENTY

Three weeks later, I'm headed out to sea to scatter my mother's ashes. It's the first clear morning we've seen since the fogs of summer rolled in with the tourists that flock to our shores in equal number each season. The sun is posing for its glamour shot on the red carpet that's rolled out along the horizon above the hills to the east, and a cool sea breeze is blowing from the west. The boat we're on is an old rust bucket of a fishing trawler belonging to a friend of Stan Cruikshank, who was introduced simply as "Captain Jack." I stand at the helm, flanked by Arthur and Ivy, keeping a firm grip on the railing as we ride the swells. I'm thinking about how my mom loved the ocean. When my brother and I were little, she'd take us to the beach on her days off from work, weather permitting. Or she'd go on solitary walks along the shore, collecting her thoughts, I imagine, along with the seashells she gathered. It's fitting that it be her final resting place.

It's fitting, too, that Stan be here. Mom would've wanted it. Whatever else he was or wasn't, I know in my heart he was the only man she ever truly loved. And he felt the same way about her—she was the love of his life. As for McGee, I asked him along because I know Mom would've been grateful to him—if not for him, the ashes about to be scattered might have been mine.

When we're a few miles out to sea, the sun riding the hilltops and casting a golden glow over the shoreline with its cluster of buildings that from this distance look like Monopoly hotels, Captain Jack pulls back on the throttle. The trawler, like a rambunctious dog brought to heel, stops its bouncing and settles into a sedate bobbing. I retrieve the urn containing my mother's ashes from the duffel bag at my feet and straighten to find my brother peering at me anxiously through the ocean spray that coats his Clark Kent glasses. Standing tall, with his dark hair slicked back and an errant lock forming a comma on his forehead, he could be Superman himself in disguise.

His gaze drops to the urn. "Um. Should we say something?"

"That's the idea. Why don't you go first?"

He takes a step back, looking slightly panicky. "Me? No. I wouldn't know what to . . . that is, what I meant was . . . a prayer. We could say a prayer. Like in church." Arthur hates being the center of attention, which is more than a little ironic considering that's usually where you'll find him. I take it as a positive sign that he's feeling self-conscious. He doesn't notice other people staring when he's in what our grandma used to call a "state." It seems his stay at the "puff" did him some good.

"It doesn't have to be a speech," I tell him. "Just say whatever's in your heart." I realize I'm asking for trouble in encouraging my brother to speak freely—it can be like opening an unmarked package of suspicious origin. But he should be allowed to express himself as he sees fit.

He looks dignified in his suit and tie, his wool overcoat draped over his shoulders like a cape. Earlier, when I arrived to pick him up and found him dressed as if for a church service, I didn't suggest he change into attire more appropriate for an outdoor ceremony. I think it's nice that he wanted to look his best. The last time he wore that particular suit was in court, two years ago when he was up on an assault charge (he thought he was defending himself against an attack by a Greenpeace activist who'd buttonholed him, wanting him to sign a petition), and I like to think he's in a better place now than he was then. He has his ups and downs, but I see signs of improvement.

Captain Jack thrusts his grizzled head from the cabin just then. He looks like the guys you see in AA meetings who took their sweet time getting sober, his ruddy cheeks and bulbous nose a roadmap of broken capillaries. "Want me to take her out a bit farther, or will this do?" he bellows at me over the throaty chortling of the engine and sound of waves slapping the side of the boat.

"This is good!" I call to him. To Arthur I murmur encouragingly, "Whenever you're ready."

He draws a breath, straightens his shoulders, and with his eyes shut, begins, "Mom, it's me, Arthur. I don't know if you're listening or if there's even such a thing as an afterlife—personally I have my doubts—but if you are, I guess what I want to say is . . . thanks. You were a good mom, even though I know I wasn't the easiest kid. Oh, and if you're worried about us, don't be. Tish almost got killed, but that's a whole other story—and you probably know it, anyway—and apart from that, we're okay. She looks out for me. She's bossy, but she's a good sister. She doesn't let the bad guys get us." He cuts me a sidelong glance, a corner of his mouth turned downward in the faintest hint of a smile that lets me know he's rooted in reality. For the moment, at least.

I wipe moisture from my cheeks that isn't just from the salt spray. Then it's my turn. "Mom, we miss you. A lot. It was never the same after you went away, but I know now you didn't mean to leave us. That you would have come back for us if you could have." I pause to clear my throat, glancing over at Stan who has his head bowed as if in prayer. He cuts a striking figure with his thick, silvery hair scuffed into peaks by the wind, his blue eyes squinted in a show of manly restraint. Like my brother he's wearing a coat and tie, though his jacket is made of leather and the tie is a silver-and-turquoise bolo. Spaghetti-western Clint sporting his Sunday best.

"Anyway," I go on, "now you can finally rest in peace. We have Stan to thank for that. He took his time and picked a funny way of making it happen . . ." He lifts his head to give me a chastened look. "But I know his heart was in the right place, and it was a good thing in the end because it led to . . ." I catch myself. "Like Arthur said, that's a whole other story. And we're here to say good-bye."

Ivy takes my free hand, lacing her fingers through mine. She's a bit green around the gills—she's prone to seasickness—but, true to form, she's hanging in there. I look past the choppy waters off the bow to where the sun has beaten a golden path over the whitecaps. Closer to shore, the distant figures of surfers, seal-like in their wet-suits, paddle on their boards or ride the swells.

"Amen," murmurs Stan in a voice husky with emotion.

When I glance over at McGee, his eyes are bloodshot. I choose to believe it's not solely due to the fact that he's hung over, if the odor of stale beer emanating from him is any indication.

Arthur and I take turns scattering ashes before I pass the urn to Stan. As I watch the last of my mother's earthly remains swirl like smoke over the water, I think of the line from the poem, *Gather ye rosebuds while ye may.* In my mind I see the bouquet of roses, that Stan had placed inside her makeshift coffin, crumbling to dust. What seemed a macabre touch I now know to have been a last, romantic gesture. At least Mom knew true love in her lifetime, which is more than I can say for myself. My relationship with Daniel ended much the way it began: amicably and with little in the way of fireworks. It was sad, of course, and he was hurt, though at the same time I sensed a certain relief. The media blitz sparked by the Trousdale scandal was more than he could handle. It hasn't been easy for me, either. I've been fielding calls from reporters and talk-show producers, and I had TV news crews and tabloid stringers camped outside my house for the first week or so, until they moved on to another story. One morning, as I was leaving for work, I found one of the more enterprising stringers pawing through my garbage cans, looking for God knows what—evidence that I cheated on my taxes? I almost pitched my travel mug of coffee at him.

I'm told Douglas Trousdale is cooperating with the authorities. It's doubtful he'll ever be charged in connection with his father's crimes much less be sent to prison—he retained Grant Weathers as his criminal defense attorney—but he'll be tried and hung in the court of public opinion, which, for a guy like him, is punishment enough. As for Joan Trousdale, who's currently under house arrest, it's only a question of whether she'll be wearing orange or a strait jacket. The charges she faces include kidnapping, attempted homicide, and assault with a deadly weapon. I could almost feel sorry for her, except that it's people like her who give the mentally ill a bad rap.

I haven't seen or spoken to Bradley since the story broke. I left a couple messages on his voicemail, which he didn't return. I wish now I'd acted on my impulses when I had the chance and carpe-diemed the hell out of him in the sack, instead of dragging my heels in breaking up with Daniel and letting my inferiority complex where Genevieve was concerned get in the way. Who knows what might have come of it? Maybe we would have weathered this storm together.

By the time the trawler pulls into its slip at the marina minutes later, we're all starving, having skipped breakfast to get an early start. We jump in our respective vehicles and head over to the Bluejay, where we consume a gallon of coffee and mountains of food: pancakes and waffles, scrambled eggs and house-made sausage, the chicory beignets for which the café is renowned both locally and throughout the foodie blogosphere. A little known fact about funerals that no one will ever admit to: They leave you ravenous. I have yet to attend a wake at which deli platters weren't demolished like pizzas at a football team's post-game bash. I think it must derive from the primitive need we all have to be reassured in the face of death that life goes on. For me, at one time, it was also an excuse to drink, though today I'm content to drown my sorrows in maple syrup.

At one point Arthur looks up from plowing his way through a stack of blueberry-cornmeal pancakes to ask of Stan, as he's regaling us with tales of his travels, "What was the worst place you ever lived in?"

Stan doesn't miss a beat. "Coyote, Texas. Hands down the meanest place on Earth. Ain't nothin' there but dirt, flies, and rattlesnakes."

"Ever kill a rattlesnake?" My brother eyes him with interest.

"More'n one," he says darkly, and I wonder if that includes the two-legged kind.

"What was the worst job you ever had?"

"Claims adjustor for an insurance company. I'd sooner muck out stalls for a living than cheat honest folks outta what they got coming when they're looking at a pile of sticks that used to be their home."

"Did you love my mother?"

This last question comes out of the blue. Stan looks a bit startled, but to his credit, he doesn't hesitate. "Yeah, I did," he answers softly.

Arthur nods, satisfied.

When the table is cleared and the bill settled—Stan insisted on picking up the tab—we exchange good-byes before going our separate ways. Ivy and Stan both head to work, as will I as soon as I've dropped Arthur off at the senior center on Fredericks, where he's now a part-time volunteer, teaching computer skills to seniors. It was Dr. Sandefur's idea, and to my surprise and delight, Arthur not only agreed to it but has embraced his new role. You'd think it was an executive position at a Fortune 500 company from how proudly he carries himself walking through that door. He even has his own set of gray-haired groupies in the older ladies who flock around him.

"Will you stay on at the ranch?" I ask of Stan as we're strolling to where our vehicles are parked, Arthur lagging behind while he texts his friend, Ray.

"For the time being. Who knows where I'll be this time next year?" he answers, with the ease of someone who's comfortable living out of his suitcase. "Colorado, or maybe South Dakota. I hear there's good money to be made in the oil fields."

"It's not about the money, though, is it?"

"No." A pained expression scuds like a low cloud across the rugged terrain of his face. "Which is why it wouldn't have worked out with your mom and me. I never could stay put for very long."

"I have a feeling she'd have followed you anywhere."

"I used to think that. But whenever I picture her, she's right here." He pauses, pointing toward the ground next to where I'm standing. I feel my throat tighten. "Thanks for today—it meant a lot," he says in a gruff voice when we reach my Explorer where we part ways. My hand is engulfed in his manly grip, then he turns to continue on. I watch him round the corner and disappear from view. I wonder if we'll ever meet again. Probably not, though he promised to stay in touch.

Ten minutes later, I'm pulling up in front of the modern blue-and-white frame building that houses the Trousdale Senior Center (named after its founder Leon Trousdale—the final twist of irony for me) and is conveniently located next to a multi-storied medical complex. "You don't mind that it's not Microsoft?" I ask as Arthur's getting out. I worried at first he would miss his old job.

He pauses to consider this. "No. It's nice helping people instead of always being the one who needs helps." He smiles crookedly. "Also, it's kind of nice not always being the craziest person in the room." He's talking about the seniors in the early stages of dementia.

"Well, there is that."

"'Things don't have to change the world to be important.'"

"Steve Jobs, right?" He's fond of quoting his idol.

He nods. When I reach over to straighten the knot in his tie, he pulls away, saying impatiently, the busy executive running late for a board meeting, "Tish, I have to go. I can't keep them waiting."

It's standing room only when I arrive at St. Anthony's for my AA meeting on Thursday evening. Every chair is filled, and I see a lot of new faces in amongst the usual suspects. Before I can wonder about this sudden outbreak in sobriety or the curious looks I'm getting, I'm distracted by someone motioning to me from the last row. McGee. I slide into the empty seat next to him as he retrieves the jacket folded over it. He smirks as he states the obvious. "Saved you a chair."

"Thanks. I wasn't expecting to see you here." Except for the bit of tissue stuck to his cheek where he nicked himself shaving, he looks presentable for a change, wearing clothes that aren't rumpled and fit properly—tan chinos and a striped button-down shirt that covers the tattoos on his forearms. "To what do we owe the pleasure? Don't tell me you finally recognized the pitiful and incomprehensible depths to which you have sunk?" I paraphrase from the Big Book.

McGee flashes me an unrepentant grin. "Not a chance."

"Speaking of 'pitiful and incomprehensible' . . ." I look around me at tonight's unusually large assemblage. "I didn't know there were this many drunks in town who were looking to get sober."

"They ain't all here to get sober," he replies.

I utter a curse. "Unbelievable. This is a new low even for them."

"I wasn't talking about the press." He goes on, at the quizzical look I wear, "In case you haven't noticed, you're a celebrity, Ballard—our very own Kim Kardashian. You're good advertising."

"That's ridiculous. If being on TV was all it took to be famous, Joan Trousdale would have her own perfume label." It wasn't even on purpose, my being on TV; it was only when some reporter shoved a microphone in my face.

He shrugs. "What you're selling, money can't buy."

"I'm not selling anything!"

"Sure you are. It's that little feathered thing called hope."

Now he's quoting Emily Dickinson? I must be hallucinating. "What are you talking about?"

"Human nature. People need heroes. Because they're looking at you and thinking to themselves, 'That could be me shaking the hand of the mayor and cashing that fat check for the reward money.'"

"What reward money? And I've never met our mayor much less shaken his hand."

"Figure of speech." Up front, tonight's chair, old-timer Gavin L., is approaching the mike. The smokers who were standing outside puffing up a storm when I was on my way in start to straggle back inside, stinking of nicotine. "Own it, Ballard. All Kim did was give birth to Kanye's kid. So the fuck what? Anyone can have a kid. Not everyone has a set of brass balls like you."

"Wow." I rock back on my spine to regard him. "That's a first. I didn't even know I had a set of balls."

He pats my knee and treats me to another of his snaggle-toothed grins. "Whatever. You did good."

"I couldn't have done it without your help," I remind him.

"Maybe, but it's your name in the papers, not mine." He was mentioned only as the "retired NYPD police officer" who'd been at the scene. His choice, not mine. He prefers to keep a low profile.

"You think I'm enjoying this?"

"I wouldn't go that far. But, you gotta admit, it had its moments."

"Hardly." I snort. "If this is what being a celebrity is like, I'm never having Kanye's baby."

"I meant the adrenaline rush," he clarifies. "From playing cops and robbers. It can be addictive."

I stare at him. "You think I intend to make a habit of this? That it's every day I stumble on a dead body?"

"If anyone would, it's you."

"Jesus. I hope not."

He gives another low chuckle and rasps, "Don't worry about it." It comes out sounding like one word as he rolls the consonants together in vintage Brooklynese fashion. "I got your back, Ballard."

"Yeah, I know. That's what worries me." It seems I created a monster in coaxing him out of his retirement from law enforcement. "First, it was you making a few calls. Then I'm buying myself a gun and you're teaching me how to shoot it. What's next? A police band short-wave and a Kevlar vest?"

Before he can respond, the meeting is called to order and the first speaker is introduced by Gavin L. A young woman with an old face and short, spiky hair dyed the color of India ink, Carol D. tells her tale without a trace of self-pity in her voice. At her lowest point she was a prostitute, turning tricks to pay for her habit. Her tough-girl demeanor cracks only when she talks about losing custody of her nine-month-old son. At the end, she steps away from the mike to a round of applause and shouted affirmations. Others take turns sharing. The chips are presented to more rounds of applause, the cheering no less enthusiastic for the newcomer who put together thirty days than for Gavin L. marking his twenty years of sobriety. The principle of "one day at a time" in action. Then we all join in reciting the Serenity Prayer. *God, grant me the serenity to accept the things I cannot change . . .*

There are things I would change about my life. I wish I could drink like a normal person. I wish my brother weren't mentally ill. I wish every candy bar I ate didn't go straight to my hips. But I don't dwell on those things. What I'm working on now is accepting that there's no future for Bradley and me. I'll never see him again unless it's in a courtroom. Over before it began, really. Sparks snuffed out before they could catch fire. The thing is, the heart wants what it wants. And my lady parts? They're like a room full of raucous drunks; they won't shut up. I glance toward the church sanctuary on the floor above as the Serenity Prayer is drawing to a close. Is it too late for me to become a nun? On second thought, God probably wouldn't have me, either.

CHAPTER TWENTY-ONE

If I had my own reality show, it wouldn't remotely resemble *Meet the Kardashians*. I don't possess a single article of clothing that isn't off the rack. I favor Sketchers over Manolos, and, if my key ring holds more house keys than the average person's, it's not because I own multiple homes in various, exotic locales. In short, my life is fairly boring. When I'm not solving crimes or getting shot at by psychotic society matrons, that is. I'm not even getting laid these days.

On Friday, I deal with the ant infestation at the Oliveiras'. I follow up on a report of an overturned trashcan at the Iversons' split-level, where I catch the culprit—a raccoon—foraging for food in the strewn garbage. At the Willetts' Cape Cod I catch a minor leak under a bathroom sink before it can become a major flood. I tend to the bromeliads at the Russos' midcentury modern. The big drama of the day was my finding the ninety-year-old lady who lives next door to the O'Briens wandering around their front yard, looking for her cat that died the year before. I had to promise to find and return Pumpkin before she would allow me to escort her back to her house.

And yet I wouldn't trade my life for Kim Kardashian's. Being a small business owner isn't easy and I won't get rich from it, but I earn enough to get by with a little extra to set aside for a rainy day. I love that I don't have to dress up for work or deal with office politics that make me itch to throw a stapler at someone or spend entire days chauffeuring annoying people from one property to the next while they natter in my ear. Lately, too, my job has been a welcome distraction from the dark thoughts that crowd my head. Physically I'm fine, my wounds healed, but I still have nightmares and not just when I'm asleep. The only remedy is to keep busy, keep moving.

It pales compared to what Bradley must be going through. Imagine finding out your mother is criminally insane, your grandfather a serial killer, and your father possibly an accomplice to those murders? It'd be enough to make you go at the family tree with a chainsaw. I wonder if he's turned his back on his parents or if he's being the dutiful son. I have no way of knowing. He hasn't gotten in touch. Nor has he given any interviews to the press—being a canny newsman himself, he's apparently wise to their tricks. I'm told he's only speaking with the authorities.

And soon he'll be in another war zone halfway across the world.

If I think about that, I'll cry.

My last stop of the day is the Kims' Asian-style ranch house, where, after I've done my walk-through, I feed the school of piranha disguised as goldfish in their *koi* pond. It's dark out by the time I head home. Ivy phones to invite me over for Tandoori takeout and a DVD of my choosing. She's been hovering over me like a helicopter mom since the night she dubbed "Cypress Bay Chainsaw Massacre," but I beg off this once. I want only to curl up on my sofa in my snuggies and zone out in front of the TV. *Free Willy* is airing on AMC tonight. That sounds about right.

I arrive home to find a present from my cat on the doorstep: a dead and partially disemboweled mole. Ugh. I know Hercules is only exercising his feline instincts—also, what's one less mole with the legions that are forever digging up my yard?—but I so do not need this right now. I grab a roll of paper towels from inside and, minutes later, I'm headed for the garbage cans along the side of the house with the corpse, wadded in paper towels, when I hear the sound of a car pulling into my driveway. I wasn't expecting company so I can only surmise it's a reporter. Crap. Another thing I so don't need. Most of them have moved on, but a few of the more persistent stringers—dingle berries of the media, as I call them—don't take "no comment" for an answer. Before I can retreat to my house, however, a shadowy male figure rounds the corner of the detached garage. I halt in my tracks when I see who it is, my heart leaping.

"Tish." Bradley calls out my name. For a few seconds we stand there staring at each other, separated by a dozen feet of lawn. The shadow of the roof overhang accentuates the new sharpness of his cheekbones and hollows of his eyes. He's unshaven and appears to have dropped a few pounds; his jeans aren't quite as snug and the leather jacket he's wearing can't hide the pared-down look of a man who's weathered the family equivalent of a category-five hurricane.

When I finally find my voice, it comes out high and breathy. I sound like I did when I was thirteen making awkward conversation with Zach Mancusi, the boy I had a crush on in eighth grade. "Oh, hey. I wasn't expecting . . . um, did you call? I haven't checked my voicemail yet."

His face creases in consternation. "Sorry, I should have phoned. Is this a bad time?"

"No, I was . . ." I hold out the wad of paper towels before remembering what's in it. I quickly lower my hand. "Nothing. I wasn't doing anything special, I mean. I just got home. It's . . . it's good to see you."

He starts toward me. "Can we talk?"

"Sure. Let's go inside. If you'll excuse me a sec . . ." I dash to the nearest garbage can and toss the dead mole before we head up the walk. "Can I get you something to drink?" I ask when I'm ushering him into my living room. "Coffee, a soda? Sorry I can't offer you anything stronger."

"I'm good," he says, though he looks as if he could use a medicinal shot.

"Have a seat." I gesture toward the Morris sofa as I lower myself onto the other end. I'm nervous and feel a childish urge to put my hands over my ears so I won't have to listen when he lists all the reasons why it wouldn't be a good idea for us to see each other again. Starting with his parents.

"I apologize for not returning your calls," he begins. "It's been kind of crazy lately, as you might imagine."

"No shit." I glance down to see my cat sitting at my feet, eyeballing Bradley as a bouncer in a bar would a potential troublemaker. "You must be looking forward to the relative peace and quiet of the Middle East."

"You have no idea. Unfortunately it'll have to wait until the dust settles." Radioactive dust in the aftermath of a nuclear blast, to be precise. "But that's not what I wanted to talk to you about."

"I know what you're going to say, and it's okay. I understand," I jump in, wanting to get this over with as quickly as possible. The sooner I rip off the Band-Aid, the sooner the wound will heal.

"You do?"

"I get it," I plow on. "You're looking at an epidemic and I'm patient zero. Your own personal Typhoid Mary. Oh, I know you don't blame me. But that doesn't change the fact that I'm a walking reminder. And they're still your parents, no matter what. So if you came to say goodbye, I—" I break off, registering the look of confusion on his face. "Wait. Why *are* you here?"

"I came to ask your forgiveness."

I stare at him in astonishment. "What? You didn't do anything."

"Not directly, no. But I knew Mom was having problems. She's been acting strange ever since she and Dad split up. But she was seeing a shrink, so I assumed everything was under control. Wishful thinking on my part," he adds bitterly. "I should have acted sooner, before it was too late."

"What could you have done?"

"I don't know. Something. Anything." His balled fists are matched by the tightness in his face. His eyes glitter with unshed tears. I only wish I could take away the blot on his life like I did the stain on his shirt, the night of Ivy's gallery opening after I accidentally spilled red wine on him.

"You had no way of knowing how bad it had gotten. Your mom was good at hiding it. Even *I* was fooled, and remember, I have a mentally ill brother, so I'm no stranger to delusional behavior."

"I'm her son. I should have made it my business to know. I ignored the red flags." He pauses, his gaze turning briefly inward. "Though I have to admit what she said about my dad doesn't seem so farfetched, in light of everything that's happened since. He swears he had nothing to do with any of that other business—" He pales, looking physically ill— "and I'm giving him the benefit of the doubt for the time being, but between you and me, he's far from off the hook."

I have my own opinion, but it would only cause further distress, so I don't voice it. "We all want to believe the best of our parents."

"A fatal error in my case. You could have been killed!" he cries in a strangled voice.

"True. But I wasn't. I'm still here, aren't I?"

"Thank God for that. It's the one thing out of this whole fucking nightmare I can be grateful for."

"Have you been to see her?"

He nods unhappily. "She was heavily sedated, so she wasn't very communicative. Just as well. I don't know what I would have said to her. I could hardly bring myself to look at her. That's a horrible thing to say about your own mother, but whenever I think of what she did to you . . ."

"She's not in her right mind. That night . . ." The memory hits me like a punch in the stomach, bringing a sharp intake of breath followed by a wave of dizziness, "she told me some stuff I never knew. About what it was like for her growing up. It sounded pretty awful. And we both know her marriage was no picnic. Then with the divorce . . ." I can't believe I'm making excuses for Joan, but however much grief as she caused me, I can't bear to see her son suffer. Besides, I'm not saying anything untrue. "Look, I won't deny what I went through was horrific, but the fact is, your mom isn't . . . well. And mental illness is no different from any other major illness, in one sense. No one *asks* for it. Take my brother, for instance. He's really, really smart, but the wiring in his brain is messed up. He often thinks he's being followed by secret government agents." I refrain from pointing out that, unlike Joan, he's not a danger to society. No need to rub it in.

Bradley regards me in wonderment. "After what she did to you, you can still find it in your heart to forgive?"

"'To err is human, to forgive divine,'" I quote loftily. I've never been called upon to forgive someone who terrorized, then tried to kill me, but I'm prepared to be generous for his sake.

"You're one in a million, Tish Ballard," he says softly.

Our eyes meet and we stare at each other wordlessly. The silence is like a held breath, and I'm aware of every beat of my heart. Then in a sudden movement he closes the gap between us, I'm in his arms and we're kissing. And I'm on fire. Not a contained fire, an accelerant-fueled blaze that has my blood sizzling in my veins, my body alive like never before. I'm acutely aware of each and every sensation. The chafing of his beard stubble against my face. His soft lips contrasted with the rock-hard muscles of his arms and chest. The tip of his tongue playing over mine, and more insistent, the bulge in his jeans pressing against my thigh. We're going at it like horny teenagers alone in a house with no adults present—bodies entwined, mouths fused, hands tangled in each other's hair and clothing—when a loud crash from the next room causes us to jerk apart.

I jump up and run into the kitchen to investigate.

"Talk about lousy timing," I moan to Bradley as I survey the damage. Ceramic shards and potting soil are strewn over the countertop where my cat knocked over the flowerpot that was on the windowsill—in a fit of pique, I imagine, at his being ignored in favor of another male.

Together, Bradley and I clean up the mess.

"Maybe it was a sign. The universe letting us know the last thing either of us needs is another complication," he says, pulling me into his arms again, this time with tenderness rather than passion.

I tilt my head to look at him. "Since when does a manly man like yourself spout New Age-mantras?"

"Since the universe took a big crap on my head."

"You're sure it wasn't a seagull?"

He smiles, and says with regret, "Tish. This is a bad idea and you know it."

"Uh-huh. Whatever you say." I brush my lips over his neck. He smells pleasantly of well-worn leather and the soap from the guest bathroom at the La Mar house and the deeper, muskier scent that is his alone.

He moans. "You're not making this any easier."

"It's complicated, I know. So what? Life is complicated."

"Seriously, Tish . . ."

"Is it because you're still in love with Genevieve?"

He pulls back to look at me, dark brows drawing together. "What gave you that idea? I told you, we broke up."

"Ex-girlfriends are like missiles. Always ready to be deployed in a crisis."

He chuckles. "You certainly have a way with words. One of the many things I love about you."

"You still haven't answered my question."

"No, I'm not still in love with her. I don't know that I ever was, at least not to the same degree as her feelings for me. You're right about one thing—she *did* want to fly out. I declined the offer."

"Oh." It an effort to contain my glee at learning it's really and truly over with him and Genevieve. Also, he used the L-word. Spoken lightly, and yes, I know "love" has as many meanings as "Twinkle, Twinkle Little Star" has musical variations, but whatever, I'm reveling in it.

"Speaking of breakups . . ." He tosses the ball into my court with an arch of his eyebrows.

"You heard about Daniel and me, huh?"

"He told me. He seemed pretty bummed."

"He couldn't be too bummed. He's already seeing someone else." Her name is Jillian Harper, a professor of women's studies whom I'd long suspected of having a crush on him. My suspicion was confirmed when Ivy reported that she'd spotted them together, strolling hand in hand along the sidewalk in front of the Gilded Lily.

Bradley whistles softly. "Wow. He didn't waste any time."

"I'm happy for him. Honestly. It was never going to work with us. Even before I met you." I smile at him before closing my eyes, lips parted in invitation. But instead of the feel of his mouth on mine, there's the pressure of his finger against my lips. When I open my eyes, I see tears in his.

"Tish, no. Think what it would mean."

"Is it because of your parents?" To say they hate me is putting it mildly. I'm sure Joan, in her deranged state of mind, imagines herself to be the victim. And Douglas? God knows what's going through that man's mind.

"No. They don't get a say." Bradley's voice turns hard. "I'm talking about the press. They'd be all over it. You wouldn't have a moment's peace."

"Kind of like how it's been, you mean?"

"Much, much worse. This would cause a feeding frenzy." I picture the *koi* at the Kims', snapping at my fingertips. "And, believe me, nothing is off limits to the bottom feeders. Your mentally ill brother . . . a sexy photo your boyfriend took of you in high school . . ."

I feel a stirring of unease, recalling the stringer whom I'd caught pawing through my garbage, even as I argue, "My brother's mental illness is hardly a secret. And I didn't have a boyfriend in high school." I either sat home alone on Saturday nights or got so trashed at parties, even the boys who might otherwise have expected to score with the "school slut" cut me a wide berth. "If there are any questionable photos floating around, they're of me drunk."

"That, too," he says, grim-faced. "Believe me, they'll stop at nothing. And whatever they can't dig up, they make up."

"Whatever. They can say what they like." He groans as I press my mouth and body to his. I sense him weakening. Then, with what seems a supreme effort, he draws back, gripping my shoulders.

"No. You've been through enough. I can't let you get hurt again. Especially when I won't be around to protect you." I feel a pang, remembering: He's leaving soon. All the more reason to *carpe diem*.

"I don't need you to protect me. I'm like you—I'm not afraid to take risks."

He smiles sadly. "Which brings us to the other reason this is a bad idea. My work has me overseas nine months out of the year. We'd only see each other when I was between assignments."

"We can always Skype."

"Easier said than done. When it's daytime for me, it's the middle of the night for you."

"Back in my drinking days the party didn't get started until after midnight."

He groans again, his resistance crumbling. "You're not making this any easier."

"I'm not trying to."

"This will only lead to trouble."

"Which we both know I find impossible to resist." With that, I turn and lead the way to the bedroom.

AUTHOR'S NOTE

I've led a storied life in more ways than one. I've gone places and done things that astound me, looking back on it. Where did I ever find the courage? The willpower? Much of it I would advise against, were I to go back in time and have a heart-to-heart with my younger self. But good or bad, it was all grist for the mill, so I regret none of it. (Though I feel fortunate not to be haunted by compromising photos of myself online, having come of age in the pre-Internet era). The beauty of fiction is you can reshape past events however you please. I wasn't popular in high school but got to hang out with the cool kids when I wrote for the phenomenally successful teen series Sweet Valley High in the early years of my career. Trust me, you wouldn't have wanted to live through some of what I lived through, but hopefully you've enjoyed the novels that came of it.

If you Google my name, you will see my Cinderella story: welfare mom to millionaire. Every word is true, though the reality is I was a starving artist for a much longer period of time than I was on welfare. With two young children to support on my own, I often had to forgo buying office supplies and stamps to send out the articles and short stories I wrote on spec, in order to put food on the table.

The lean years were the making of me, though. When I wrote

my first adult novel, *Garden of Lies*, the story of babies switched at birth, one of whom grows up rich, the other poor, I knew what it was to go hungry. I knew what it was like for Rose putting on the skirt she wears to work every day, ironed so many times it's shiny in spots. *Garden of Lies* went on to become a *New York Times* bestseller, translated into twenty-two languages. I attribute its success in part to my having suffered.

I've also had my share of romantic ups and downs. More grist for the mill and the reason my fictional characters tend to be of the folks-this-ain't-my-first-rodeo variety. I've been married more than once. At one point, I was married to my agent. His client list boasts some notable names, and just recently I was struck by the realization that I had dined with two of the famous people depicted in the movies *The Theory of Everything* and *Selma*: professor Stephen Hawking and Coretta Scott King, respectively. How extraordinary! I witnessed history and saw it reenacted on film.

I met my current and forever husband, Sandy Kenyon, in a Hollywood meet-cute, which seems fitting given he's in the entertainment business, as a TV reporter and film critic. He had a radio talk show in Arizona at the time. I was a guest on his show, phoning in from New York City, where I live. He called me at home that night, at my invitation, and we talked for three hours. It became our nightly ritual, and when we finally met it was love at first sight, though we were hardly strangers. We married in 1996, and he became the inspiration for talk-show host Eric Sandstrom in *Thorns of Truth*. Though, as Sandy's fond of saying, he never killed a coanchor while driving drunk.

I have many people to thank for the support and guidance I've received along the way.

First and foremost, my husband, Sandy, who's been there every step of the way and who reads multiple drafts of my novels. He's patient, kind, and wise. He understands when I'm there in body but somewhere else in my mind, and doesn't get too upset at having to repeat himself more than once to get through to me. From him I learned the true meaning of romantic love, which has enriched my fictional love stories immeasurably. He's also partly the reason I'm still walking this earth. More than once it was his hand on my arm, pulling me to safety, that kept me from stepping into the path of a moving vehicle while in one of my preoccupied states.

To my children, Michael and Mary, for being the quirky, loving individuals they are. Whenever I beat myself up for having been a less-than-perfect parent (which pretty much describes every single parent), they tell me they couldn't love me any more than they do. They also both have a wicked sense of humor, which they get from me. When I was exploring the idea of having another child, with Sandy, I was told I'd need an egg donor. Which led to the what-if scenario that would have me giving birth to my own grandchild (and writing the bestseller that would come of it!), at which point my daughter remarked dryly, "Mom, would you like that over easy or sunny side up?"

To friends and family who have made their vacation homes available to me through the years. Their generosity has allowed me to go away for extended periods of time to write in solitude amid serene settings. Bill and Valerie Anders. Frank Cassata and Thomas Rosamilia. Miles and Karen Potter. Jon Giswold. Thanks to my friend Jon, I was introduced to the scenic wonders of northern Wisconsin and befriended by the good people of Grantsburg, which I now consider my home away from home.

To my friends and author pals, who are my cheering section. Whenever I'm at a low point or feeling blue, they're always there to offer a hug, a pat on the back, or a word of encouragement. I wouldn't be where I am today if not for them.

I smile, and brush away a tear, whenever I think of my oldest friend, Kay Terzian, who had every single one of my titles, in multiple editions, when she passed away. She would always say she was my biggest fan. I never doubted it.

To my publisher, Open Road Media, and its smart, happening crew led by the visionary Jane Friedman who saw the future of digital publishing. Special thanks, too, to my editor, Maggie Crawford, who helped shaped my most recent titles and make them better for it. She's living proof of why an author needs an editor.

I am also blessed to have many loyal readers. They range in age from fourteen to ninety-four and come from all walks of life and all parts of the globe. One, a prisoner doing time on a drug offense, sent letters commenting intelligently on my novels, which I was happy to know were available in prison libraries. Shortly before his release, he sent me a Mother's Day card. I had written a few times 'in response to his letters, but would hardly describe myself as a pen pal, let alone a surrogate mom. I think he regarded me fondly because he felt he knew what was in my heart, which I pour into the pages of my novels. That is the greatest compliment of all and the best part of what I do for a living, worth more to me than fame or fortune.

Thank you for taking this journey with me. If you've enjoyed what you've read, leave a comment on Amazon or Goodreads to help spread the word, so I can keep doing what I do.

Eileen Goudge

ABOUT THE AUTHOR

Eileen Goudge (b. 1950) is one of the nation's most successful authors of women's fiction. She began as a young adult writer, helping to launch the phenomenally successful Sweet Valley High series, and in 1986 she published her first adult novel, the *New York Times* bestseller *Garden of Lies*. She has since published twelve more novels, including the three-book saga of Carson Springs and *Thorns of Truth*, a sequel to *Gardens of Lies*. She lives and works in New York City.

THE CYPRESS BAY MYSTERIES

FROM OPEN ROAD MEDIA

OPEN ROAD

INTEGRATED MEDIA

INTEGRATED MEDIA

Find a full list of our authors and
titles at www.openroadmedia.com

FOLLOW US
@OpenRoadMedia